P9-DUJ-605

Out of the patient silence . . .

The man behind the curtain waited. He had all the time in the world. He listened. Mrs. Sloane blew her nose, murmured, wiped her eyes. "It reminds me"—she faltered again—"of a day in early May."

She was weeping, all at once, like a spring torrent. "I can't bear living any longer!" she cried. "I can't bear it!" She clenched her hands on her knees and was horrified at the echoing sound of her outburst . . .

The Listener

Another spellbinding triumph
from the pen of Taylor Caldwell

TAYLOR CALDWELL
THE LISTENER

BANTAM BOOKS · TORONTO · NEW YORK · LONDON

All the characters in this book are fictitious,
and any resemblance to actual persons,
living or dead, is purely coincidental.

This low-priced Bantam Book
has been completely reset in a type face
designed for easy reading, and was printed
from new plates. It contains the complete
text of the original hard-cover edition.
NOT ONE WORD HAS BEEN OMITTED.

THE LISTENER

A Bantam Book | published by arrangement with
Doubleday & Company, Inc.

PRINTING HISTORY

Doubleday edition published September 1960

2nd printing . September 1960		4th printing .... July 1961
3rd printing .. December 1960		5th printing ...... January 1962

Serialized in EXTENSION *Magazine 1960*

Doubleday Book Club edition published March 1961

Bantam edition | September 1962
10 printings through April 1969
New Bantam edition | May 1971

2nd printing ...... October 1971	7th printing .... March 1975
3rd printing .... July 1972	8th printing . September 1976
4th printing .... February 1973	9th printing . September 1976
5th printing .. September 1973	10th printing .... May 1978
6th printing .... August 1974	11th printing .... October 1978
12th printing .... December 1980	

All rights reserved.
Copyright © 1960 by Reback & Reback.
Cover art copyright © 1980 by Bantam Books, Inc.
This book may not be reproduced in whole or in part, by
mimeograph or any other means, without permission.
For information address: Doubleday & Company, Inc.,
245 Park Avenue, New York, N.Y. 10017.

ISBN 0–553–14230–5

Published simultaneously in the United States and Canada

Bantam Books are published by Bantam Books, Inc. Its trade-
mark, consisting of the words "Bantam Books" and the por-
trayal of a bantam, is Registered in U.S. Patent and Trademark
Office and in other countries. Marca Registrada. Bantam
Books, Inc., 666 Fifth Avenue, New York, New York 10103.

PRINTED IN THE UNITED STATES OF AMERICA

21 20 19 18 17 16 15 14 13 12

Dedicated
with all humility to

THE LISTENER

THE LISTENER

For who listens to us in all the world, whether
he be friend or teacher, brother or father or
mother, sister or neighbor, son or ruler or
servant? Does he listen, our advocate, or our
husbands or wives, those who are dearest to us?

Do the stars listen, when we turn despairingly
away from man, or the great winds, or the seas or
the mountains? To whom can any man say—Here I
am! Behold me in my nakedness, my wounds, my
secret grief, my despair, my betrayal, my pain,
my tongue which cannot express my sorrow, my
terror, my abandonment.

Listen to me for a day—an hour!—a moment!

lest I expire in my terrible wilderness, my
lonely silence! O God, is there no one to listen?

Is there no one to listen? you ask. Ah yes,
there is one who listens, who will always listen.
Hasten to him, my friend! He waits on the hill
for you.

For you, alone.

Seneca

FOREWORD

This is a true story. It may be your story, but certainly it is your neighbor's story. You may find your own face here, and it may anger you. I hope so. Anger is a cleansing agent.

The most desperate need of men today is not a new vaccine for any disease, or a new religion, or a new "way of life." Man does not need to go to the moon or other solar systems. He does not require bigger and better bombs and missiles. He will not die if he does not get "better housing" or more vitamins. He will not expire of frustration if he is unable to buy the brightest and newest gadgets, or if all his children cannot go to college. His basic needs are few, and it takes little to acquire them, in spite of the advertisers. He can survive on a small amount of bread and in the meanest shelter. He always did.

His real need, his most terrible need, is for someone to listen to him, not as a "patient," but as a human soul. He needs to tell someone of what he thinks, of the bewilderment he encounters when he tries to discover why he was born, how he must live, and where his destiny lies. The questions he asks of psychiatrists are not the questions in his heart, and the answers he receives are not the answers he needs. He is a sealed vessel, even when under drugs or while heavily drinking. His semantics are not the semantics of anyone else, not even the semantics of a psychiatrist.

Our pastors would listen—if we gave them the time to listen to us. But we have burdened them with tasks which should be our own. We have demanded not only that they be our shepherds but that they take our trivialities, our social aspirations, the "fun" of our children, on their weary backs. We have demanded that they be expert businessmen, politicians, accountants, playmates, community directors, "good fellows," judges, lawyers, and settlers of local quarrels. We have given them little time for listening, and we do not listen to them, either. We must offer them concrete help and assume our own responsibilities. We forget that they are men also, frequently very tired, always unappreciated, sometimes disheartened, quite often appalled, worried, anxious, lonely, grieved. They are not supermen, without human agony and human longing. Heedlessly, we neglect them—unless we wish them to serve us in material ways, when their ways should be exclusively God's. We demand of them what we would not dare to demand of anyone else, even ourselves. We give them no time to listen, when to have someone listen, without hurry, without the click of a clock, is the direst need of our spirits.

Until we free our shepherds from our insistence that they be our servants, let us remember that there *is* someone who listens. He is available to all of us, all of the time, all of our lives. The Listener.

We have only to talk to him. Now. Today. Tonight. He understands our language, our semantics, our terrors, our secrets, our sins, our crimes, our sorrow. He will not consider you sentimental if you speak fondly of the past, if you are old. He will not turn you away if you are a liar, a thief, a murderer, a hypocrite, a betrayer. He will listen to you. He will not be impatient if you become maudlin, or cry in self-pity, or if you are a coward or a fool. He has listened to people like this all his life. He will continue to listen.

While he listens, you will find your own problems solved. Will he speak to you, also? Who knows? Perhaps. Surely, if you ask him. If you listen, too.

Taylor Caldwell

THE LISTENER

The newspaper reporters were wild with curiosity.

"Oh, come on, sir!" they said to old John. "Who's behind that curtain? A clergyman? Clergymen on shifts around the clock? The—what do you call this, anyway?—is open twenty-four hours a day, isn't it? How much did it cost you? Is it true that you put your life's savings in it? Real Carrara marble, isn't it? But who's behind that curtain?"

Old John Godfrey was eighty years old. A mediocre lawyer in a large city rarely made much money, especially if he was honest, and John had been both mediocre and honest. He was a widower. Beyond a few, a very few, devoted old friends, his name had not been known widely. He had never wanted to be a lawyer in the first place, but his mother and father, who had worked so hard to educate him, had chosen that profession for their only child. They were immigrants; they had never learned to read and write. In the old country a man of law had been a man of consequence, even more esteemed than a physician. He had been the man to approach for help in leaving the

1

country and going to America; he wrote out the applications, the forms; he made mysterious journeys to the big town where he no doubt consulted grave authorities and consuls. He had been the man who could approach the clergy easily for baptismal certificates, and the police for a letter stating that the would-be immigrant had no bad record. A friend of the mayor or burgomaster, it was not difficult for him to obtain exit visas or passports. If he frequently took a man's last cow or pig in payment for his benevolent and necessary services, what did that matter? Men become rich in America, almost overnight.

John, whose surname was not Godfrey but something beyond the tongue of Anglo-Saxons to pronounce, never told anyone that he had always wanted to be a poet. He had been born in this large American city only two months after his parents' arrival. One of his teachers, a shy young girl, suspected his ambition and his natural endowment, and she had timidly encouraged him. But she had been the only one. His parents would not have understood, and he was their only child and he loved them, and above all things he would never disappoint them. So he became a lawyer, and disliked every minute of it.

He had made an adequate living. Naturally austere, he had not longed for many material pleasures. Books of prose and poetry and history, a small organ, four acres on the edge of town where he built an undistinguished clapboard house, but where he had a magnificent garden, a dog, a cat, two canaries, and a few friends, were

2

more than enough for any man, particularly John Godfrey. He had no taste for the flamboyant part of law and confined himself to a prosy practice which did not occupy his mind but left it free to think and pray and meditate and plan his garden. Freedom, above all things, of soul and mind and body, was the stuff of life to John Godfrey. He early became acquainted with the writings of Emerson and Thoreau, and he had his own Walden Pond on his four acres of land.

When he was thirty he married the daughter of old immigrant friends of his parents, and there were no children. Few ever saw Mrs. Stella Godfrey, who bore a strange resemblance to the shy young teacher who had first known that John was a poet, when he had been only six years old. Stella, though American-born and educated, always retained a strong but soft accent, and she was extremely reserved and gentle and timid. Even John's few friends had found her colorless. When she died, ten years after the marriage, they hardly missed her. John rarely mentioned her; his friends believed that he did not miss her, either. She lay near his parents in "that queer old foreign cemetery," and if he visited those three graves his friends did not know. He had a quiet serenity of manner, a charming smile, and was not loquacious. He preferred to listen to others. None of these characteristics altered or dimmed after his wife's death, so it was decided, with relief, that "poor Stella" had left no mark in John's life.

There was one odd thing about John Godfrey. No one, not even the closest of his friends, Walter

Baker, ever called him "Jack." He was always John, dignified yet kind, helpful and thoughtful, never disturbed, rushed, hurried, or harassed.

The city grew up around his four acres of land, but he would not sell them for any price. Apartment houses rose within sight of his living-room windows; a school and its yard lay beyond his walled garden; a busy street hummed not far from his bedroom. But he kept his acres, and he painted his old-fashioned house, mowed his own lawn, and attended his own flowers—even to the day he was eighty years old.

He told no one, not even his best friend, Walter Baker, the city's leading urologist, of a dream he had held for fifty years. But the day after he was eighty, four architects, with blueprints, called on him and stayed with him for hours. They left, smiling but silent, wonderingly shaking their heads at each other. No one knew anything until John Godfrey moved into a small residential hotel nearby and the old house was demolished. Friends questioned; he only smiled. When the finest of white marble arrived, carefully crated, the newspapers took their first notice. John refused to answer any questions, gently but firmly. The foundation was dug. People came to stare and wonder, and speculate. A private library, museum, music school? No one knew. John, who was retired now, stood and watched, a tall old white-haired man, his hands under his coattails, his face attentive, a cigar in his mouth. For the first time he seemed mysterious.

It was soon evident that the building would be square and that it would have only two rooms, a large front entrance and a small rear one. One room would be about eighteen by eighteen feet, the other a little larger. The white marble slabs rose to a flat roof. The gardens expanded, dying trees were replaced with tall young saplings, red gravel paths laid out, flower beds enlarged. "A kind of little church," said some neighbors disdainfully. "Is he going to preach in there?" But no one knew.

The curious, peering through the doorway— there were no windows at all—saw that the floor of the smaller room was being covered with a deep blue carpet, thick and soft, and filled with comfortable chairs, tables and lamps, all quite expensive. They could not see beyond this room, which had a wide, tall oaken door. The front door, of bronze, imported from the old country, was set in place, and over it, in an arch, was inlaid in gold letters: "The Man who Listens."

And set deeply in the white marble floor was a brass plate: "In Memory of Stella Godfrey."

Now it was complete, and John Godfrey let the press enter, for it was necessary that the public know. The young reporters surged into the pleasant and serene room with its glowing lamps, its glass tables covered with magazines and flowers in pots and vases, its white marble walls on which there were no murals or pictures, its thickly carpeted floor. It was very restful here, and quiet, and waiting. But for whom did it wait?

John, smiling, touched a bell near the oaken door at the end of the room. It chimed gently. He pointed out a slot near the door. "For requests to be heard," he said. The door automatically opened

5

after ten minutes, while the reporters fumed with eager impatience. Then they entered the room beyond and stared.

There was nothing whatsoever in the room but a tall marble chair covered with blue velvet cushions. The chair faced an arched alcove hidden by thick blue curtains. At the side of the alcove was a brass plate: "If you wish to see the man who has listened to you, touch the button above. You will see his face. He will be glad if you thank him, but it is not necessary."

So the reporters asked, "A clergyman? Shifts around the clock?" They knew that the building would never be closed. John did not answer except with a smile. The newsmen flashed their cameras on him, the sitting room, the empty marble room which was lighted obliquely by a soft and muted light falling from the white ceiling. One reporter, very young and brash, went to the button near the thick blue curtains, but John said with unusual sternness: "No! Not yet, not yet, for you."

He showed the reporters the box which lay below the slit that opened in the sitting room. "People may deposit their requests here, to be heard. Then, after touching the bell, they must wait ten minutes. Then the door will be opened, for one at a time. He then leaves by the rear entrance."

"A lawyer, perhaps, or a social worker, or a psychiatrist?" wheedled the young reporter. But John only smiled. "Of course," said the reporters, "the people who come here will tell us all about

6

it. It won't be a mystery very long, you know, Mr.
Godfrey." John only smiled.

"What do you expect people to say in here?"
asked another reporter, taking another flash of the
old man. "They will know before they come," said
John. He paused and said gently, "One of the most
terrible aspects of this world today is that nobody
listens to anyone else. If you are sick, or even
dying, nobody listens. If you are bewildered, or
frightened, or lost, or bereaved, or alone, or lonely
—nobody really listens. Even the clergy are hurried and harassed; they do their best and work
endlessly. But time has taken on a fragmented
character; it doesn't seem to have any substance
any longer. Nobody has time to listen to anyone,
not even those who love you and would die for
you. Your parents, your children, your friends:
they have no time. That's a very terrible thing,
isn't it? Whose fault is it? I don't know. But there
doesn't seem to be any time."

"And you think the man—whoever he is—will
have time?" asked the impertinent reporter.

John appeared to consider this gravely, his tall
old head bent. Then he said, "Oh yes. I think he'll
have time. All the time there is." He looked at the
reporters and repeated: "All the time that's left."

They thought him old, prosy, and enigmatic.
They were certain that they'd have the whole
story very soon from any man or woman who
came here to talk, alone in this white marble room
with the soft light and the shut curtains. They
looked at the bronze box below the slit. It was
very uncomplicated. The simple-minded would

7

drop their illiterate little notes in there and a hidden clergyman or social worker or psychiatrist would read the notes, retire behind the curtain, and give ponderous advice. Some of the older reporters said it was very nice, and modern. The man behind the curtain couldn't even see the speaker, and so it would all be very confidential. Silly old men and women would talk their heads off, in solitude, and go out comforted. For who ever listened to their complaints, anyway? The reporters would soon know, they reassured themselves. A new kind of psychiatric treatment, without charge.

No one ever told. Two months after the building was opened to the public John Godfrey died. His wants had been meager; he had left a large fortune, for he had speculated for his dream. His friends laughed affectionately and said, "Who would have thought that old John was in the stock market?" His fortune was given to his building for perpetual care. Cleaners who became curious found that they could not move the blue curtains in the alcove. It was as if the velvet had been woven of steel. It was finally decided by everyone—with some truth—that it was the voices of the desperate which operated some kind of electrical impulse that opened the curtain after they had finished their confidences and had touched the button. But those who came with false confidences, out of curiosity, found that even when they touched the button the curtains did not part. It was discovered, months later, that old John, over long years, had studied electronics.

8

Only the genuine voice of sorrow and grief and loneliness and despair could part the curtains.

The button was only an added impulse.

It was noted that those who slipped through the rear exit had radiant faces, or peaceful ones, or thoughtful. Some were in tears. Some walked resolutely, as if about to take a journey. Some cried aloud, "Oh yes, yes! I'd forgotten!"

The reporters went to the clergy, Catholic, Protestant, Jewish. "What's all this flim-flam?" they would ask. "Do you approve of it?"

The clergy would answer only with smiles. Some would say they really knew nothing of the man who listened behind the velvet-steel curtains. Some would frown and talk of "superstition in this modern age of the hydrogen bomb and science." A very modern clergyman said, "I know nothing about it and want to know less. Have you read Professor Blank's latest book on the nature of the physical universe? Very enlightening. But only for intellectuals, of course. He explodes superstition for all time. Not that I am against religion," the clergyman added hastily as he lit an excellent Havana, "for, after all, I'm a clergyman, am I not? But Things Advance, and Knowledge Grows."

A very old minister said briefly, "I myself have talked to the man behind the curtain. He answered me fully. He made it possible for me to continue when I thought it was impossible."

"What did he say to you?" asked the reporter.

The minister looked at the young man thoughtfully. "Why, he said everything."

9

National newspapers sent their reporters to the city in droves. They learned nothing more. The Man in the Street was interviewed and his sage opinions recorded. Sure, the guy behind the curtain was a psychiatrist. The mother of the lady next door had gone to that place, and after she'd told all about her old goat the doctor had given her some good advice. And there was that girl in trouble, two blocks down the street. Social worker had told her what to do and where to go for help. And there was this widow with five kids. One was one of these juvenile delinquents. The social worker had helped her, too. And there was this man who had cancer and was scared to death. The worker had sent him to a hospital, free, and he was cured. Oh, sure, the guy behind the curtain was a priest. He'd told a feller to confess his crime to the police. Say, was old John Godfrey a Catholic? Somebody said he was a Jew, and there was Jewish scrolls behind that curtain. What did the Jews want, anyways? Don't you believe it! The guy behind the curtain's a Christian Scientist. Can cure anything with the Bible, see?

Other opinions, equally sage, were advanced. Oh, there was a recording machine behind the curtain. Some Communist or other. Or maybe the guy was a Socialist, or Republican, or Democrat. You kind of have to watch things these days, don't you? Propaganda everywheres. Say, did you hear about that lady comes out and goes out of her mind? Had to take her to the state hospital. Me? I wouldn't go there on a bet! Somebody should burn the place down. Know what real estate values are around there? We need a new school—or something.

A priest said to a reporter, "Have you gone there, yourself, in the proper spirit?"

"What is the proper spirit—sir?"

The priest smiled slightly. "I'm sure you'll find out, yourself, someday."

A rabbi said to a reporter, "I haven't been there as yet, myself. But some of my people have. No, you can't ask them. They won't answer you."

A psychiatrist said, "I don't know what is behind that curtain, and one of my most difficult patients went there, and he won't tell me, either. But one thing I do know: he's cured now."

There were attempts to break into the sanctuary, because there were rumors that the people who visited if left money "in the box." But for some reason the doors resisted all kinds of pressure and force. And, of course, there were no windows to break.

SOUL ONE

The Confessed

*And the priest shall bring her
near, and set her before the Lord.*
Numbers 5:16

Mrs. Merrill Sloane entered the sitting room
with resistance. She wore severe tweeds and a
sable scarf and carried a leather purse soundly
closed. She was fifty years old, gray and sharp
of face, neat and trim of figure, and had a hat that
was at least five years old and good for another
five years. It was of felt, with a dipping brim. Her
no-nonsense shoes set themselves firmly on the
carpet. She walked and moved with precision and
stared haughtily at the others in the room. They
did not look at her. Murmuring distastefully to
herself, as if ashamed of her own emotions, she
took a sealed note from her purse, marched to the
slit in the wall near the oaken door, and dropped
the note through the opening. She waited. Nothing
happened. Men and women of all ages were reading the magazines and slim books of poetry which

13

had been laid on the tables. She sat down, very stiffly.

Why had she been so stupid as to come here? Restlessly she removed her gloves and looked at the large diamond on her finger. But she was more concerned with the fact that her hands appeared to be withered and grasping and deformed. All the women in her family had always had soft, smooth, white hands, even in their eighties and nineties. Why were hers so dry and parched, and with such big knuckles? She looked again at the others in the room. It was warm and fresh in here, though it was March outside and there were no windows or any visible source of heat. A spring day! Suddenly she thought of a spring day, and the room blurred before her eyes and she dropped her head. She forgot her silent companions. Vaguely she was aware that one by one they rose, were admitted beyond the oaken door. Finally she was the last. Then she heard the bell chime for her, and she stood up on legs suddenly weak and entered the other room.

Only a white, softly lit marble room, with a marble chair covered with blue velvet cushions. What was that tall alcove hidden by blue curtains? Mrs. Sloane frowned. Nonsense. John Godfrey—she had never met him—was a European, and possibly decadent, too. She remembered all the rumors. She sat down in the chair, as straight as an oak. She waited. The soft silence waited also. Oh yes, she recalled, she could say what she wished and someone behind that curtain would listen. All at once she was crying.

"Please pardon me," she murmured. "I have a

14

slight cold. Prevalent this year. Or a sinus condition. I've just come from Dr. Bundy's. He isn't very competent, I'm afraid. A very painful affair, this sinus condition. My head aches all the time. Sometimes I think I am just one ache. This ache—"

The man who listened behind that curtain could not be interested in her sinus condition, which was due to the seasonable fogs and the melting snow. One must be dignified. "I should really tell you," she said with severity, "that I don't know why I am here. I'm sure my clergyman would not approve. He does deplore superstition so. Certainly he would not approve of my visiting you. I don't know why I am here. So foolish."

The patient silence waited. There was no hurry, no bustle, no rustle of clothing. No sound of traffic or of jet liners or of feet. No subdued opening or closing of doors. No clock. No ticking. No impatience. "Very restful," said Mrs. Sloane approvingly. "It reminds me—"

The man behind the curtain waited. He had all the time in the world. He listened. Mrs. Sloane blew her nose, murmured, wiped her eyes. "It reminds me"—she faltered again—"of a day in early May."

She was weeping, all at once, like a spring torrent. "I can't bear living any longer!" she cried. "I can't bear it!"

She clenched her hands on her knees and was horrified at the echoing sound of her outburst. She looked about the marble room, cringing. Mrs. Merrill Sloane screaming like this, Mrs. Sloane who managed the Junior League ruthlessly, the

Rheumatic Hospital League, the Debutante Cotillion, the Town Club; Mrs. Merrill Sloane who said, and said finally, who should be admitted to the very core of the city's society, who should be chosen for the League for the Philharmonic, the Crippled Children's Hospital Board, the Green Country Club—— Mrs. Merrill Sloane whose husband could buy and sell the whole city.

Buy and Sell.

The man behind the curtain waited. She stared at the curtain, which did not move or stir. But she could feel the great patience, the great sympathy. "Are you someone I know?" she said. The man waited. "I suppose not," she murmured. She paused. Then she exclaimed, "No one knows me!"

She had the strangest sensation that the man behind the curtain knew her very well, and with affection and understanding, and that she could trust him. She said, "I hope I can trust you. After all, I have a position—— May I trust you?"

Did a voice answer "Yes"? She was never sure. "Very silly, really," she said as the tears ran down her gray cheeks. "I shouldn't have come. But there is all that talk. You listen, they say. No one ever listens any more. My mother did, but she died when I was ten years old. I've never found anyone to listen since then. Certainly not my children!"

She leaned toward the curtains urgently. "Mine is a silly story. I've talked with my doctor. He's indulgent! Indulgent! Does he ever know how much his indulgence is like slamming a door in one's face? I've talked with my clergyman too. He's very elegant. He delivers the most erudite

16

lectures—I mean sermons. Are you a clergyman? I didn't mean to offend you. But lectures—— I tried to talk to him; he murmured something about 'my time of life.' Is there a 'time of life' when one isn't in agony? No!"

She twisted her gloves in her sweating hands. "I've thought of killing myself," she said, and looked at the curtains fearfully. They were not agitated; there was no stir of protest behind them, nor reproach.

"A very silly story," she said. "I don't know why I am wasting your time like this. I have an appointment at——" The man did not speak behind the curtain. "An appointment," she repeated. Then she cried out, "What does an appointment mean! It means nothing at all! People all have appointments! With what? With whom? Why? With death?"

She paused. She said in a very low voice, "That is very strange. It has just occurred to me that we all have appointments with death. I never thought of that before. Death. Death. When you think of that, everything else seems very foolish. Except a spring day in May. That is all that matters.

"You see," she said, "my family is very old, and very distinguished, in America. Scholars, professors, lawyers, doctors, financiers. There are three governors in my family, too, and four senators. My father could walk in and out of the White House any time he wished; he had only to announce he was going to Washington. I have sent his letters to the Library of Congress, and all the letters of the Presidents, too. My aunt married an English peer. We are very distinguished."

17

If the man behind the curtain was impressed, he gave no sign. Mrs. Sloane became smaller in her chair, like a girl. "One has obligations," she offered. The pale warm light beamed down at her from the ceiling. "One has duties," she offered again. "One mustn't consider just oneself, must one?"

Did the man say "No" in a very gentle voice? She leaned toward the curtain again. "You do understand, don't you?" she said. "Really, I am taking up a great deal of your time with my silly story. What did I say earlier? Oh yes, an appointment with death." She considered. "Once I read somewhere that when we love we have become acquainted with death. I am very irrelevant, am I not? I am ashamed of myself, too. My husband has at least eight million dollars; why should I complain of anything?

"Oh yes, that day in May. You see, I'd known Clyde Bennett since we were children together. He was of a very distinguished family too. He built a tree house on the land of our summer home. We used to climb up there together and talk. About the most childish things. A leaf, perhaps, from the elm. Full of veins. It was very wonderful, thinking of the sap in the leaf. Clyde had a magnifying glass. We'd look at things through it. The leaf. Green and living. An insect. We'd stare at it, and it would be frightened, just like a child, and we'd be sorry and let it go. I wonder what it felt. I'm sure it must have felt something. I never thought of that before; I never wondered if insects—and people—felt anything important. What is importance?"

18

She waited. There was no sound. But a sense of vigor came to her, like a memory of her childhood. She laughed tearfully. "Why, everything's important, isn't it? Certainly. Everything in the sight of—of——" She put her hands over her face and whispered, "God."

After a long time she lifted her head and faced the curtains resolutely. "I really don't know why I am complaining! Clyde's family lost their money; so did ours. So marriage was out of the question! I remember that last day I saw him. We were in the tree house, and it was spring, and May, and it was raining. Do you remember what rain sounds like in a tree, with the leaves rustling and dripping and gleaming about you, and no sound at all but the rain? And everything green and hushed and safe? Clyde and I were eighteen then. He asked me to wait for him. He had an uncle in Hartford who might help him. I never knew. I only knew what my father had said that last night, 'Clyde is going away, perhaps for a long time. Our family is very distinguished, and famous. You have a duty; you are my only daughter and you have three younger brothers who must be educated to live up to our standard in life. Old families must never wither away; they owe a responsibility to their country. Only money can save them, and we have no money.

" 'But there is Merrill Sloane in my office. A country bumpkin, the son of a rich buccaneer. No family, of course. Pirates. Blackguards. But they have money. He wants to marry you.' "

Mrs. Sloane bit her lip. Her tears were like acid on her cheeks. "I knew Merrill. A big, awk-

19

ward, stumbling, bumbling young man. A university graduate; I simply don't know what education is coming to when a man like Merrill can graduate —with honors! Summa cum laude. Think of that! I always thought that universities were above bribery, but now I simply don't know! Besides, he didn't have Clyde's elegance and delicacy, and sensitiveness of character. A dull brute."

She looked at the curtains. "A man of no family, no background; a family without learning and tradition. Peasants, really. Summa cum laude, as if he were a wise man! Isn't that ridiculous? A wise man—Merrill! At least he had the intelligence not to try to appear wise; he was very quiet when I would see him in Papa's office. Did I tell you that Papa had a lumber company? His father acquired it as a sort of joke; Grandfather was a banker, and he foreclosed on a fine farm with much timber on it. That is how Papa became interested in lumber—if he really was. But Papa really preferred Meissen china; he had quite a collection. Of course it sold for practically nothing. I never cared about it, myself.

"Merrill came in as Papa's assistant. Such a joke in the family, the lumber, and then Merrill. Of course I must admit that Merrill had—has—a feeling for wood. He carves almost lovely things in his spare time. He has no social graces whatsoever; he belongs to no clubs, except nominally. Yet people seem to like him; I don't know why.

"Oh, please forgive me. I forgot to tell you that I married Merrill when I was nineteen. For his money. For Papa. He saved all of us. My brothers went to Harvard and made excellent marriages.

Merrill—I must give him credit again—didn't seem to care much about all the money he had. He gave my brothers large, permanent allowances. Settled trusts on their children. That was quite unnecessary, you know. They could have tried to do something for themselves. One must have a little independence. I think Merrill really did that—" Mrs. Sloane dropped her wet handkerchief, and her gray face became strained and startled. "I think Merrill did that for me! For me! To please me! I never thought of that before!"

She burst into wild tears and bent her head. "I never thought of that!" she sobbed. "To please me, to do something he thought I wanted!"

She shrank deeper into the chair. "Merrill! I married him because he said he loved me. And I despised him. I have despised him—all these years. Only a dull brute with dirty money he had inherited from his father. I couldn't talk to him about anything—why couldn't I? Summa cum laude. I thought that was such a joke. Was it a joke? Oh, God, was it a joke?"

She stood up and approached the curtain, and she was trembling. "I was so lonely all these years! But now I am wondering if Merrill hasn't been lonely too. The children—our children. They all love Merrill; they talk with him. I never could. I say to them, 'What can you talk about with your father?' And laugh. They never laughed back. They looked at me—they look at me—as if they despised me, as if I were dull and stupid—— Oh, God, are you listening?

"My children hate me! They have nothing to say to me. The girls avoid me; the boys are in-

21

different. But they are always with Merrill. I have no one. I hear them laughing with him, and talking, talking, talking. I'm so lonely! I'm so terribly lonely!"

She stammered, sobbed, wept. "Merrill. Are you lonely? What did I ever give you but scorn? Merrill! Poor Merrill! Why were you so patient? Why did you not leave me long ago? What am I to you?"

She went closer to the curtain, and it was within reach of her hand.

"What am I to you, who've offended you so? Can you ever forgive me? Oh, God, can you forgive me?"

Her shaking hand reached out and touched the button. The curtains stirred. She could see them through her tears. They blew as if in a slight wind. They separated, and a light shone out. Now the curtains rolled apart swiftly, and Mrs. Merrill Sloane stood and looked in silence. The light shone all about her.

"Yes, yes," she whispered, gazing at the man fully revealed to her. "You forgive. I hope Merrill will too."

She looked again and murmured. She walked through the rear exit, and she walked as a girl walks, running to someone who is waiting for her, and she is free, and full of joy and love. In the springtime.

SOUL TWO

The "Underprivileged"

*'Tis not in mortals to command success,
But we'll do more, Sempronius—we'll deserve it.*

Addison

"Well, it's like this," said Tab Shutts sullenly, clasping his callused hands together on his knees. "O.K. Listen. You can listen your head off, see if I care. Bet you never worked a day in your life. I know you guys, college grads. I never went beyond seventh grade. Maybe you don't understand fellers like me, huh? Well, anyway, they say you listen. God damn it, who listens anyways? Nobody I ever heard of. So, you listen. You're goin' to get an earful, mister. You and your college!

"I never had a chance. First thing, after school, I get a job. Know what comes then? The goddamn Army, that's what. But maybe I'd better tell you about my folks.

"Dad never had a chance, neither. Worked twelve hours a day, six days a week. Then he fell

23

in bed. That's all. Eight of us kids. Don't know how he got them, workin' like that." Tab grunted. "Mom worked too. Doin' washin'. Could be they just passed in the doorway. What doorway? The whole place was full of us kids, doorways too.

"The priest comes around and says, 'Why aren't the children in school?' Mom says, 'Father, they work around, just like Joe and me.' And the priest looks sad, and he's no well-fed specimen, either. Thin and young, and pale like a ghost. And he says, 'Our Lord worked around too.' Kind of silly, wasn't he, the priest? Christ knew He was God, but what do we know? The priest says, 'He was a carpenter.' Stupid answer.

"My name ain't really Tab. It's Timothy. A saint. I ain't no saint. Ain't been to confession or Mass for years. What for? What's a guy like me got to live for? Here I am, thirty-two, and putter around in a factory, can't even operate a machine. There's automation too. No use for us guys any more. Where they goin' to sweep us?" He chuckled. "Under the carpet? Maybe."

The soft white light beamed down on him, and he looked at it and shifted uneasily. "Oh, they tell us they'll train us! They'll make jobs for us. What do I need trainin' for, at my age? All I want is just to work, like always, and earn a decent livin'. No fancy stuff. Hell, come to think of it, why work, anyways? Factory stiff. A nobody. Kids yellin' for television, and I'm loaded up to here in debt for the refrigerator and washin' machine. Only fun I get is goin' for a glass of beer and talkin' with the other guys who got gripes too.

"About my folks. Dad dies when I'm fourteen.

24

Law says I got to go to school until I'm sixteen. I got a paper route, and I wash cars at the gas station. And there's this chick. Dad's a factory bum too, but she's got lipstick and jeans and a big fat can. I met her when I was seventeen and she's fifteen. Same class together, with Sister Mary Dominic, and is *she* tired! No wonder, all those kids. Oh, we ain't hungry. Who goes hungry, with the Welfare and all that stuff? We got our orange juice and vitamins and hot lunches and milk. We're big as horses; make our folks look like midgets. Sister Mary Dominic's half our size. Guess she never had a chance, neither."

Tab paused, and his big tanned face darkened and became more uneasy. He shifted impatiently on the marble chair. "Nobody's ever got a chance," he muttered. "Hey, you, behind that curtain, what chance did you have? Your folks had money, eh? Sent you to college? Sure! So you can sit there and listen to jerks like me and smile to yourself. We ain't nothin' to you. Anyway, you're paid to listen, ain't you? All the time in the world!

"About my folks. Mom keeps up the laundry, then all at once she dies. I'm seventeen. Never did know why she died. Eight of us, some younger than me, some older. Who cares? We get the hell out. I've got this job, and it pays me fifteen dollars a week, spare time. Not enough to live on. Then I go into this factory. New war's on. Make big money. All the money there is. War's going to last forever. That's what the foreman says. Then they pull me out for the Army. What chance does a guy have?

"I don't know what the hell I'm doin' here talk-

25

in' to you. But Fran—she's my wife, she's the one with the jeans and the lipstick and the big fat can —she tells me to go talk to you. What've I got to lose, shootin' off my mouth? At least *you* listen. What're you doin' behind that curtain, anyways? Listenin'! What d'you know about jerks like me who never had a chance?

"So I'm in the Army. What's the Korean war about? Who cares? Had a hell of a good time. Tokyo. All those places. If I'd had an education I could've stayed there in one of these houses, with maids and everything, and big pay from the gov'-mint. But I never had a chance, and they shipped me back, and there's this chick, waitin' for me. Oh, we fooled around. She's kind of pretty, if you like a kid who shows all of her upper teeth and her tongue and squints her eyes and tries to look like Hollywood and the movies. First thing you know, there's a kid comin' along. I wanted to duck the whole thing, but she brings around a priest, not the young, sick kind I used to know, but a big guy, and he won't stand for no foolin'. Big hams on him; like to break your neck if you say anythin'. Well, anyway, we got to get married. And then this priest says, 'What about the G. I. Bill?' Well, what about it? Here I am, married, though I don't want to be, and a kid comin', and my dad had three of us at my age. Who wants to get educated and sit around in an office drawin' maybe thirty bucks a week? I can go in a factory and get three times that, with fringe benefits. So I go, and Fran howls, and I slam her in the jaw, and the cops come and I get a suspended sentence. Nobody made a big noise when Dad slammed Mom around, except

26

us kids. Jesus, how we howled! I remember I bit Dad in the leg, and I was only four then."

Tab grinned, then scowled. "Why'd he hit her, anyway? She was doin' her best, wasn't she? And she half his size. Wonder what makes people do the lousy things they do. Maybe they never had a chance."

Tab looked belligerently around the room, one hand clenched on his knee. But there was no one there. The light flowed down upon him, warm and soft. "Hell," he muttered.

"Well, now I got three kids, and they want everythin'. Fran says they can't have it. She's got this budget. Baby-sits, too, as if she ain't got enough work to do without that. She thinks money in the bank's somethin' everybody should have. Why? Money's made to spend and have a good time on. But not Fran. Come to think of it, she ain't so pretty any more. Gettin' old, though she's only thirty. Maybe that's old for a dame, I guess. And she's always readin' and listening to newscasts. Hates sports. Ain't that somethin'?

"What do I get? I can tell you this: I get more than the schoolteachers, even if I'm only a factory stiff! Yes sir! Think that one over. Is Fran satisfied? Oh no. Not my old girl. She wants me to go to this automation school the factory has. Learn somethin', she says. And she shoves her damn books at me from the library. You know somethin'? Women make me sick. Always tryin' to be bigger than they are, and not the way you think, either! They never know a guy don't have a chance these days."

The warm and mutely lit room was silent. Tab

27

glared at the curtain. "One of those headshrinkers, huh? Listen and then write books about us poor jerks who never had had a chance. What'm I here for? Well, I've had all there is. I'm pullin' out. I'm on my way, and Fran and the kids can go on Welfare. Why not? That's what taxes are for, ain't they? Anyway, the way they're throwin' the atom bombs around, there won't be no world soon, anyway. Or maybe it's the hydrogen bomb. Or missiles. So why not live it up? Well, Fran seems to know what I've got in mind, and she says, 'Go to that place Mr. Godfrey built.' I say no, and she begs and cries, and what the hell can you do with women? Hey, are you a priest back there? I hear you're a Jew. Know what I think about Jews? There's this guy in the Army—— Hell, who cares? I'm filled right up to here, never havin' a chance or anythin'. One guy tells me the Jews've got all the money cornered. And the factory's full of niggers and Puerto Ricans. A white man don't have a chance these days."

He scowled surlily at the curtain. "Maybe you're thinkin' about the bonus I got from the state. That wasn't Fran's business. Had a good time on it; four hundred dollars. A guy's got a right to have a good time once in his life, don't he? What've I got to live for? Bet you never saw a lathe or a saw or a hammer in your life. What do you guys know about workin'? I work forty hours a week, and then I fall on my face." He paused, then grinned sheepishly. "Hell, my dad worked twelve hours a day, six days a week. The sucker. Wonder how he did it. Yeh, I wonder how he did it. Did you ever work twelve hours a day?"

28

The silence of the room appeared to enlarge and to hold him. He rubbed his jaw. "Hell, Fran ain't a bad kid. I'm not complainin'. It's just I never had a chance. Maybe Fran didn't, neither. She worked, too, in this diner. And now there's these kids. Molly's kind of cute, but the two boys just yell all the time." He laughed shortly. "Just like me and my brothers yelled. No wonder Dad and Mom used to clip us. But Molly's kind of cute. She was real cute in that Christmas bit at St. Aloysius. An angel. She looks kind of like Fran. Yeh. Come to think of it, women don't have such a hot time, do they? They get pretty and then they marry——"

He looked at the curtain. He was a big and burly young man; he stood up, his hands hanging at his sides, his face thrust forward. He said softly, "And then they marry jerks like me. That's what they do. They marry jerks like me."

His face changed, became heavy and sober. He rubbed his chin again. He said, "Poor Mom. Poor Fran. Poor Molly." He moved toward the curtain and said earnestly, "But I guess you don't have a mother now, do you, and I guess you don't know about women."

The curtain did not move. He looked at it uncertainly. Then he cried out, "Why don't you talk? Why don't you tell me what to do? I've got Fran and Molly, haven't I?"

He ran to the curtain and pushed the button savagely. The curtains rolled apart swiftly, and the inner light rushed out upon him. He looked, and stood in utter silence. Then his eyes filled, and the tears ran down his full cheeks as if he were a child again.

29

"Yeh," he whispered. "I guess you do know about women, about Mom and Fran and Molly. Yeh, I guess you do. Say, do you think there's a chance for me? I mean, a real chance for jerks like me? I sort of forgot about Mom. But you didn't, did you?"

His hand stretched forward, and the sullen and hostile face softened. "I guess I'd better be goin'," he said. "It's too late for Mom now, but Fran's waitin'. You won't forget me, will you? You won't forget? I'm goin' to that automation school to-morrow. I'm sorry I said you don't know nothin' about work. You sure worked hard, didn't you? All your life. For jerks like me."

SOUL THREE

The Despised and Rejected

". . . despised and rejected from among men."

It was an extremely hot day, but the air was pure and fresh and cool in the sitting room. The young man entering was dressed in black. He paused on the threshold as the bronze door began to close on his heels. He glanced about at the waiting men and women and waited, himself, for the inevitable stare of repudiation or disgust. But the others appeared not to notice him. They were sunk in engrossing thoughts of their own. He hated himself for apologetically tiptoeing to the slit in the wall, where he dropped a sealed note. Then he threw back his shoulders, carefully chose a chair far from the others, and sat down and waited. The others did not look at him. He picked a magazine from a table and riffled through the pages. He could not concentrate. He lifted his head, and though he coolly scrutinized the waiting room his eyes were timid.

He wondered what the man behind that door would think of his note. He smiled disdainfully. What did it matter what anyone thought now? Why had he come here? A chance word, a half-remembered line in the newspaper? This was no place for him.

If only there were some pictures on the stark white walls! But no. A man, apparently, was to be left solely with his thoughts. Now, that was very pleasant! His thoughts. They stared back at him from the shining surfaces like questions. He tried to answer them angrily; they remained. He tried to keep his anger, but it became a question too. He studied his companions furtively. Why were they here? What troubles did that rosy fat man in the fine summer silk suit have, or that young woman with her pretty white face and light hair? Or that young man with the brief case at his knee? Or that comfortable matron who was knitting? What agony could they have, compared with his?

The chime sounded, and one by one they rose and went into the mysterious room behind the oaken door. The young man strained to hear voices, one complaining, the other complacently soothing. There were no voices. Was it a chapel in there? If so, he would stalk out. There was no place in a chapel for him, or in hypocrisy, or breezy common sense. He himself was a curse. He hated himself and hated those who hated him.

Then the chime sounded for him, and he started, looked about the empty room, and rose. He began to tiptoe, then put his feet down solidly and wished the carpet could register his step. He held his good hat in his hand. He stalked to the oaken door and pushed it open and saw only gentle light and the marble chair with its velvet cushions, and the curtained alcove. Seeing the latter, he smiled grimly. A psychiatrist, as he suspected, or one of those busy social workers, or a clergyman. He sat down.

"Good afternoon," he said in a beautiful voice. There was no answer, but all at once he felt that his greeting had been returned. Never mind! He was tired of their politeness, their vigorous pretending that he was not what he was.

"I am a Negro," he said coldly. "I am twenty-five years old. My name is Gideon Cowles, and I was born in this city. I was graduated from the university here four years ago. With honors." He paused. "I work in the kitchen of the best hotel—as a part-time cook and full-time dishwasher."

The room waited. He could feel peace and alertness about him, and a listening. "Oh yes," he said, and tried to laugh. "They call you 'the Man who Listens.' It is engraved over the door. Splendid. I am glad you are listening. No one ever listened to me before, not even in the orphan asylum where I was brought up. Not even a clergyman. I hope you are not offended—if you are a clergyman. I know how busy you all are; there aren't enough of you. Sometimes I wonder if that isn't the trouble with the world. There are not enough clergymen." He bent his head and considered this with a kind of wonder.

"But then," he said in a thinking voice, "who wants to be a clergyman these days? You are poorly paid; you are held in low esteem; you have no influence and no money. You don't know any powerful politicians. You go through the streets of your parish, calling to your flocks—who do not listen. Forgive me; I come of a poetic race. Did you know that Negroes are naturally poetic? Indeed they are.

"You clergymen call at the gates, and no one opens them for you. You cry in your pulpits, and they yawn. You speak of the Fatherhood of God and the Brotherhood of Man, and they nod, and go home to hate their neighbor. You go up and down, and no one hears your footsteps. Many of you are desperately poor—as Christ was poor—and no one cares. You stand at your altars and look at empty pews. You are a voice in the wilderness, and you may as well be voiceless. You offer Communion with your God, and the lips that take it are profane. You sing the Psalms of David, and the women think of the Sunday dinner and the men of baseball. The children wiggle and are restless; there is television waiting. There is a whole, evil, boisterous world outside your churches, ringing with bells and pounding with horns, and shattering with drums and whining with wheels, and shouting with silly bouncing voices. What effect has your voice against all these? No more than a bird's call.

"What do your people want? They want everything. Except you. And your God. You are despised and rejected among men."

He put his hands over his eyes. "As I am despised and rejected among men."

The silence waited. The young man sighed and dropped his slender dark hands on his knees. "My own people laugh at me. The university graduates among us are sour and disgruntled. Do you blame

34

them? They have no place to go with their degrees. Except to the meanest work. What nice house will shelter them? What intelligent white man will welcome them and drink and eat with them? Many of them become Communists, out of bitterness, because the Communists lie to them and assure them that in the coming Soviet world they will be equal. Equal to what, to whom? We are the despised and the rejected. We know what liars men are.

"Do you know what it means to be despised and rejected, turned away, laughed at, cursed, hated? Did any man ever treat you like this—as I have been treated? Did you ever feel a blow or see a look of disgust? Did you ever hear catcalls and jeers? Did any man say your people were less than animals? Were you ever driven away or refused food or shelter? Did you ever cry to your God, asking why He had forsaken you?"

Gideon stood up and cried aloud, striking his hands together in the utmost despair.

"Did you ever feel your own blood on your face and in your hands? Worse, did you ever feel your heart bleed helplessly? Did you look for one single accepting face? I tell you, I can't live any longer!"

The silence hovered over him, and the light, like a presence of pity and love and understanding. He began to cry helplessly.

"I'm sorry," he stammered. "You are a clergyman, a preacher. I can feel it, even from behind those curtains. I've insulted you. I'm sorry. But still, as a white man, you can't know what it means to be despised and rejected."

He moved slowly to the curtains and timidly

touched the button. The curtains rolled back, and he saw the light and who stood in the light.

He burst into deep sobs. He extended his hands.

"Forgive me," he groaned. "For you know, don't you?"

He waited humbly. Then he whispered, "I've always known that I wanted to be a clergyman, to speak to my people with the authority of faith and with the love of God. But I was angry against man —and God. How could I tell my people of the goodness of God when they daily saw the hatefulness of man? There is a theological seminary here and they won't reject me—you've made me see my own heart and what I really wanted, and where I was needed, for you've never despised us."

He smiled, and the smile was now neither haughty nor timid. It was the smile of an accepted son whose father has always loved him.

SOUL FOUR

The Betrayed

I do not know this man you are talking about.
Mark 14:71

The man who sat in the marble chair was neither middle-aged nor old. His winter tweeds were good, if worn; his shoes were handmade, if beginning to crack. His expensive tie showed signs of constant ironing. He sat with dignity, his gray hair smooth, his quiet face rigid and bitter.

Then he smiled with faint contemptuousness at the curtains. All this childish superstition! This amateur psychiatry, this self-diagnosis! He, Clive Summers, knew all the psychiatric jargon and the proclaimed methods. You "talked" out your problems to an allegedly sympathetic ear—paid for by the expensive hour—and you found your own solution in the babblings of your own tongue. The new confessional! The most modern way of discovering your foolish self, as if it were precious! Hadn't he tried it? He had tried three thousand

37

dollars' worth, and God knows he couldn't afford that much waste of money now. It had been a long time, in fact, since he could afford much of anything. And of curse there were Celia's chronic doctors' bills for her arthritis, and there was his idiot son—— Well no, George wasn't quite an idiot, but pretty close, with his enthusiasms.

The white and utterly silent room waited. Mr. Summers looked about him curiously. Where did the heat come from, this harsh winter day, and the light? He could hear no ventilating fans and see no warm-air outlets. He had never known John Godfrey, a small-time lawyer who had never entered through the door of the Summers Metals Company. He would not have gotten past the reception clerk, except with a subpoena, if even that. Yet he had had the money to build this trumpery pseudo-temple and create this maudlin religious atmosphere. For whimpering housewives and failures and clerks and petty mystics who needed an ear as others need a laxative. Well, then . . .

He spoke in his tight and careful voice. "Good afternoon."

No one answered. He said, "I am Clive Summers. If you are a resident of this city you'll recognize the name; everybody knows me or of me."

He looked at the curtains, and squared shoulders which had taken on a tendency to sag these past five years. The curtains remained shut and still.

Mr. Summers thought of the psychiatrists he had known socially and the one he had known both socially and professionally. His thin cheeks reddened. One of them was behind that damned curtain! Could he be trusted? You could not trust a man unless you had bought him. And often, not even then.

"I hope," he said coldly, "that everything that is said in here is confidential? By the way, I have deposited twenty dollars in your—offering—box, with the suggested note, which no doubt you have had time to read now. The money is not meant as an offering, which I understand is never requested. But, as I have paid for your time as a professional consultant, you are ethically obliged not to reveal confidences of your—patients. Not that I am, in any sense of the word, a 'patient.' It is just that I know that I am going blind, in spite of what the doctors say."

There was no answer. Mr. Summers wished to be irritated, but he found himself, instead, relaxing in the chair. But he spoke warningly. "I have ways of discovering who betray my confidences, I assure you."

Again he waited. Mr. Summers laughed shortly. "'The Man who Listens.' Who does, except a paid psychiatrist who hardly regards you as human if you have problems? You are a case then; you are a 'disturbed mind.' You are 'emotionally involved.' Therefore, not quite sound. You see, I know all about your profession. Well, listen."

But he could not speak for a while. He listened for the scratch of a pencil in this profound quiet, the rustle of paper, the shift of feet, the creak of a chair. There was nothing. No rumble of traffic reached this room, no footstep, no voice. He sat in a silence that was like eternity. His clenched hands loosened.

He said, and it was easier to speak now: "I am going to destroy a man. Utterly and completely destroy him. So thoroughly destroy him that he'll have to leave this city, and penniless, if I have my way. It's possible that a man such as he is will kill himself when I reach him, which will be soon. I hope so! That will be the final pleasure, the complete satisfaction. Yes, I hope so. For you see, he betrayed me."

He looked at his watch. "I assume twenty dollars will pay for at least half an hour? If not, you may send me your bill." He spoke arrogantly, but the arrogance fell into the quiet as ineffectually as a feather. "I still live on Humberson Avenue." He paused. "But not much longer, I am afraid. It is going to be sold for—for—taxes." Now his voice broke with despair.

"Celia and I built that house. She was a schoolteacher, and therefore had very little money. I was a young chemical engineer, working for thirty-five dollars a week. It was the Depression then. We were fortunate, in a way: we had a little flat, and we ate enough, and we had just enough clothing. Just enough. We both hated poverty. Do you know what it means to be poor? Hopelessly poor? Our parents were that poor. We know what poverty is, grinding, black, crushing. The majority of men don't mind it, because they have no imagination. But Celia and I had imagination. On Sunday afternoons we'd walk on Humberson Avenue— it's never deteriorated—and we'd look at a few empty lots and plan for the day when we'd have one of them and build our own house on it. We planned every room, the color of every wall, the trees in the rear gardens, the exact shade of stone we'd use, the fountain, the bedrooms, the nursery, the hall with its great chandelier.

"It took me many years, but we finally fulfilled our dream. I had invented a new metallurgic process—I won't bore you with the details, which would mean nothing to you. I had many offers for the patent, but I kept it: I believed in it. I started out with a small shop, employing one man besides myself. Up to five years ago I employed five hundred. We had our house, we had one child, our son George, who is also a chemical engineer. He never would go in with me, and it was a terrible disappointment. He's a fool, full of enthusiasms. He says he wants to begin as I began."

Mr. Summers' voice broke again, and he did not know that there was a sound of reluctant pride in it.

"Celia and I couldn't afford a family until it was almost too late. All our savings went into my first shop and into equipment. We wanted children, but there was no time, no money. We needed every penny. Celia continued to teach, and I worked day and night, and I'd forget to sleep or eat. Then Celia was suddenly thirty-eight and I was forty-one, and we had our lot and we had the money for our house. And we were rich! It was only on Celia's birthday, when she was thirty-eight, that we had time, all at once, to realize the fact that we were rich.

"We also realized that Celia wasn't young any longer, and if we were to have any children at all we must begin immediately. And so we had George, but Celia could have no more children. She almost died when George was born; she was a little old to be having her first child. The house wasn't quite finished when we moved in. But women are sentimental. Celia wanted George to be born in our own house, for which we'd worked so many years."

He chuckled dryly, then started at the sound and put his carefully tended fingers to his lips, as if he had uttered an obscenity. But he shook his head over and over, musingly, and his dry smile lifted the corners of his bitter mouth. "It was winter, and only four rooms could be heated; the entire equipment wasn't yet in, and the plaster was still wet, and there was no wallpaper or paint. It was, in a way, like the life we'd had as children, huddled together for warmth, a big black old stove temporarily heating the bedroom, a bare table in the kitchen, no curtains at the windows. Makeshift. I never heard Celia laugh so much. She never laughed again quite like that."

He laughed himself, a rustling murmur like the crackle of parchment. He forgot where he was, remembering. Then he came to himself and stared at the shut curtains. He said a little huskily, "You're very patient, I see. Thank you. I can't remember when I've talked like this. I was always so busy, too busy for conversation. It must have been lonely for Celia, even with the clubs she joined after we became rich, and her community activities, and only one child who was cared for by experts, No illiterate nursemaids, you see. Yes, it must have been lonely."

He paused, struck and frowning, and shook his head again. "That's a stupid remark," he said. "Celia now had everything she'd ever dreamed of: furs, cars, leisure, effortless living, travel. Of course I was too busy to travel much with her; she had an older sister, a widow, and she would travel with Ethel. Then Ethel died; that was about ten years ago. And then Celia had no one."

Again he paused, and now he shifted violently on the chair. "Nonsense. I must be losing my mind. Celia had everything. And everyone. Friends, house buzzing with women's meetings, the church affairs, the Philharmonic Women's Committee, the various hospital boards. Of course Celia was always a little shy; 'the schoolteacher's personality,' I would say to her. It was hard for her to mingle easily. Then of course she was at some disadvantage. All the other women had been in these things from girlhood, and Celia was a late arrival, and I believe there was some social snobbery—— People are fools, aren't they? But I suppose you know that only too well in your practice. Fools."

The word echoed back from the gleaming white walls like an accusation. Mr. Summers said hurriedly, "Celia began to develop arthritis, or perhaps it was neuritis. At any rate, it is hard for her to walk much now, and she's only sixty-four. Damn those doctors! They can talk about miracle drugs and new treatments, but, so far as I can see, people are as frequently and mysteriously sick as they were when I was a boy. Celia spends a lot of time in bed now, poor girl. And——" He hesitated, then spoke in a shamed voice. "We have only a maid of all work, as we used to call them,

43

and she only part time. We can't afford even that now."

He waited for a superior murmur from behind the curtains, a condescension. But there was no sound. However, Mr. Summers became suddenly and acutely aware of a deep listening, a weighing, a kind measuring, a sympathy. He took off his glasses and rubbed them, for they had dimmed. "I hope," he said a little hoarsely, "that I'm not going to lose my eyesight into the bargain. That would just top everything, wouldn't it?" He coughed, and the cough was like a sob.

Then his words rushed out. "I wish I could do something for Celia! Damn it, do you know that I didn't really see her for nearly twenty-five years, until just recently? Now you'll think I'm out of my mind. I mean that I was always too busy to 'see' her. She was just Celia to me. Perhaps it was six months ago or less when I 'saw' Celia. It was a shock to me. Sixty-four isn't a great age now, you know, what with vitamins and exercise and beauty parlors. But when I saw Celia, she was old, very old. Not so much physically——" He stopped. "What in God's name am I talking about! 'Not so much physically.' Of course it was physically! Her hair was dyed, and her skin was smooth— you know all those creams women use—and her body was slender. But she was old." He stopped. "Even older than I. And that's a damned funny thing. She's three years younger. Of course women age earlier. But there was something strange about it. It was as if Celia had become lifeless. That's the word. Lifeless. And I had the peculiar sensation that she'd been that way for a long time. God! I must really be going out of my mind! Or blind."

His voice rose, became harsh and brutal. "I can see now. It was all that worry over me. Celia's afraid. She's afraid of being poor again. And that's what Henry Fellowes did to me—to Celia. He made us poor again. Poor Celia. Poor Celia!"

He stood up in his powerful hate and rage and began to walk up and down the room, his footsteps echoing on the marble floor. The turmoil of his spirit filled the room.

"I don't know why I've been blabbering like this, when the most important thing in my life is still unsaid. What has Celia to do with it, or George, that young idiot? I had no intention of telling you about Celia and George—wasting your time! If I hadn't stopped myself, I'd be telling you now that I never even saw the gardens we planted. They were pictured in that big national magazine; Celia was so proud of them; she worked side by side with the gardeners. George and Celia stood there together in the photographs, and I thought to myself—you can see how things had affected me—'Is that actually my son, George, near Celia, with his arm around her shoulder?' I didn't recognize him at first. I hadn't 'seen' George for years, not really 'seen' him. There was never any time for anything but work, but George had everything I could give him. Everything. Ungrateful, too. He never once thanked me. He's been pouting for years because I didn't have the time to go to Boston when he was graduated from Harvard. Children are very ungrateful these days. I tried to explain to him that I had a government contract, but he shrugged it off. Now he has a government contract—a very small one, no importance—himself——"

He took off his glasses and wiped them vigorously. "Damn it! Am I getting cataracts? Everything seems a little dim."

He sat down in the chair with determination. "I'm taking up too much of your time. Just send me your bill. It's very relieving, though, to talk. I haven't really talked to anyone for years. I was brought up in an age when a man valued every hour and knew he must accomplish something. I remember what I learned in Sunday school about the talents the king gave his servants, and how he damned the one who was afraid to invest the talent he was given and buried it in the ground—where it certainly didn't breed other talents! You must utilize every minute." He stopped. "And now I can utilize nothing."

His hands made fists. "Henry Fellowes. I didn't tell you. He was the first man I took on. He was my partner, a school chum; was graduated when I was graduated. Chemical engineer, like myself. (By the way, did I tell you that I received an 'E' from the government during the war? Where is that flag now? I don't know, and I don't care.)"

His voice became deep, almost groaning. "'E' for excellence. What excellence? I'm getting old too. Never mind. Henry Fellowes. You don't need the details. I trusted Henry, more than a brother. My partner. Worked together, denying ourselves everything. Together, we became rich. Henry made a mess of his life. Divorced one stupid woman after another; five of them. They only

46

wanted his money. I'd try to tell him. 'Marry somebody like Celia,' I'd say. But no. Henry had been poor, as Celia and I had. He wanted glittering women, all teeth and flounce. He was like a kid who has no money but stares through the window of a candy store. And when he gets some money he runs in and gorges. And makes himself sick. Henry isn't a fool, not normally. But those women of his! Bleached, hard, singing, chattering, flashing. He must have a vulgar streak in him somewhere. He couldn't have enough of the bitches."

Mr. Summers laughed briefly. "It's very funny. He thought, each time he married, that the woman would become like Celia—I suppose. Settle down in a nice house and have children. They never did, of course. They wanted his money, and rich furs and jewels and travel and dancing. And lovers. He always found out. But he had a juvenile personality. Celia wanted to help him, to introduce him to friends of hers, lonely widows. I told her, 'Mind your own business, Celia. A man always knows what he wants. Henry wouldn't be interested in your well-bred friends.' I was right, of course. Henry wanted something they call 'glamour.' " Mr. Summers paused. "At least I think he wanted that. He'd never had any gaiety in his life when he was young. He had no discrimination. He had no one like Celia to give him a sense of values."

He became aware of what he had said, and stared blankly. Then he frowned, and his face blackened. He struck the arm of the marble chair with his fist.

"What has all this to do with anything? I had no intention of telling you all this rot. All you need to know is that Henry's paying alimony to at least five women, all childless. Such women are expensive. They're like leeches—on Henry. Sucking his blood. Naturally it serves him right. But he was always the hopeful, buoyant type, like a kid. And then it happened, inevitably. I had pneumonia five years ago, a bad siege. I was out for five months, then we went to Montego Bay so I could recover. When I came back I found that Henry had swindled me, ruined me, practically sold me out. He had a team of very shrewd lawyers. The details don't matter. What does matter is that he betrayed me, his friend, the one who gave him a start, who helped him to become rich in the first place."

Mr. Summers started forward in the chair, his face fierce, yet wounded and bewildered.

"When I asked Henry to come in with me he was making twenty-five dollars a week. He never did have any sense of direction. But we were old friends. He was like a child. 'Be a partner with me,' I said, 'and we'll do big things together.' He was doubtful. 'We'll have the whole world,' I said. 'I'm counting on you, Henry, to help me establish something.' I must have reached him finally, for he looked at me trustfully. 'You mean that you want me?' he said. 'More than anything else,' I told him. 'Come with me.'

"He did. And then he betrayed me. The details don't matter. Now I have less than five thousand dollars in the bank. I have no company—my company. All my friends have deserted me. I'm all

48

alone. Betrayed. By Henry, whom I trusted, on whom I built. Do you know what I heard recently? He was in one of those clubs I formerly belonged to but which I can't afford now. Someone said to him, 'What's become of Clive Summers, your partner? He was your partner, wasn't he?'

"And he said, 'Clive Summers? Clive Summers? Oh, Clive Summers. I don't know.' And then he walked away. That's what someone told me. He didn't even know me, after all these years, and after what I'd done for him! He actually implied he hadn't even known me!" Mr. Summers again beat the arms of his chair with his fists. "He hadn't even known me, the man he betrayed!"

He stood up and shouted: "Do you think they believed him? No! One of my old friends—he doesn't know me now—said, 'Why, you and Clive were in partnership for years! Wherever I saw you, I saw him.' And he denied it. We weren't friends; it was just a loose business association. Only an association, in passing. Who did he think he was deceiving? Henry Fellowes. Why, I loved him as if he'd been my brother; we couldn't have been closer." He said in a lower voice, almost whispering, "We couldn't have been closer."

Mr. Summers walked almost within touching distance of the immovable curtains. "But what do you know about betrayal?" he challenged. "Oh, in an academic sense, no doubt. As one of the facets of the human personality. But did anyone betray you? Do you think it was just the money he defrauded me of? No. It was his denial of me, his desertion. That was the worst, the most terrible thing. He'd not even known me!"

The curtains did not stir. The room seemed to smile deeply in its whiteness. Mr. Summers cried, "What do you know? About betrayal? Who ever betrayed you, you, smug behind that curtain?"

He plunged his finger on the button, and the curtains whirled aside in the overwhelming light. Mr. Summers stepped back, staring, and then he bent, as if broken. He could not look away from what he saw.

After a long time he said, "Yes. Yes, of course. You know all about betrayal. Who, more than you, should know? Forgive me."

His legs felt boneless and weak, and he fell to his knees and covered his face with his hands. Another long time passed. He could feel the light all about him. Then he spoke again, whisperingly, and with pauses.

"I'm sorry for Henry. You see, I can ruin him now. I have the facts. At first I was too sick and stunned. Now I have the facts and the lawyers. I can have him prosecuted, thrown into jail, for fraud and misappropriation of funds, and a dozen other things. But I am not going to do it.

"He has another wife, and I've heard she is worse than all the others, and he's desperate, even with the money he took from me by fraud and manipulation. He's almost out of his mind. Perhaps he's remorseful. After all, he is as old as I am. A man doesn't get younger. He must be lonely. He must be as lonely as Celia and George.

"Whatever Henry did, he must live with it. At least I'm clean of anything like that." Mr. Summers took his hands from his eyes. "Are you still

50

listening?" he asked humbly. "But you always listen, don't you? Aren't you ever tired?

"'As lonely as Celia and George.' That's a strange thing to think of, isn't it? I am beginning to remember Celia before we built that house. She used to laugh and sing in our little flat. She would agree with me that it would be wonderful to have that big house—someday. Do you know? I don't think she cared; she was just kind, and she went into the dream with me because she thought that was what I wanted too. Perhaps I did, when I was younger. And then I had it. But I didn't see Celia any longer. I didn't even miss her. Until everything I had was gone. I didn't notice my son, with his governess and his tutor, and then his boarding schools, and then his university. I was proud of his reports, yes. But I never really saw him. I buried my one talent in the ground. I wonder if it is still there."

He dropped his hands. "There wasn't any time, no. Not for worthless things. There never was."

He stood up resolutely, like a young man. He laughed a little. "George has some radical idea about the conversion of energy through manipulation of metals. But you know more about these things than we do, don't you? He's tried to interest me. He's looking for a partner. I am going to be that partner with my five thousand dollars. I'm going to work in a shop again with a young man, and he's my son and he'll never betray me. Never. My son. My son will never betray me.

"I must go home now and tell Celia. I've just had the most peculiar idea. I think when I tell

51

Celia she'll get out of bed and she won't be sick any longer. I often wonder at the patience of good women. And your mother? Was she patient too? Yes, yes. She must be the most patient of all. Please give her my love."

SOUL FIVE

The Father's Business

*Did you not know that I must be about
My Father's business?*

Luke 2:49

"So, you listen, huh?" said Barney Lefkowitz heavily. "A doctor. One of them psychiatrists.
So, what's there to listen to? Me, I've been listening for forty years. I've got this butcher shop,
kosher. 'Barney for Beef.' That's what it says over
my door, just like your ad. Listen, I can pay. I
don't take anything from nobody, free. Worked
all my life, even in Russia. Ever been to Russia?
Communism. That's what they call it. This
schnook, Khrushchev. He's just one of the old
czars. Czar Alexander, Czar Nikita. What's the
difference? Different names, same people. That's
what I try to tell my customers. But no. They
read the newspapers. Me, I don't have time."

He was a short stout man with a round bald
head, a big red face, and large, intense blue eyes.

"Yeh. I've been listening. To my customers. Neighborhood store. Once I hear this opera about a feller called Figaro. Figaro this, Figaro that, Figaro, Figaro! That's me. I hear all their troubles, mostly the women. Have they got troubles! Who hasn't? The ones don't have troubles you can count on the fingers of one hand. But nobody's got troubles like me."

He pulled out his handkerchief and wiped his brow. "I got real troubles. Only thing that's good about it, my wife's dead. If she was here, it'd be worse. I'd have her to worry about too. You see, it's our boy, Morris."

He shifted weightily in the chair. Again he wiped his forehead, as if he were weeping at every pore.

"Every Yiddisher mother wants her boy to be a doctor or a lawyer. A dentist, maybe. But a doctor's the best. We saw them in the old country, in their carriages, with horses, and coats with fur collars, and fur gloves. A doctor. He's like a rabbi, see? One's for the soul, the other's for the body. Don't know which one gets hurt more easy. (You a psychiatrist, huh, like a lot of bright Jewish boys?) Well, that's new. Morris, he's just a specialist. Cancer. All those big machines, like a factory. Thirty-five years old. Never got married. Too busy taking care of everybody else."

He sighed and looked about the white and shining room. "Kind of like a temple," he said. He glanced down at the hat on his plump knee. "Well, I hear you can come in here and you listen. All the time in the world.

"Bertha and me, we work so Morris can go to

this doctor college. Bertha works by the store too. Every cent in the bank, for Morris and the college. A nice boy, Morris. A good boy. Even in school the teachers say he's a good boy. A fine scholar. Not like me. Never a word that ain't good. No screaming, like other kids. And even when he's little, he come in here for the meat and takes it to the customers. Polite like a king, and some of those women——!

"I should complain! If it wasn't for the women, Morris wouldn't have gone to the college. They ask every year, 'How is the bank account for Morris?' No, we don't complain. Times are bad, we give credit. When times get better, they pay. That's poor people. There's this big fancy store on Shelton Street where the rich ladies go. They pay when they think of it, and they don't think often. Money don't mean anything to them.

"Maybe you got all the time there is. I don't. I got to be back for the phone. Well, it was three days before Morris graduated, with that funny hat they put on. And Bertha's shopping for a new dress, and this kid is driving and he runs her down, and that's all. She says to me in the hospital, 'Never mind, Barney. You go to the graduation like I was there. And maybe I will be too.' So, after the funeral—maybe you don't know about this, but I'm Orthodox. We bury the dead before sunset. Morris is eight hundred miles away, and he can't get a plane for two days. The holidays. Easter. Well. What does it matter? Bertha wasn't there anyway. What an angel. So, we do it the way she wanted; she had a right to say, didn't she? And I was there, and after the graduation Morris

55

breaks down in my arms, and then we go to the temple and he says kaddish.

"Morris, he wants to be a cancer specialist. Eight more years. I work, and he works, and it's eight years. Then I say, 'What about a nice girl, Morris?' And he only smiles. He has work to do. He don't have an office; he goes in one of them big hospitals. Intern. Another two years. Then he's on the staff, with a nice salary.

"You should see my boy, Morris. Dedicated, like they say. Eyes like a prophet. 'We'll have a breakthrough, Papa,' he says, all excited. 'Then we'll know what causes it and how to cure it. You should see the kids who come to this hospital, Papa. People think cancer's just for old people, but do you know something? More kids die of cancer before they are fifteen than of all the other diseases put together! We need more money. There's this cyclotron, and the isotopes. We'll have a break-through.'

"You'd think he was doing it all by himself. He never stops working. His salary gets bigger. He gives most of it to the cancer funds. I wouldn't take a cent, though he offers. What do I have now but Morris? And I keep hoping he'll find a nice girl and there'll be kids. A man needs a grandson. I keep hinting. And he just smiles and talks cyclotron and the need for money. Hospitals always need money. Why, Morris says, what people spend on popcorn every year would build big cancer hospitals! Popcorn! That's a funny thing. Death— and popcorn. When you think of it, it seems like it was always that way, don't it?"

He cocked his head. He thought that he had

heard a murmuring, sad assent. "You say something?" he said politely.

He waited. His hands were wet, and his face, and he scrubbed them with his handkerchief.

"I don't know why I'm wasting your time, Doctor. You hear these things every day. It's an old story. It don't get any better, though, does it?

"And now Morris is thirty-five. When he comes home for the holidays a year ago I notice he looks sick, but he's smiling. Sick and thin. Like he has consumption. I get scared. They don't feed him right in the hospital. 'No, Papa,' he says, 'I'm perfectly all right.' And he talks cancer some more. You'd think there wasn't anything else in the world. But I think about Morris. And so I get this young fellow to be by the store and I go to Morris' hospital. I know the old doctor there, chief of staff. I say to him, 'My boy's sick. Tell me. Don't keep me in suspense.'

"The doctor's an old friend. Loves Morris like a son. And so he tells me."

The room was silent. Then suddenly it was broken by faint cries and the sound of weeping. They went on for a long time.

"It's what they call occupational hazard," stammered Barney. "Excuse me. A grown man shouldn't cry like a baby. But Morris has got cancer; in the brain. They can't do nothing about it. All those cyclotrons and X rays. Maybe Morris got careless. Nobody knows. The cancer's slow-growing, they tell me. Maybe a few months more, maybe another year. They pat me on the back, and the old doctor breaks down, and I got to comfort him! Funny, eh, and Morris is my boy!

"Morris? He's still alive. I go to see him last week, and I says to him, 'Morris, come home. You look like a skeleton. Come home with Papa, Morris.' And he says, 'Papa, don't you know I must be about God's business?' That's what he says. And what can I say?

"I can't sleep. The telephone's by my bed. I look at it in the store. Any day. Any minute. They don't know. And Morris is working in the hospital, like he's in good health. 'God's business!' Any minute. He'll work till he dies. Saving people. With all that pain! And knowing he's going to die. Any minute."

Barney folded his arms on his knees and bent his head upon them and moaned over and over. The light increased about him. He looked up, dazed.

Then he got to his feet. "Anyway, I feel better, just telling you, you a doctor, too. I've got to go back. Maybe there's a telephone call. Who knows? I tell you, it's like something bleeding away inside, waiting. Only a father can understand. You a father? Only a father, watching his son suffer, waiting for him to die. Because he lived for other people and not himself. You know something? I can't go to the temple now. I'm scared I'll start screaming."

Barney hesitated. He looked shyly at the curtains. And then at the button. Then slowly he approached the curtains and pushed the button.

The curtains flowed aside instantly, and Barney stepped back, trembling. He stood and looked, with the tears on his cheeks.

He said very gently, "Yes, I guess your father

58

knew what it was like. Just like me. Yes, I guess so. So, I guess I'm not alone, after all."

He gravely put on his hat. "I see, Landsman, that they put another kind of yarmilke on you, didn't they? They always do. They always do."

He went to the door, turned and looked at who stood in the light. "I guess, maybe, I'll go to see my rabbi. The store can wait. Even the telephone. God and me, we've got 'business' too."

SOUL SIX

The Magdalene

Wherefore I say to thee, her sins many as they are, shall be forgiven her, because she has loved much . . .

Luke 7:47

Mary Lanska came softly into the sitting room, carrying her flowers. It was almost midnight, and, as she hoped, there was no one else there. She dropped her little note in the box and sat down to wait. It was so warm and pleasant here, this Holy Saturday night before Easter. She looked at the flowers in their large porcelain holder with that funny sort of stuff, she thought, like cotton, they put in there to keep the water. She bent her head to smell the flowers. They had cost all her tips in the restaurant for the past week. Beautiful! She loved flowers. They were much better than a lot of people. She did not know the names of all of them, but she recognized daffodils and iris and white lilies and innocent fringed daisies. They exhaled a sweet deep perfume in the lighted quiet. She hugged them to her gently, kissed the cool lip of a lily. They had cost her a lot, but flowers were expensive at Easter. She hoped the man who listened in the other room liked flowers too. They were all she had to give him.

He must be a good man, she thought. She'd read about him in the papers. No one had ever seen him, or if they had they hadn't told. But he was very kind, and he never lectured anybody. All he did was listen. Well, that was enough; it was more than enough. He'd help her find out what to do. She was sure of it.

She sighed. It would be nice to go home to Mass tomorrow. But Father Stephen was dead now. Besides, he would be angry at her. She hadn't fulfilled her Easter duty for—how long? Ten years. Ten long years. How could she tell a priest that? Why, she was probably excommunicated by now! And she was afraid of the priests in this big city; they looked so sure and sharp and quick. Enough to scare a country girl to death. Very educated, not slow and easy and kind-looking like Father Stephen, who had all the time in the world to listen to you and help you. If she went to one of these big-city priests now—why, he'd probably drive her away! Not that she didn't deserve it, at that. He'd be right. Still, she wished everything could be O.K. Nothing had been O.K. since she was sixteen years old, when Mom died and Pa just disappeared and all the little kids were sent to the orphanage. Maybe they got adopted by nice people. She hoped so. She, their sister, hadn't anything to give them. She'd always wanted to have something to give, but it never happened that way. At least now she had these flowers for the Man who Listens.

She was twenty-eight years old, and plump and pretty, with thick yellow hair, light blue eyes, and a square, tender face full of delicate color. She did not know she was pretty. She had scoffed at Phil when he had told her, and at Francis. Francis. Tears came into her eyes, and she fumbled for her handkerchief. The chime sounded softly, and she got up and carried her flowers into the white and empty room.

She did not know what she had expected, but certainly not this suffused quiet, these white walls, the blue curtains over the alcove, the waiting marble chair. She sat down fearfully, clutching her flowers.

"I hope," she murmured, "that someone's here. They say someone always is. You, I guess. How could you be here all the time? Did you read my note?"

There was no sound; it was like a church when there was no one there. But all at once Mary knew she was not alone. She smiled tremulously.

"I shouldn't be here," she said. "Not a girl like me. You won't want me here when I tell you. My name's Mary Lanska. I sort of feel I should change it to Maggie or something. It's a crying shame my name's Mary."

A large tear, hot and burning, ran down her cheek. She gulped.

"It was after Mom died and the kids went to the orphanage. I was sixteen and kind of independent,

63

and I looked eighteen, almost. Mom was a good cook, and she taught me to keep house. So I got myself a job as a maid. Oh yes, that was in the little town where I come from, eighty miles from here. Rich people by the name of Mallon. He was a banker, Mr. Mallon, and owned practically everything in town. He wasn't a *good* man, in the way I mean it. I don't mean he drank or ran around—after all, he was kind of old, about fifty. And he didn't beat up his old lady, the way my pa beat up Mom, and he didn't wallop Phil around, either. But Phil—that's his son—was nineteen, and too big, I guess. Four girls in the family, but Phil was the only boy. I never liked any of them but Phil. He was the only decent one. I still say so!" And she lifted her square and dimpled chin firmly.

"No, Mr. Mallon wasn't *good!* Mean, and never smiled except at the bank when he had a good customer. He did a lot for his church, too, I heard, but you can't buy God, can you? Sister M. Benedict said God was the only thing you couldn't buy in this world. She was sure right!

"Well, anyway, Phil wasn't the strong type. So he didn't go away to school; he had a tutor and then went to the private school in the town. And then it was time for him to go to college. How old lady Mallon cried! You'd think Phil was going to his own funeral. And I cried, too, when I was alone at night. What would I do without Phil?

"For you see, Phil and I loved each other. We really loved each other. No one can tell me different, no sir!" She shook her head vigorously. "I loved him the minute I saw him. A real doll. Big and thin, with dark eyes like a girl's and thick black curly hair. And how he could talk! It made stars sparkle in your heart. When he kissed me for the first time—it was a few days after I started to work there—I thought I'd die. I really did."

The tears were coming faster now, but unheeded.

"No one in the world had ever kissed me before, except Mom, and that was when I was confirmed. No boy, no man. Nobody but Mom and Phil. I thought I'd die. Oh, I'd read the movie and romance magazines, and I knew all about love, even if I didn't get all the big words in the magazines. Why, it was better with Phil than I'd ever dreamed! It was like a dream, and I mean it."

Her voice dropped. "I guess it was all wrong, if you think about it, but nobody'd ever told me. Mom had too many of us to take care of; she never got around to it. Why, do you know, I was a big girl of sixteen, looking almost eighteen, and I didn't even know how a lady got a baby! Honest, I didn't. I just never thought of it; that shows you how stupid I was, with all the kids we had in the house. I never gave it a thought.

"Well, Phil started coming up to my room after everybody was in bed, and it was like a dream. I was so happy. I guess that was what it was—I was happy. I'd never been happy before. And in that little town they didn't keep kids in school until they were grown, the way they do now. Especially not kids like us. I left school when I was thirteen; Mom needed me. So all at once, there was Phil, and stars and being happy, and love. Sometimes I thought I'd burst, I was so happy.

"Well, still, I had a sort of idea after a while that this wasn't right. So I stopped going to confession. Anyway, Father Stephen was dead by then. I couldn't go to confession and say to the new priest, 'I think maybe I'm doing something wrong.' And then tell him. I was afraid he'd tell me I had to stop, and then I wouldn't be happy any more. I couldn't live without that happiness, and Phil, and him stroking my hair on the pillow and telling me I was pretty and that I was all his love and there was never going to be anyone else. And I'm sure he meant it! Yes sir, I'm sure of that! We were going to be married when he was twenty-one and out from under his old man's thumb, and with a job. I'd say to him, 'Your pa won't want you to marry me.' And he'd laugh and say, 'Who cares? Besides, I'm only nineteen, and I can't marry without his permission, so let's forget everything but us.' He was always right. It was the only way."

She paused. Her blue eyes widened as she stared at the curtain, and she shrank. "Oh! Maybe you're a priest! Maybe you want me to get out after what I told you? Should I get out?"

The light beamed all about her. She listened intently. No voice answered her, but she was suddenly reassured that she could stay. She sighed over and over. "Well, thank you," she murmured.

She looked at the flowers on her knee, tall and fresh and sweet, and she smiled sadly.

"Then Phil had to go way to college. 'Don't write me,' he said. 'If you do I'll have to answer, and someway they'll find out. Just remember I love you, and I'll be thinking of you every minute.' Of course he was right. So I'd lie alone at night, dreaming of him. I wanted to pray for him, too, but I was afraid that God would be offended. I was beginning to be scared of Him, anyway. I guess that's the way you feel when you know you're doing something wrong. I'm not saying I didn't know by then; I did. I wrote to this woman in the newspaper and didn't sign my name, just 'Polly.' And she answered it in the newspaper and she said I should leave 'your place of employment at once! Go to a relative, or a close friend, or your clergyman.' That's what she said. The only thing was I didn't have no relatives or close friends, and if I went to the priest he'd tell me never to see Phil again, and how could I stand that? I loved him; he was all I had.

"I thought he'd be home for Thanksgiving, but there was this football game, and the whole family went to the college town to be with Phil and see the game. You wouldn't believe it! He was playing football! They came back, and I'd listen, and they'd say, 'What a wonderful improvement in dear Phil.' That was his mother and sisters. The sisters were all older'n me and had a lot of boy friends, and one was engaged. About time, too; she was twenty-six, the oldest. Married one of the men in the bank.

"Well, there was Christmas coming, and Phil would be home. Except he wasn't. You'd think the family would be mad, wouldn't you? But they weren't. It seems like he'd met some son of a big shot from Philadelphia, and they'd invited Phil for the holidays. He was Phil's best friend. But old man Mallon puffed up and grinned and said his boy was coming along and it was an honor, and

67

though the old lady cried the girls jumped around as if they'd just got diamond bracelets or something.

"And then I got this pain in my chest. It wouldn't go away. It ached all the time, day and night. Mom died of heart trouble, and I went to a doctor. He charged me five dollars, and I was only getting ten a week. He said I didn't have a heart condition. 'It's all in your mind, young lady,' he joked, and pinched my cheek. 'Some boy, eh? Well, go home to Mother and play the field. I don't approve of this going steady at your age. Seventeen? Too young. Just you go out with all the nice boys you can, and dance and have fun and wear your pretty clothes and stay close to Dad and Mother for some time yet.' Much he knew about me! Anyway, the pain wouldn't go away. It was like something eating at my heart all the time.

"Did you ever have a pain like that, loving somebody so hard? A friend, maybe, or your mother or your father? And wanting to see them like mad, and you couldn't? Well, it was that way with me. And Phil didn't come home for the spring vacation. He didn't come home until June. Nine long months.

"But the minute I saw him I knew he still loved me, and that's all that mattered. He came up to my room the very first night he was home, and it was like he'd never gone away. Every night, the whole time he was home, when he could. He'd filled out; he was a man and not a boy, twenty years old. I was so proud of him, and so happy. Why, even the air had sparkles in it! And we had only one year to go before we could be married."

Mary wept deeply into her handkerchief. She could not stop for a long time. Then her face was flushed and swollen. She glanced furtively at her cheap watch. Why, it was half-past one! It was Easter morning. "Oh, God," she whispered.

She smoothed a leaf of the flowers. "That boy he met at college, he came in the summer, and Phil was out a lot with him, showing him off, his sisters said. The youngest sister sure had her eye on him, and she had no looks at all. Like a plucked chicken. She used to stare at my hair, and she said I bleached it! I never bleached it in my life, and then the old lady swooped down on me and examined the roots of my hair. Like I wasn't human, or something, and she could do what she wanted to me. I wanted to kick her hard. But that meant I wouldn't be there any more, and maybe new people would find out about Phil and they wouldn't let him come and stay with me.

"Well, it wasn't like the first summer. Phil was out and around; the family made him go. And then in August he went off to sail on that boy's father's yacht, and you'd think, by the way his family acted, that he'd been elected President. But before he went he came up to my room on the last night, and it was like in the very beginning, and he kept whispering how much he loved me. And he gave me the first present I ever had. The prettiest compact. I bet it cost all of six dollars, maybe even more. It looked like gold and silver. I still got it.

"Phil didn't come home that Thanksgiving, either, and then the whole stupid family was invited to Philadelphia, and you never heard such a

69

noise. Laughing and yelling and hugging each
other. That was for Christmas. And Phil didn't
come home in the spring, and then not in June.
The family was whispering around, but I couldn't
hear what they said. He came home in July for
just four weeks. I was eighteen then, and he was
twenty-one, and we could be married."

The handkerchief was wet and useless, so Mary
let her tears flow, down onto the flowers, down
onto her cheap but sturdy winter coat and neat
dark blue dress.

"Again it was like the beginning, those four
weeks. And I'd say to him, 'We can be married
now, Phil.' And he'd kiss me hard on the mouth
and say, 'Just be patient.' And I was. And then
at the end of that four weeks his engagement to
that boy's sister showed up in the newspaper."

Mary's color ran from her cheeks at the remembrance of that old agony.

"I thought I'd lose my mind," she said, her voice
hoarse and low. "I thought I'd just lose my mind.
I couldn't work. I said I was sick, and I went up-
stairs to my room and lay down on the bed. Maybe
I fainted, or maybe I slept. I don't know. But I
kept waking up and saying, 'Oh, thank God it was
just a nightmare!' Only, it wasn't. It'd come back
to me, like a knife in my chest. I kept thinking I
was dying, and then I was scared, thinking of God
and how angry He was with me, and this was my
punishment and I'd end up in hell for sure. No one
wanted me now, not Phil, not God. Nobody."

She could see the curtains through her tears.
"Well, all that day I was sick and just about dying.
And then I couldn't go down and get dinner, and

I could hear the old lady grumbling. I'd lift my head, and then I'd have to run into the bathroom and throw up. Phil wasn't around. I waited and waited, and it got dark, and then the house was full of company; I could hear them laughing and shouting; I could hear Phil, too. I sat up and told myself it was a mistake. If it was true, and the old man forcing him into this, then we could run away together. I'd saved a little money, and Phil had a big allowance. I just had to wait for Phil.

"And right about one in the morning he came to my room in his pajamas, like always, and I was in his arms, and I was almost out of my mind again. He kept putting his hand over my mouth and then trying to close it with kisses. He kept saying, 'Hush, hush, it'll be all right. You'll see.' And I was so sick, and so tired. Then suddenly I was happy again. Phil would take care of everything. I'd just about fallen asleep, I was so tired, when the light flashed on, and there was the old man."

Mary shuddered and cringed and squeezed her eyes together.

"It was awful," she whispered. "I pulled up the sheet around me, and Phil jumped out of bed and pulled on his pajamas, and the old man looked like he was going to go up in flames. And he looked at me! I never had anyone look at me like that! And he said, 'The evil woman taken in adultery. You dirty tramp, in a better age than this they'd stone you to death. Get out of this house at once, you filthy creature.'

"And Phil kept saying, 'Now, Dad, please, Dad, it's all right, Dad. Don't shout like that. You'll have Mother and the girls up here. Please, Dad.

It's all right.' And all I was afraid of was that the old man would punch him. But he didn't. He kept looking at me, like he hated me like death, and he said, 'My poor boy, seduced by this vile wretch who dared to sleep in a house where innocent young girls are sleeping. My poor boy. Go to your room.' I almost laughed; I never wanted to laugh so much in my life, though I was crying by now. And Phil said, 'You can't put her out now, Dad. It's almost morning. What will people say?' And the old man nodded and said, 'You are quite right. But you,' he said to me, 'be out of the house before my daughters get up.' "

Mary sobbed, her yellow hair flying about her face. "You know what I said to him? 'Mr. Mallon, I've got my savings in your bank. Three hundred dollars.' And he said, 'Be there when the bank opens, and if you are in this town by five o'clock I'll have the police after you.' And he meant it, too. And I said to Phil—he was looking so white and sort of green around the mouth—'I'll be in the bus station at four o'clock,' and I tried to smile at him so he wouldn't look so sick."

Mary looked at the curtains again in vague fear. "You are listening, aren't you? I could sort of feel you listening. And look, it's half-past three. Easter morning. When Our Lord rises from the dead. Oh, I shouldn't even speak about Him! I've got no right to, a woman like me. Why, He'd turn me away, wouldn't He? Like—like—it was something I read in the Holy Bible—— No, He didn't turn the woman away. I wish I could remember the whole story.

"Well, I got my money out of the bank, and I

72

was in my best dress, with a short white coat and hat, and I had my suitcase, and I was happy again. Phil would meet me at the bus station at four, and we'd leave town at five. I ate a big breakfast, then I was sick at the stomach again and had to throw up in the ladies' room. But I was happy just the same. I sat in the bus station the whole day, reading a magazine. And then it was four o'clock. And I went to the door and watched for Phil. And then it was half-past four, and quarter to five, and they were loading the bus for this city. And Phil didn't come. So I ran to the telephone, and the old lady answered it, and though I tried to disguise my voice she knew it, and she screamed at me about the police and hung up, and I knew Phil couldn't come; maybe they had him locked up in his room and they wouldn't let him out. I got on the bus and I came to this city, and I found myself a room in a cheap hotel, and then I wrote to Phil, telling him where I was.

"But they must have opened my letters. He never wrote me, and he never came to me. And after a month I knew I'd never see him again. I got a good job as a waitress. That was ten years ago."

She leaned back in the chair, exhausted. "Maybe everything would have been all right except—— Well, in a couple of months I found out I was going to have a baby. I couldn't believe it! I still didn't know how it happened, I was that dumb. Phil's baby. So I went to a doctor, and I asked him what was the matter, and he told me, and he said, 'Mrs.——?' And quick as a wink I said 'Mrs. Mallon.' And then it hit me. I don't even remember getting back to the rooming house where I lived.

"I thought and thought. God didn't want me. Phil couldn't come to me. I didn't want to hurt him. His father would have killed him. I even thought of killing myself. And then I got this good job I have now, and I told people my husband was in the Army and I was Mrs. Mallon. I was, in my heart. All the time. And that's what they know me as now. And I had my baby, a dear little boy, and I called him Phil, after his father, and the people in the hospital mailed letters I wrote to Mr. Phil Mallon in the Army. But I didn't put any return address on them. I was getting smart by now. And I paid everything myself.

"I got my little boy out in the country, where all the little kids should live, with the grass and the trees and flowers and fresh air. I pay good for him, too. He's a darling little boy. And everything would be all right, except that a year ago I met Francis Lewis. He's a young farmer, and it's a big farm, and he's all alone on it since his dad died a couple of years ago. He came in the restaurant; he'd just brought his beef cattle in. And right away we liked each other, and he came back and took me out."

Mary shivered. "And now you're really going to hate me. I told Francis I was a young Army widow with a little boy, and he believed it. It didn't matter at first. And then I sort of began to think of him. He's so good and kind. I don't feel for him like I felt for poor Phil, who couldn't come to me and who doesn't even know he has a little boy nearly ten years old. Imagine that! Not knowing you have a child! I just ache for Phil.

"Then Francis asked me to marry him, and I thought of being his wife, safe on that nice farm, with somebody to care about me again, and how wonderful it would be for little Phil, and we'd be all together. And then I thought what a cheat I was, and so I had to tell Francis, and I knew that would be the end. But do you know something? It wasn't! No sir, Francis is that kind of man; he's thirty-two. It's just that he hates Phil—not my little boy—my Phil. And he said, 'It doesn't matter, Mary. I will just be marrying a young widow with a child. We'll have to keep that up, for the boy's sake and ours.' That's the kind of man Francis is."

Her young face suddenly glowed, and she smiled. Then her smile went away. "But how can I do that to Francis? He deserves a better girl than me, somebody good and nice. We'd have to be married in the Church, and I'd have to go to confession, and what will the priest say? He'd say just what God would say, and old man Mallon. So I'm holding off, and I won't take a ring yet, and here I am."

She waited. The room was still shimmering with light, and it was almost dawn. "Tell me!" cried Mary in despair. "Tell me that I must be real strong and send Francis away, and that God wouldn't want him, either, if he marries me! Tell me! All at once I feel I love Francis, but I can't do this to him!"

There was no sound. Mary stumbled to her feet.

She extended the flowers. "I brought these for you. They're so pretty; Madonna lilies, too. Take them."

She crept to the curtains, read the brass plate, then touched the button, her whole body shaking. The curtains fell apart, and she fell back, uttering a great and terrified cry.

She looked at the man before her, and she trembled more and more. The light appeared to grow stronger, more triumphant. Mary bowed her her head.

She whispered, "Will you take my flowers? They're all I have to give you. Maybe, because of all my sins, I should've given the money to charity or something. But I want you to have them. Will you take them? Please?"

Closer and closer, blinded by tears, she approached him again. She put the flowers tenderly at his side. "You did listen," she murmured. She straightened up, weeping reverently. "Why, you always listen, don't you? Look! It's Easter morning! It's dawn outside. And you—you——"

She knelt down and clasped her hands. "I remember now. The woman wasn't turned away. 'She loved much.' I remember now. Yes, I loved very much, and I love again.

"You want me to have Francis and my little boy, don't you? Yes, that's what you want! Oh, I'll be so good to them both!" She swallowed her tears. "And there was another Mary, and a man she thought was the gardener—— And now I know no priest will ever turn me away. He wouldn't. He wouldn't!"

She bent her tired head and pressed it against

76

the man's feet, and suddenly she slept for a little while.

The bells of the churches began to ring. "The Lord God is risen! He is risen!" And Mary slept, and the flower scent filled the room. He watched over her, in her safety, and her golden hair covered his feet. They kept the vigil together.

SOUL SEVEN

The Betrayer

All things betray thee, who betrayest Me.
Francis Thompson: "The Hound of Heaven"

"I hope," said the young man coldly as he looked at the curtains this warm, late spring day, "that you aren't a psychiatrist. You see, I was in analysis, myself, for over a year, and I know only too well now—as I did even before that—that I am in the wrong profession, maladjusted, a round peg in a square hole, and that so long as I remain in my—profession—I will be emotionally disturbed and troubled and will continue to have my psychosomatic headaches. Which are really disabling, I assure you, even if there is no physical basis for them." He laughed disdainfully.

"So I won't waste your time if you are a psychiatrist. Frankly, I am a little tired of the jargon. In the light of what I've learned, the jargon seems puerile to me, though of course I'd never tell my——" He paused abruptly. "Are you a psychiatrist?"

The room stood about him in its fresh white silence. He waited. Then he nodded, relieved. "I'm glad you're not. So you must be a physician. But then you may be a marriage counselor. I am not married, though I am thirty-eight years old. The girl to whom I was engaged—— We had a violent disagreement, and the engagement was broken. Her ideas, to say the very least, were childish. Of course there are men in my profession who would disagree, especially those of the Roman persuasion, but after all, the majority of young men in my profession, in these days, understand that we've advanced beyond the kindergarten era."

He looked down at his well-kept hands, his dark blue trousers and fine shoes, and he dusted a speck from the sleeve of his excellent blue and brown sports jacket. Absently he examined a new callus on his right palm. He had been doing a great deal of golfing recently. The greens were fine this year, the club smarter, the people more suave and cultured and better-mannered. That was, of course, because of new and younger members. He was very popular among them and saw them regularly, and not only at the club. In fact, he had never been so popular. It was a mark of a well-rounded personality if people liked you; at least he was no neurotic. Even Dr. Bergson had assured him of that. "You could do much better as an executive," Dr. Bergson had said, "or a consultant in human relations. Eminently fitted for that, I'm convinced. Especially that. Personnel work. You know people and their problems; there's a big demand for your specialized sort of work."

The young man put his hand to his forehead; another of those damned headaches. He was a tall and slender man, with a long, intense, ardent face which he kept under control constantly; he knew his secret tendency to ardor and passion and all the other disheveled emotions. Once or twice, lately (but only once or twice!), he had forgotten to keep his voice modulated in the club when some ass had made a gently sneering remark and had mentioned "bad taste, these days." The young man's heart had suddenly pounded then, his cool face had flushed, and he had been guilty—that was the only word for it, guilty—of raising his voice a little vehemently. The older men in the locker room at the club had looked disturbed but serious, and one or two had nodded; but the younger, his close friends, had appeared startled and embarrassed and had hurriedly changed the subject, as if to spare his shame and cover up his social blunder. His social blunder.

"Did you speak?" he asked, suddenly aware of a change of quality in the atmosphere of the silent room. "Did I hear you say, 'A social blunder?' in a questioning tone of voice?"

No one answered him, but he was convinced that he had heard those words. He said as if his thoughts had been spoken aloud and heard in entirety: "Of course, there in the locker room, I was guilty of a faux pas. In a way. That was no place for discussion. My study is the place. And my pulpit. For you see, I am a minister, and I have

81

one of the largest and most desirable parishes in this city. I am the Reverend Mr. Anson Carr. So if you are a clergyman you will see we have much in common." He laughed with a carefully cultivated ease.

It was strange, and purely imaginary, certainly, that he should have the impression of a gentle smiling, a sense of brotherhood. But it made him laugh with genuine ease now, as if in the company of an older colleague to whom he could speak frankly.

"I was right to come," he admitted. "I suspected that you were 'of the cloth,' as my grandmother used to call it. There is a Mrs. Merrill Sloane in my congregation, a lady for whom I had had little sympathy two years ago because of her various personality defects. A most remarkable change has come over her, and I hinted I'd be interested to learn what had accomplished this. She told me only that she had been here to see you, and then she said—that was a month or more ago—'Do go yourself, Mr. Carr. It is just what you need.' I must admit that I was disturbed at this; I wasn't aware that I 'needed' anything. Not anything that was visible to my congregation, at least. If a woman once so self-centered as Mrs. Sloane was aware of my 'need,' then it must be flagrantly evident. I hope you are not offended, but that is the reason I am here: to find how to conceal some of my— thoughts—from my congregation."

He paused. His headache was becoming very ferocious. He took a beautifully enameled pillbox from his pocket and slipped a tablet on his tongue and swallowed with a little difficulty.

82

"Not that I will have a congregation much longer," he said, clearing his throat. "I have no right to it. For you see, I am dry. Dry as death, dry to the very marrow of my bones. Like David, I cry out to my God from the darkest depths, and there is no answer. Have I lost my faith? I don't know. Perhaps. It is as if I've been working for years on a desert, excavating parched bones and presenting them as living forms. A desert. Dry bones. A minister has no right to a church and a congregation when he experiences that dryness, has he? He is, in a most important way, a total fraud. So I am doing more than merely considering leaving the ministry. I intend to resign in September—and accept another position. Money is no object; I have a private income from my father's estate, and Mother has her own income. She is living in Florida with my sister."

He looked about the room with pain in his gray eyes. "It's very strange," he said. "My family was very pious, even though my father was a successful businessman and very popular and belonged to all the best clubs in this city—I am a member too. We had prayers every evening, as well as prayers before our meals. Father used to lead us in the Bible reading and in the prayers. He was, I suppose, a very old-fashioned man. I worshiped him. When I told him I wished to be a minister and not take over his business later, he—well, he became very emotional in the way of Victorians. I wasn't embarrassed, but after all, I was only seventeen then. One doesn't expect men with high self-esteem and a sense of individual worth to burst out crying with joy—not in these days! I think we

83

have better control of our emotions now, don't you? If I were a father, for instance, and had a son who told me he wished to enter the ministry, I'd say to him, 'You must give a great deal of consideration to this and weigh the advantages and the disadvantages thoroughly. I think we should consult an expert on aptitude tests and then a psychiatrist before you commit your life to any—profession.'"

He waited. No one answered him. Then something rose in him like the high and thundering swell of a wave. He fought it down, but it rose higher and higher, and out of its smothering he cried, "'Profession!' I call it 'profession'! But it is a calling—a calling!—isn't it? That is what my father said—'a holy calling'!"

He put the heels of his hands hard over his eyes. "Oh, my God," he murmured. "To think that there were people long ago who thought God 'called' them! Now we gravely consider the impulse we have toward the ministry and wonder if we are well rounded enough, and fully psychologically educated, and adjusted, to become ministers of the Gospel! Are we good administrators? Do we like people? Do people instinctively like us? Are we excellently grounded in the social ethic? Do young people naturally gravitate toward us? Are we expert businessmen? Do women like us? Are we liberal in our ideas? Do we have good voices which inspire confidence? Can we meet men on their own ground easily and confidently, whether it is the golf course, the broker's office, the club, the family living room, the parish hall, the community activities, the schools, the theater, the good restaurants? In short, are we 'good fellows, sweet guys, regular people'? Are we enthusiastic about sports and take an active part in them? Are we 'broad'? Men of 'diversified' interests? Conversant with television? Are we on the board of this and that? In short, are we 'active'?"

He stood up, looking about him with a kind of wild hopelessness. "In short," he cried, "must we be everything but ministers of the Gospel?"

The white walls were lined with his questions. He stared at them. He shrank. He fumbled for the chair and sat down again. He was breathing in short gasps. He looked at the curtain. "You probably know," he said. "As a clergyman, you probably know. You can see, surely, what confronts every minister, a pastor, a shepherd."

The room appeared to become cold, the light glacial. "It's not my fault," said the minister. "Not my fault. It is what they want. I give it to them. And it is killing me." He added in a groaning voice, "It is killing me."

He waited. Then he said roughly, "You are probably a very successful clergyman. Your people love you, admire you, and talk over your lectures—I mean, your sermons. You satisfy them. You give them what they want, easily, silkily. You never tell them about their 'sin'! You never rebuke them. No minister would dare, these days.

"Do you know that no one speaks of sin these days? Except, of course, the Roman Catholic priests and perhaps a scattered Orthodox rabbi here and there? There is no 'sin.' It's a matter of environment, of conditioning, of lack of opportunity, of society's 'oppression.' Of broken homes.

Of racial discrimination. Of bad housing. Of slum conditions. Of 'rejection' by parents. Of physical disability. Of not being able to adjust to the 'peer group.' Of lack of conventional clothing, or money, or recreational advantages, or luxurious schools, or unsympathetic teachers, parents, neighborhoods, ministers, priests, rabbis. In short, 'sin' is not the fault of the individual. It is not his responsibility. He has 'rights' and 'claims,' but he has no duties. Not to himself, his community, his church, his parents, his wife and children, his pastor, his country. He has 'rights.' And," said Mr. Carr in a low and desperate voice, "he has no sin. There is no sin. Man, as Rousseau said, is sinless. Only the institutions around him provoke anti-social behavior, for which we must be compassionate, surrounding the sinner with 'help.' But we must never blame him. We must never say, 'Rise, and sin no more.' We must never call evil people a 'brood of vipers,' as John the Baptist called them. We must never call them liars and hypocrites, as Christ called them. This would give the 'victim' a trauma. We must, at all costs, reassure the sinner that he has been sinned against."

His voice rose, stammered. "Above all things, we must never say, 'You are evil; you have an immortal soul which is in danger. God will not be mocked. You are black with sin, a sinner. But you can be saved. Repent, and do penance, before it is too late.' No, we can't say that to our congregations. Not our congregations who gather on Sunday morning well shaved, well brushed, well dressed, well furred, happy with themselves. And those of us who are ministers to the poor dare not call our people 'sinners,' either. The damned social workers would be rushing in, in droves, in their fluttering black skirts and ballet slippers and fierce little faces, screaming about 'discrimination' and what 'chance' did our congregation have in this competitive society."

Mr. Carr stood up again, straining tensely toward the curtains, which did not move.

"Who is the competent receiver of all this? The government? With its slips of green paper recoverable in more green paper at the bank? What value is in that? Who will 'recover' our world for us? Who will teach us to say, as we all ought, 'God, be merciful to me, a sinner?' How can we pastors call our congregations vipers, liars, hypocrites? There would not be a church standing if we dared to say that!"

He dropped his head. Then he said, "But first we must say that to ourselves. Yes, first of all to ourselves, we the false shepherds, who led our people into the papier-mâché valleys of complacency, who laid mirrors in the earth, instead of living water, so that our people could contemplate themselves with self-congratulation, who spread carpets of artificial green grass for them, steam-heated, on which they could bask and forget the earthquakes rumbling below them. But which will never feed their hunger."

He moved toward the curtain, his face damp and very white under the tan.

"Do you know what I said in that locker room, where I embarrassed the men of my age who were preparing to shower and go home for the nightly drinks, the well-served dinner out of the deep-freeze, and the hi-fi afterward, and the television, and their badly behaved and godless children? And the urbane programs which featured, in long and boring detail on a wide screen, the houses, jewels, furniture, dresses, shrill aspirations, simperings—and, God forgive me!—the evil nonsense of actresses, 'public personalities,' politicians, songsters, and dancers?

"I said to my friends, 'This also is vanity.' I don't know what made me speak! I said, 'What have you done today for God? What did you do yesterday for God? What do you intend to do tomorrow for God?'

"If they were appalled—after all, it's socially unpardonable to speak of God these days except in church, and then only in passing—I was even more appalled. No wonder they were embarrassed. I was even more so, though the older men nodded seriously. My friends covered up for me quickly, for which I am grateful. I had exhibited myself as a kind of Fundamentalist screecher, and that is not the picture I have of myself at all."

He leaned sideways against the tall marble chair. He could hardly get his breath. His head pounded violently. It was some time before he could speak, and then only faintly. "What picture do I have of myself? A community leader, a sportsman, a good fellow, a shaker of hands, a soother of aggressive women, an adviser on problems on which I consider myself a psychological expert, a co-ordinator, a raiser of funds, a sweet patter of heads, arms, shoulders, a fine partner at bridge, an adolescents' pal, an arranger of parish amusements, a smiler. God forgive me! Always a smiler! Forever and forever a smiler!

"What does Shakespeare say about that? '. . . Smile and smile, and be a villain.'"

He fell into the chair, slumping forward, his hands between his knees. "A villain," he repeated. "That is what Alice called me when she broke our engagement. 'What do you tell them of God, and the Laws of God, and penance and repentance, and their immortal souls?' she asked me. 'Do you ever say to them, "This night your soul will be required of you"? Do you ever tell them why they were born? Why do you let them believe that all will be forever sunshine for them on this earth, that they will always be young, their children forever children, their money always available, their health unfailing, their legs always strong and their hearts always brave, their security unshakable, their lives ever eager and full of food and entertainment and dances? Why don't you tell them all that tonight, perhaps, but tomorrow, surely, their souls will be required of them, and that all the dancing they did and all the fun they had, and all the bells they rang, and all the money they made will be nothing at all, not even a memory?' "

The room waited, as if for an answer. Mr. Carr, waiting also, could see vast answers shaping in his spirit, and he cringed before them.

"Yes," he said finally. "It is all my fault. The desert I live in; the dry bones I offer my people. For I am the desert and the dry bones. I am the liar and the hypocrite. I never had the faith to tell my people the truth, nor the spirit, nor the cour-

89

age. I am the guilty. I not only never had a flock, I am not even a shepherd."

He pushed himself to his feet, tired to the very heart, aching like an old man. He said to the curtain, "Do you understand? You are a clergyman too. But did you ever have a flock like mine, resentful of the truth, liars to themselves, complacent, hurrying, grasping, smirking, preening, authorities on everything, greedy, betrayers, hardeyed, coveting social honors, doubters, atheists, hypocrites, adulterers, sportsmen, lovers of the trivial and the passing, sheepish before the mention of God's name? Did you? If you did not, then you can't answer me and you can't help me!"

He ran to the curtains, his head roaring, his finger outstretched toward the button.

The curtains rushed aside. Mr. Carr stood and looked in the light. Then he stepped back slowly, foot by groping foot.

And then he fell to his knees.

"Yes," he said, "of course you did. That is the flock you had, and that is the flock I have. We have them together; we have them together. Until the end of time, we have them together. You and I.

"But you never had to say to yourself, 'I am the guilty,' as I say to myself now. I am the guilty. God, be merciful to me, a sinner.

"Give me strength to tell my people the truth. If they reject me, as they rejected you, what does it matter? There is only the truth. Forgive me. Above all things, forgive me. For betraying you in trivialities."

SOUL EIGHT

The Condemned

Because I could not stop for Death,
He kindly stopped for me;
The carriage held but just ourselves
And Immortality.

We slowly drove, he knew no haste,
And I had put away
My labour, and my leisure too,
For his civility.
    Emily Dickinson: "The Chariot"

Eugene Emory walked stiffly into the sitting room, saw those waiting in silence, and hesitated. How placid they were, like cattle, some reading a magazine, some only staring at nothing. Like people in an anteroom of the Salvation Army! Why had he come here? That specialist who had given him the irrevocable news, finally! What had he said? "I think you'll find some peace there. We're very proud of old John Godfrey's place. I've seen some remarkable things. No, I was never there myself. But you must have read about it."

He had. In one of the big national magazines. A beautiful square building, set in flower gardens, with trees and arbors—the finest architects had built it. It was open twenty-four hours a day to everybody and anybody. "The Man who Listens." The reporter in that magazine had been a very amusing boy, full of mocking wide-eyes and arched brows and rounded, contemptuous mouth. "Ooh," he seemed to be saying in every clever paragraph. "Ooh. Ooh! The lame, the halt, the blind—come one, come all. Find your particular nostrum here, your own face, your own voice. That's what they say. Your reporter did enter the inner sanctum of sanctums and asked a lot of questions aloud. That big, bright, melodramatic curtain just wouldn't open! It couldn't be pried open. I know; I tried. Velvet over steel mesh, apparently, which could only be parted by electrical impulse, and the boys had shut the juice off. Everybody welcome, except a reporter whose job it is to expose sham, cheapness, brash popularity, vulgarity, and pretense. Why the clergy haven't denounced it is one of the continuing wonders of the years."

The colored photographs, however, had been exceedingly handsome, the pictured gardens exquisite, the paths carefully tended, the trees luxurious. No walls or fences guarded the four acres of land, and though the grounds were in the very center of a very populous part of the city, it had never been reported that any vandalism had been committed here, except an attempted robbery a few times, scattered over the years.

The reporter had been particularly annoyed and skeptical, because no donations were solicited and none accepted. He scattered a few dark rumors for public speculation. The governor of the state, after reading that article, had ordered an "investigation," though he knew all about old John's structure, for he had been there himself one quiet night. But the public "clamored" for the investigation, the governor said apologetically, though he failed to notice that the clamor did not come from the city itself, or even the state, but from towns and villages and cities in far parts of the country. The governor found "nothing wrong." It was a quiet, restful place where you could think, he announced.

A quiet, restful place, thought Eugene Emory as he sat down. Just what I need now! A quiet, restful place, closely resembling a grave. And these are my companions, these dolt-faced women and men, waiting. He saw that one by one, in perfect silence and composure, they rose at the chiming of a bell, opened the oaken door, and disappeared from sight. That was all. My God, what am I doing here? thought Eugene Emory, thinking of what he must tell his wife tomorrow, and his children.

He was forty-nine years old. He had worked all his life, worked while going to high school, worked while going to the university in his home city. He had known nothing but work all his life. He had not resented that until a month ago, or was it two months? Then his resentment had reached fury. He had been so enraged that he had lost two of his easiest cases in court, and the judge, his friend, had looked at him with concern. Three days later he had looked at him sternly and had called him to account with a threat of punishment for contempt of court. Emory, Dean and Hartford had lost face through him, he who had established the firm. Jack Dean, his best friend, had told him that he looked sick and that he was perhaps too tired. "I've been feeling like a sick pup," he had finally admitted. "I suppose I need a vacation. Haven't had one in eight years; no time. You ought to know that. I'll talk to Emily tonight, and maybe we can plan something, a cruise or a trip to Europe."

His wife had been joyful over the idea, but first she had insisted that he see the family physician for a thorough examination. "I hardly know the man," he had protested. "I only know his bills, and that's enough! What are you doing here, running a hospital?" But Emily could not be turned aside and, fuming, he had gone to the physician. "I have only an hour to spare," he told the doctor immediately on entering the examination room. "I'm very busy, you know. How are you?" he added as a belated thought. Had he ever seen this competent youngish man before? He seemed vaguely familiar. At the club? In his house?

"I'm all right. But I don't think you are," said the doctor, looking at the ghostly face of his patient, the gray lines under his strenuous blue eyes, the clefts about his mouth, the ashen color of his thin lips. "Well, we'll soon see."

Tests, tappings, soundings, breathings, bendings, listening. The hour was up, but the doctor had not finished. "I must go," said Eugene impatiently.

"Yes," said the doctor with grave thoughtfulness. "But just to be sure, I want you to see Dr. Hampshire in this same building. He's the blood specialist, you know. I want to be absolutely sure."

94

"Of what?"

"Of something I suspect. Of course I may be wrong. I hope I am. How long, by the way, has it been since you had that attack of tonsillitis?"

"Two months ago. How did you know I had that attack?" Eugene became alert.

The doctor said evasively, "And you had swellings under your jaw line, too?"

"Yes! What was it? Strep? I took some of the penicillin tablets you left for one of the kids. Look, do I have to go to this Dr. Hampshire?"

"Yes. Right now. You may call your office from here, if you wish, and tell them you've been delayed. And I'll call Dr. Hampshire."

"Can't I make it next week, or after we come back from our cruise?"

The doctor did not say, "You'll probably never come back from that cruise." Instead he said, as if after giving the matter thought, "No, I'd feel better about it if you had the examination now. For Emily's sake. She's been worried about you for weeks."

This was another surprise. So they were on a first-name basis, were they? And why had Emily been worried? Of course he had lost some weight, suddenly and very recently, and he had been feeling sudden exhaustions and palpitations, and there had been that day when he had vomited after breakfast and had thrown up some blood. Ulcers. Well, that was the badge of success, as they said.

"Ulcers?" he said to the doctor.

"Why do you ask that?"

"Never mind." If he told about that blood

95

there'd be more delays, and barium meals and X rays; he knew all about it. Young Hartford had ulcers, and his descriptions had been graphic.

"I've never been sick a day in my life," said Eugene as he dressed.

"Good," said the doctor. He waited until he was certain that Eugene was on his way to see Dr. Hampshire, and then the young doctor called his older colleague. "Eugene Emory," he said. "I've known him for years, but he hardly notices anybody. He's tough. He can take it. Leukemia. But I'd like to make sure. Acute, I'm afraid." He attempted to laugh, feebly. "Try to make it chronic, will you, Ed? Then perhaps we can prolong his life."

The doctor thought about all the advances made in the treatment of leukemia. Sometimes life could be prolonged, even in such devastating acute cases. But it was a life under absolute sentence of death. Of course, thought the doctor, we all live under sentence of death, but so long as we aren't aware of it all the time we can forget it. People with leukemia, though, can never forget it. Not even in fantasy.

Less than an hour later Eugene Emory returned. He sat at the young doctor's desk, and there was death in his face. He said, "I don't believe it."

"You must, Eugene. If you have any affairs that need putting in order—you can't evade the fact that you are going to die. And too soon, I'm afraid."

Eugene said nothing. He lit a cigarette with pale thin fingers. He stared over the doctor's head.

"We begin to die the moment we are conceived,"

said the doctor. "Sooner or later, we die. I may die tonight, under the wheels of an automobile, or next year, of a coronary thrombosis, or tomorrow, falling down those damned steep steps at our club. Death is something we can't escape. The only thing that's wrong with it is that we don't begin to tell our children about it in the very earliest childhood, so that they will live with the fact and think of it regularly, so that it becomes familiar to them and not something terrible, or something which, through mysterious luck, they can avoid. Not to tell a little child all about death—and the hell with the 'psychic trauma' of it!—is about the most cruel thing you can do to the child. To tell him soothingly that only the very old die is to make a liar of yourself, and the child will soon find out and despise you. And children are born tough and resilient; they aren't fragile flowers who must be protected from life. They can take the fact of death easier and more naturally than we can; it becomes harder for us every year."

He added, "Death is as much a part of life as birth."

"I never lived," said Eugene, as if talking to himself. "I never knew how to live; I only knew how to work."

He stood up. "How long?"

"A month, perhaps. With luck, perhaps two months. But no longer."

"There's nothing you can do?"

"Various things. But they're not too successful in acute cases; they work best in the chronic. How do you like the idea of going into the hospital today, for blood transfusions, radiations, and so on?"

Eugene gave it thought. His face became more ghastly by the moment. He passed his hand over his fading light hair. "Why should I?" he said.

"Well, it might make you a little more comfortable—"

"And that's all? And then I'll just linger around there until I die?"

"Yes."

"Then, no. I'll keep on going until I have to stop. It will make it easier on my family, too. By the way, am I going to run into any—trouble?"

"Probably—I'll give you some tablets to relieve the pain. You said you've been having pain over your bones. It may or may not get worse."

The doctor hesitated. "Why don't you talk to the minister of your church?"

"I don't know him," said Eugene flatly. "I've only seen him in his pulpit at Christmas and Easter. But Emily knows him well, and the children."

"Why don't you talk to him about this yourself?"

"Thank you, no. I'm not going crawling to—— You know what I mean."

The really furious, incredulous, and helpless rage had begun then. It was all the more terrible in a man of his laconic and restrained temperament, his logical mind, his factual experiences. Always he had been able to control his life, to direct it, to fight circumstance and overcome it, to turn things aside. He knew that his juniors called him "The Univac," and it had amused him. He had only to appear in a courtroom, quick and light-footed, his face concentrated in an expression of single-mindedness, to make the opposing lawyer's heart sink. He rarely lost a case, and those only the most desperate. His life, his work were in full control, in absolute order, full of precision. He hated fuzziness. He would often say, "There's nothing inevitable."

Now he was faced with the inevitable. The rage increased. It was not a frightened, quivering rage, a pusillanimous one. It was the rage of a man who has never lived, and when he is on the threshold of living his life is taken from him.

He had known for the past two years that he must begin to give Emily more companionship; their children were almost adults now, and they would soon be leaving home. Once a son or daughter left home for school, he or she really never came home again, except as a visitor. Eugene was not a "dedicated" man, as others called him approvingly. He had wanted money only to guarantee him and his family a reasonable amount of security, and he had accomplished that now. And next came pleasure, and travel, and leisure, for himself and Emily. His wife had not been lonely or unhappy or neglected. She had known for what he was working so strongly and admired him for it. When he had suggested the cruise a few days ago she had said, "Really? Wonderful! Now we can begin to enjoy ourselves, can't we, darling? While we're still young and healthy."

They had spent hours that night planning the cruise. All over South America; they would sail in October and so would have two months to prepare. The girl and boy would be at college then. They would not return from the cruise until just before Christmas. "And then, in February, we're going to Florida," said Eugene. He had kissed his pretty wife, whose dark brown hair was so glossy and fresh. "It's time we lived. And now we've got all the time in the world. I'll get busy with arrangements at the office."

He now had no time at all.

A month. Two months. He did not tell his wife. He could so control himself that when she talked enthusiastically about the cruise and gave him more colorful pamphlets he could bring up a convincing and interested smile. They had their passport pictures taken; they applied for passports. Eugene had never been very ruddy of complexion; his deepening pallor only made his wife believe that the cruise was really very urgent. He had always been thin. She bought extra vitamins for him and gave him eggnog at bedtime. He indulged her lovingly. He could express his affection only with a glance or a touch or a quick half-ashamed embrace, but she knew how he loved her. She never saw the little tablet he occasionally took now when his physical distress was overpowering. She never knew that he went to a private hospital with his doctor for an occasional blood transfusion "to make you a little more comfortable." She thought he slept at night. He did, sometimes, after a drug.

And then one day he realized that two weeks had passed, or was it three? He had more blood tests. "We're holding our own a little," said the doctor.

"A reprieve?"

"Well—you can't always tell with this damned thing."

"The governor won't call three minutes before midnight?"

"No. Have you told Emily yet?"

"No. I don't want her to know. Until at the very last, perhaps the last hour."

"You could die in your sleep."

"All the better, for Emily."

He went to the office every day, as usual. If he spent an hour or two now and then on the couch in his office, there was little comment. He had told his partners, "I have some kind of anemia. I have to take liver shots for them. Nothing serious, but I need considerable rest. Now, the latter part of October—we have the Hadley case coming up, and I won't be here."

I won't be here.

Sometimes he thought of killing himself, in a way that would appear to be an accident, for Emily's sake. But he was a lawyer, and he knew all about the clever probings of insurance companies. And there was the police, too.

He had nowhere to turn. He had no hobbies and few friends. He tried to read, for reading had always been his best pleasure. But he would find himself staring blankly at a page for five or ten minutes at a time, unaware of it. Emily was busily preparing her wardrobe. She would put on a smart dress and turn about for his admiration. Then he would take her hand and kiss it quickly, and put it from him as quickly. Oh, God, he would say in himself, but with blasphemy.

A less disciplined man would have broken down. He almost did when Emily insisted on his buying some clothing for the cruise. "I love this dark blue

101

twill," she said. He bought it. He almost remarked in his desperate rage, "Bury me in it."

He tried to drink. His drinking had always been sparing. But he could take no more than two drinks, for then he became nauseated and he was afraid of vomiting and precipitating a fatal hemorrhage. Four weeks. He was still alive. "Still holding our own a little," said the doctor. "For how much longer?" The doctor did not answer.

Then he read of a certain blood specialist who was doing some excellent work in prolonging the lives of leukemia victims. He told Emily that he must take a short trip. "I will be back on Wednesday," he said.

He had seen the specialist. The doctor could give him no hope. He was dying. He could die any day now. He thought of Emily waiting for him in their pleasant suburban home. His strength became less. He must tell her, prepare her. Then while waiting for the time to leave for the airport he took a short walk in the late August sunlight in this city where John Godfrey had built his marble temple.

Eugene stopped to look at the gardens, then he saw the building and remembered the story of it which he had read some time ago. His white mouth trembled with disgust. He found himself walking up one of the winding red gravel paths, and then he was in the sitting room, waiting with these placid, uninteresting people. Waiting for what? The specialist had told him to come here; he had forgotten the advice almost immediately. But subconsciously he must have been drawn to it.

102

If I can come to this, he told himself, then I'm pretty far gone in my intellect.

He had a habit now of falling into brief dozes. He heard a chiming and he started, awake. He was the only one in the room now, and he knew it was his turn. The Man who Listens. Eugene stood up, then looked at the outer door and took a step toward it. He stopped. He had nothing to lose. And he might find some amusement here.

He entered the white room with its marble chair and curtained alcove. What? he thought. No crystal ball? No swami? No mystical lights and floating trumpets? And why all this light? Weren't they afraid their fakery would be discovered?

He hadn't put a note in the box. That would give "them" a clue for "the spirits," so the properly muted answer could be returned.

"I don't," he said to the curtain alcove, "believe in spiritualism. I don't believe in any life after death. I'm dying, and I know that when I am dead I am finally, thoroughly, dead."

He did not sit down. He walked about the gleaming white room as he walked about a courtroom, outlining his case, his hands in his pockets.

"I don't know who you are behind those curtains," he said. "Moreover, I don't care. Doctor, clergyman, psychiatrist. There is nothing any of you can do for me now. I am dying. I may be dead tonight, tomorrow. But I will certainly be dead within a month. I don't know why I'm here. All my affairs are in order——"

He paused, swung about, and stared at the curtains. All my affairs are in order. "What did you

103

say?" he demanded. Was his mind playing him tricks now? He thought he had heard: "Are they?"

"All in order," he repeated. It was hot August outside, but here it was as refreshing as a garden filled with fountains. It was as pleasant a place to wait as any. Or he could walk in the gardens outside; he had noted, even in his cold anguish, that they were beautifully cared for, and the trees had been exceptionally lush in this August heat, and the paths were evidently thoroughly raked at least once a day, and there had been, along some paths, a suggestion of cool green arbors waiting. Emily would like these gardens. He would—he would be dead before the first leaves fell from those trees outside. He would never show Emily these gardens, or any other gardens, anywhere else in the world.

"If I have ever had any hobby at all, it was helping Emily in the gardens at home," he said aloud. "And on Sunday afternoons. I never could understand how she could contrive to have such a massed effect at the end of the lawn, a cypress effect, with heavy shade, and a stone bench to sit on. We would go there together, to rest, to have a drink, and smoke. Sometimes when it was too hot to sleep we'd go there, and it was cool. It reminds me of a garden somewhere, I can't remember. It was a picture of some garden with cypresses, in the moonlight, and a large flat stone—I think there were some figures in the background, sleeping. And someone——" He shook his head. "I was only a child then. It must have been in some book."

His heart jumped then, as if suddenly startled

or struck, and he put his hand on his chest. His logical mind assured him quickly that this was not a physical symptom but an emotion. He could not remember having this emotion before, as of sorrow for someone deeply loved and understood and vanished. The very taste of sadness was on his tongue; the sickness of grief was heavy in his body.

"Now what is wrong?" he muttered. After a moment he began to pace again. "I don't know why I am here. I am forty-nine years old, married, a successful lawyer, and I have two handsome children, a wife who loves me, and money, and a charming home. But now I must die. I have leukemia.

"Why are we permitted, all our lives, to prepare only for life and not for death? Why do we evade the very thought of death? Our friends, parents, wives, husbands, children never talk of it. It's like an obscenity, a subject not mentioned in polite company. Yet it's around us all the time. Perhaps I wouldn't feel this way about it—this furious rage —if I had been taught from childhood to know that it was everywhere. I knew it was everywhere, of course, when I became a man, but like everyone else I had been sedulously protected from its presence. I was never permitted to see my father in his coffin, when he died when I was eight years old.

"People died all about us, and it was hushed up, like a terrible scandal. When my children asked about it, I grinned at them and hugged them comfortingly. What a fool I was. I should have said to them, 'You were born so you can die.' "

He stopped and looked challengingly at the curtains. "The child psychologists would disagree. The children must never be 'hurt.' They must be protected until they are men. And then they are suddenly pushed out of the nursery, unprepared not only for living but especially not for death. Well, I'm going to do some good with this thing I have. I am going to call my young son and daughter to me tomorrow and say, 'I am dying. Look at me very carefully and remember what a dying man looks like. Remember that he hates death, and fears it, and is enraged at it. It's an ugly thing to happen to a man. It will happen to you, sooner or later. It isn't glorious and beautiful and it doesn't inspire spiritual thoughts. It's hateful, and it's the end, and there's nothing more, except darkness and silence and never thinking again, or laughing, or working. Prepare yourselves for it and accept it. You have no other choice.' "

He clenched one fist and slapped it hard into the palm of the other hand. "No choice! We had no choice to be born, we live without a reason for living, and we die as ignorant as the day we were born. But at least if we accept it from the time we can first walk and speak, it will lose some of its terror. Do you agree?"

He thought there was a movement in the room, a flash of light or an increase in light. He shook his head impatiently. And then with wonder.

"I'm not a man of words, except in the courtroom. Why am I talking like this to you, a stranger, in a strange city? I haven't even told you my name, and I don't intend to. I am nothing to you; worse than nothing, for I am dying, and I can't stand the thought of it. For just when I can afford to live and know life, it is taken away from me. But why should I tell you?"

He waited. There was no answer. "I think," he said almost kindly, "that it's damned decent of you to sit behind that curtain and listen to any stranger who wants to come in and whimper his little tale of woe at you. At least I get paid for it!" He laughed. "I assume, of course, that you are doing this out of charity."

He heard no movement, no breath. He walked to the curtain and looked at it curiously and read the plate near the button. "Well, I will certainly not push the button and intrude on your privacy," he said. "Besides, it would embarrass me. I'd rather be faceless to you, as you are to me."

He walked again. "I don't know how old you are or how young. But, good God, do you know what it feels like to be sentenced to death? Irrevocably sentenced to death, without hope of appeal, without hope at all? No, you can't know. My mind accepts the fact, but something in me refuses to accept it, repudiates it as if it were a lie, a subornation of the truth, the blackest falsehood ever uttered by any man. That is what I can't understand. I say to myself, 'You are dying. Very shortly you will be dead and in your grave, and that will be the end of hoping, loving, life. And light.' And then something answers me as angrily as if I had another self in me and it won't even listen to reason. If there was all acceptance in me, then I could feel more peaceful, more resigned. But something won't accept the irrefutable fact that I will soon be dead and that that is the end.

"Of course," he said thoughtfully, "I suppose

that is the old will to live asserting itself in the very face of fact. It can't be anything else."

Up and down he paced, echoing step after step. He was very weary; his bones ached, and he could feel his life seeping from him drop by drop, like inner tears.

"If only there was some way to avert this, to stop it!" he exclaimed. "If only I didn't have to face this! If only I could have it taken away!"

Once again his heart was startled and struck, more deeply this time. It appeared to have a sound, reverberating, so that it filled his body as if a strong voice had spoken. And then, without any reason at all, he saw the picture of the garden he had seen as a child, a colored picture of dark cypresses against a half-hidden moon, a spread of dark grass, a stone, sleeping men wrapped in cloaks. And someone near the stone— kneeling? His mind became confused.

"If only I didn't have to die just now," he muttered. "If only this—cup—could—be—taken— from—my—lips."

He stood very still, yet rigid, trying to remember. His struggle was so intense, so concentrated, that he burst into sweat, and he felt an unendurable anguish and sorrow and fear. "I'm afraid," he whispered to the curtain. "I'm only a man, and I'm afraid. Not the actual death, but the pain of it, and the last agony. Because after that—— Do you understand how it is to feel this way, this fear, this rejection of death, this hope of life, when you know you must die? But no, how could you know that, unless you have experienced it yourself?"

He had no desire to approach the curtains again

or touch the button, but he found himself moving swiftly, and his hand was reaching forward.

The curtains swung aside at once, and the light gushed out. Eugene fell back rapidly and looked. And looked again. And could not stop looking.

Then he sighed, and there was no more pain in him, no fear, no terror, no anger, no despair. Only peace and a sense of releasing grief.

"Yes, yes, of course," he said in a low voice. "You do know how it is, the rejection of death, the hope that you will not have to accept it—and the sentence of death. The loneliness of it; the horror of it.

"Yes, of course. Now I remember the whole picture of the garden, and you were kneeling, and your companions, the ones you hoped would pray with you, slept. They, in a way, were hiding from your death, as we all hide from each other's deaths. Denying it, in sleep.

"I'm terribly sorry. I haven't thought of you since I was a child, not honestly or deeply thought of you. There was too much work to do. Work. As if it were an end in itself, as if we had all the time in the world to live as well as work. All the time in the world. But we have hardly any time at all, have we? Only enough to know why we were born, what we must do here, and prepare for our leaving. I'd forgotten that. In a welter of work that prevented me from knowing what is of the only enduring value in the world—what a waste of time! How I wasted my time!

"I know you hear me and that you brought me here. Give me a little more time, three or four weeks. So I can tell my children what I really

109

know now, so I can comfort my wife and assure her of the real truth—that there is no death."

He came closer to the man who looked so piercingly at him, and he smiled. "The truth, the one great truth we have—that there is no death."

He had made a few spontaneous gestures in his life. He hesitated, then he bent awkwardly and kissed the man's feet. "I have all the time there is," he said. "I have eternity."

SOUL NINE

The Anointed

*You have not chosen ME, but I have chosen
you, and have appointed you that you should go
and bear fruit . . .*

John 15:16

Mrs. Giuseppe Pirotti entered the sitting
room with the shy brisk air of one who is well
known, half wishes not to be recognized and half
desires to be so, affronted if not, yet relieved. She
was stout and short and rosy, with crisply curling
black hair under her mink hat, and her rotund figure bulged under her modish mink coat. She had
large and vivid gray eyes, delicate features set in
a full face, and an eloquent dark red mouth. She
did not look her fifty-four years. There was an air
of robust and hearty living about her, as of one
who enjoys every moment of living and who sa-
vors each second like a fine rich sauce, and who
has prepared that sauce.

This was quite in character, for she and her

111

adored husband owned and personally operated one of the best restaurants in the city, which served only the most delectable of Italian foods. Giuseppe had learned his art under a famous chef in Rome. They had been married when he was twenty-two and she, Agnes, only seventeen, the daughter of a restorer of old paintings. He was one of eight accomplished children, she the daughter of a bourgeois and loving family of ten.

They had come to America not to "seek their fortunes," for Giuseppe could have remained at the Excelsior in Rome at a tremendous salary, but simply out of an ardor for adventure. They had settled in this large city, where there were cousins with big families and aunts and uncles and nieces and nephews. They had been successful from the start. Reservations at their beautiful yet intimate restaurant could not be accepted less than forty-eight hours before the scheduled party, and sometimes patrons had to wait a week during holidays. Their Italian and French wine cellers were famous. If Giuseppe was not there, Agnes was sure to be found, and during most of the time they were both present. They supervised everything meticulously. Their kitchens had been photographed many times for national magazines. "Dinner at Giuseppe's" was an event. Everything was cooked to order, nothing served hastily. "If you cannot spend two hours at least with us," was politely printed on the top of their menus, "we cannot serve you well."

There had been always one table left vacant, however, for any priests who might come in. And that, thought Agnes Pirotti with bitterness, had probably been the cause of all this terrible trouble. Oh, little Joe!

There was no waiting table for priests any longer at "Dinner at Giuseppe's." A loving and obedient wife, she had had her first and terrible disagreement with her husband, and she had won. The priests understood, delicately; they did not go to the restaurant any more. Agnes would make it too uncomfortable for them.

No one recognized her in the sitting room. But then, these were all strangers, either from out of town or people who could not have afforded her restaurant, where the cheapest dish was four dollars, and à la carte, at that. She sat down defiantly. She wondered if she was committing a sin, then tossed her pretty head. It would be a long, long time! Yes indeed, a long, long time.

She had been born of a busy family, of an industrious people. She carried knitting with her. She opened her large bag and brought out a half-finished sweater of the finest black wool. She looked at it, and then her eyes were full of tears. She tightened her lips and thrust the work back into her bag and scowled before her, trying to control the shaking anger of her mouth, and her grief.

One by one the people about her rose silently as a chime summoned them, and she watched them go. She was the last; she looked at her diamond watch. She must be back at the restaurant in less than two hours. She twitched impatiently. Then the chimes sounded for her. She rose, made her

113

short body as tall as possible, and marched into the white marble room, with the light flowing down gently upon her.

Well, anyway, it wasn't a church. She sat down decisively in the chair and contemplated the curtains. Who was behind them? No one knew. A priest? She hoped so! She would never be finished with giving priests a piece of her mind. She said coldly, "Are you a priest?"

She waited. She said, "Then I don't think I should be here. I'm all through with priests, Father. I want to make that clear."

She had a rich, womanly voice with the musical accent of her people. She had learned several languages in Italy in a convent school, and she spoke English precisely.

"I'm Mrs. Giuseppe Pirotti," she continued. "We own the best restaurant in town." She paused. "And if you're a priest, which I suppose you are, then you know all about it! We used to have a table always waiting for any of you. But not now! I don't want your company or your patronage—not that we ever charged priests, not even the bishop himself. And I can't help it if Giuseppe is miserable about it. I'm not!"

Tears ran into her eyes again, but she held up her head very high and set her mouth firmly.

"Giuseppe and I were married when he was twenty-two and I was seventeen. I suppose if you are an American priest you don't know much about how we Italians feel about children. One time I heard that Italy was a paradise for children, Paris a paradise for women, and England a paradise for horses. I think America's a paradise for movie actresses and baseball players, and that's all.

"Oh, they make a big fuss about children in America! I'm an American citizen, by the way, so I can criticize. Everything's for the children in America! The best school palaces, recreation, parks, milk, vitamins, amusements, clothes. You can't pick up a magazine or a book or a newspaper that doesn't have an article or story about children. The big boys and girls, the ones they call teen-agers, rule the country. No wonder it's full of disobedient, untrained young people who are just bored to death. Yes, they are bored to death. They have 'security,' and so there's no adventure, no danger, no excitement for them, nothing unknown. No wonder they're always getting into trouble and marrying very, very young and getting divorces! Why, even when they're eighteen they think of themselves as children and have childish wants! They hate growing up, even if they're bored in their sanitary nurseries with all the parents and teachers and doctors fluttering around them like hens over giant chicks.

"Do you know something I found out recently? A very fine family, with only one child, a girl of thirteen, comes in every Saturday night for dinner. A pretty girl, that Margaret. Her age is young, but not the size! She stands five foot nine in her expensive ballet slippers, and she's fat, too. Blubbery, baby fat, and she thirteen! We like the parents, and we thought we'd lost them as customers —they give big parties on the holidays in our private dining rooms—when we told them firmly that we could not serve Margaret wine. It's the

115

law, you know, though much younger children drink wine regularly in Italy, and it never did them any harm. I never did think much of this milk fad, you see.

"I said to the parents, 'We'd lose our license if we served Margaret wine. And please don't give Margaret any of yours. It's the law.' And the girl frowned at me angrily and said, 'We kids are the law, and nobody else.' I thought she was joking, and then I looked at her parents and they had almost crossed themselves! Honestly! They looked at that big, overgrown girl as if she'd just begun to pray the Rosary!"

Agnes snorted with deep contempt. "That wasn't the worst. I wanted to soothe that discontented, impudent kid. I said, 'My, you're growing up, Margaret! You are almost a young lady. You'll be thinking of getting married in five or six years.'

"Now what was wrong with that? Nothing! But if I'd hit the girl or kicked her, she couldn't have looked more horrified and disbelieving! I'm not joking. She stared at me as if I were out of my mind. Then she shouted: 'That's a lie! I'm always going to be a child! Everybody knows that the world is full of big people and little people. I'm always going to be one of the little people! I'm *never* going to grow up! What a lie!'

"Now," said Agnes, her color high and indignant, "if the girl was stupid or one of those poor, retarded kids, I'd have understood. But she's a bright girl and gets honors in school. I couldn't believe my own ears. I looked at her parents, and her mother hurries to put her arm about the girl —the girl was actually terrified!—and said, 'Why,

116

of course, darling, you'll always be a little girl, our own little girl.' And she glared at me and said, 'How could you hurt a little child like that, Agnes? You can injure her psyche that way.'

"Well, Father, I do have a temper. I looked at that big girl who actually thought she was going to stay a child all her life, and believed it, and at her silly mother and father, and I said, very snappishly, 'Mrs. Knott, I don't know about that girl's "psyche," but if anyone is injuring it, you are! She isn't a child any more; she isn't a little girl. It's time she knew that.' And I marched away, trying to keep down my burning, and I hoped they'd never come back. I couldn't stand seeing a young person being treated like that, to the detriment of her immortal soul. I had to take a dose of baking soda for my heartburn."

Agnes flounced in the chair. "I've discovered something. All this fuss and care and whimpering and fluttering around children means only one thing: American parents don't like their children. Perhaps they even hate them. Isn't that terrible? They hate their children! If they loved them they'd think of the children as just part of the family, with duties and responsibilities to the family, and they'd love them easily and without all that strain and anxiety, and they'd know, without anyone teaching them or 'warning' them in books and newspapers, how to treat children with justice. They wouldn't have to read books or spend time at lectures! They'd just be natural, and strict, and enforce discipline, and make the kids go to church whether they wanted to or not, and they'd have prayers every night and give the kids work

117

to do at home after school. Love means teaching responsibility toward others, and reverence, and duty to God, and love for God, and love for the family, and respect for parents. If the kids have all that, they don't need big allowances and what they call 'fun,' and fancy clothes, and dances. That all means nothing. But if they have love, real love, then they have everything else that means something."

Agnes shook her head dolorously. "I don't know why I'm talking like this. I think I wanted to bring out the fact that Americans don't really love their children and so they try to make up for their guilt in other ways. You have only to look at the bold, dissatisfied faces of the American children, and see how bored to death they are, to know that their parents don't love them in the right way. How often do you see an American child who looks happy? I mean really happy and enjoying life? And I don't mean looking greedy and excited and staring after new things and running, running, running. What are the poor kids running from? I think their parents, with their cluckings, and their teachers. I don't blame them for running. But they have no place to run to that isn't filled with adults waiting to pamper and give them what they call 'care.' They want to grow up in an interesting world, and they're kept babies, with a milk bottle in their mouths. And no interest for them anywhere, only a society that is all nicely organized and has a downy niche ready for them to cuddle down into. Is that all that a soul is born for?"

Agnes smoothed the sleeve of her coat abstractedly. "A downy nest. Even when they're grown up, they just want a downy nest, always under wings, out of cold, heavy weather. They're scared to death, and no wonder."

She looked at the curtain. "But the people in the old country love their children. We have big families, and by the time a child is a year old he knows where he fits in the family and what he should do and what he shouldn't do. He knows his parents love him but that they're not going to stand for any nonsense and tantrums. So he is satisfied and feels safe. American children never feel safe.

"When an Italian boy is confirmed, he knows he's a man now, not a little child. It isn't any shock to him, Father. He's been taught to become a man almost from the day he was born. That's how it was with our little Joe."

She took out her handkerchief hastily and dried the sudden flood from her eyes. "Every Italian man and woman wants a big family of children. What else is there in life but God and a loving family? And aunts and cousins and nephews and nieces and grandmothers and grandfathers? If we have trouble, all of us are there, helping. It's not only our duty; it is joy for us.

"But Giuseppe and I—we had no children. We waited year after year. We went to shrines and doctors. We wore medals. We went to Mass every day and took Holy Communion. We prayed all the time. Our family and our friends were sorry for us, and they prayed too. But no children came. I began to think that perhaps I had offended God in some terrible way. We would sit in our nice big house, Giuseppe and I, and cry our hearts out. The

119

doctors weren't sure why there were no children; some said it was Giuseppe's physical fault or mine. I had two operations. But no children. We had built a big house, six bedrooms, all empty and silent—waiting for children.

"And then, when we had given up hope and I was thirty-six and Giuseppe was forty-one, little Joe was born!"

Her face became radiant, full of smiles and tears. She moved forward in the chair, clasping her hands.

"A big, pretty boy, as fat as butter and full of dimples. Why, he smiled before he was a month old! We almost went out of our minds with joy. The doctor said it was a miracle. It was. We were building a new church, and Giuseppe gave all its stained-glass windows, because we were so grateful.

"We brought up Joe just as we'd been brought up in the old country. All the love in our hearts. But discipline, too. Not that he needed much of that. He was a lovely boy from the very beginning, gentle, full of fun, kind, sweet, strong. But serious! Sometimes too serious. We would play with him. But when he was about twelve we found out he was playing with us just to please us! He didn't want to play any more. He was always studying. We sent him to the best schools, and he studied and studied.

"We began to dream of the day when little Joe would be married. He was fifteen then, and after school he would come into the restaurant to help us. Of course that was only right—a boy or girl should help parents from the very beginning. We began to look over our friends. Who had the prettiest, sweetest, most obedient and industrious girl? The nicest girl? Giuseppe and I would talk alone in the kitchen long after all our guests had gone and discuss each girl in turn as Joe became sixteen, seventeen, eighteen. And we'd talk about our grandchildren; at least eight of them, all like Joe.

"We had only Joe, but we'd have a lot of grandchildren, and we'd be a real family at last We could hold up our heads with the best of them. We'd fill up all the rooms in our house. Joe would follow his father or, if he wanted to, he could take up any kind of work. It didn't matter. But he and his wife would live with us, and there would be all those lovely, laughing, shouting, loving grandchildren.

"We should have known!" said Agnes with anguished bitterness. "We should have known when we saw Joe paying particular attention to the priests at the table we used to keep for them. We thought he was just being respectful and kind, as we'd taught him, and having reverence for the priesthood. He'd sit down with the priests, talking, their heads bent together. We never disturbed them; after all, it is an honor for priests to be especially interested in your children. When the priests would leave they'd say to us, 'You have a wonderful boy there, Agnes and Giuseppe. A noble soul.' As if we didn't know it! But we didn't know then what the priests meant!

"I did notice, though, that Joe would be more quiet than usual after he had talked with the priests. And I didn't know that before he came home from school he'd go first to see Father Vincent; he's the priest of our parish. If I had known, I'd have screamed to the heavens and I'd have told Father Vincent to let my boy alone!

"Joe's eighteen now. He'll be graduated from his school in June. Then a month ago he came home with Father Vincent. My lovely boy! And they told me, very gently, that Joe wants to be a priest! My son—who was to give me grandchildren—a priest! My only son! My only son! My only child! Wasn't it the duty of the priests to tell Joe that he should forget the priesthood and stay with his parents who need him more?"

Agnes sobbed desperately. "Father, in there, please don't misunderstand me. It is an honor from God if He chooses one of your children to be a priest or a Sister. But—*one* of your children! Not your only child who was born when you'd given up hope of having a child. If I had seven or eight children and Joe was only one of them, I'd say, 'Thank God that He singled Joe out for this honor, for this very great honor.' But we have only Joe, who was our hope for grandchildren. The only hope for our old age. We need him more than—than——"

She bent her whole body forward and sobbed and could not restrain herself. "My only son," she wept. "My only son. He doesn't want to be a parish priest. He wants to be a mission priest. He wants to go far away and, he says, bring those who know nothing about God to God. Like one of the Apostles. We'd never see him then, or only once in a while. Our little Joe, our only son."

She moaned over and over. "He has a vocation, they tell me. He wants to go to the seminary in

122

September. When Giuseppe and I heard about it, I collapsed. And Giuseppe gets grayer and grayer every day, but he says, 'Mama, when God calls, a man can only obey.' And Joe tries to comfort me. He said to me yesterday, 'Mama, I know how you feel. But, Mama, would you want me to ignore God when He is calling me? Mama? I can't speak to Joe, Father. I feel my heart is all bleeding ribbons. The world is such a wicked place now. What will it do to Joe?

"I think about that. What will the world do to Joe, this world that's getting darker and more evil every day? All those priests behind the Iron Curtain—they kill them, Father! When will they start killing the clergy all over the world and not just behind the Iron Curtain? Father, when you read books and magazines, nobody writes about God. Nobody wants God. They want television sets and ranch houses and new automobiles and washing machines, and bigger pay, and bowling alleys and movies and night clubs. They don't want God, Father. They want what they call 'security.'

"A mother thinks about these things. When she has an only son. She is his mother; she bore him and nursed him, and taught him, and loved him. She is afraid of what the world will do to him if he becomes a priest. She knows they will make fun of him and call him a 'Holy Joe,' and that no one will really understand him. Or want him around. If he's at a party—I've seen it myself—the people are uncomfortable until he leaves. They don't want what he has to give!"

She put her hands over her face. "They never

did, Father. They never did. And that's what is so terrible for a mother who has an only son.

"But you're a man. You don't know what a mother feels. Did your mother ever feel afraid for you? Are you her only son? Did she pray for you when you were far away? Was she frightened that they might kill you?

"Oh, if only I could talk to a mother like myself! She would understand!"

Agnes got to her feet, blind with her tears. She ran to the curtain and pushed the button.

Instantly the curtains blew aside, and the full glory of the light shone out on Agnes. She looked and looked, then slowly fell to her knees.

"Yes," she whispered. "Your mother knew. She knew what it meant to be a mother like me. With an only son. An only son. She knew what it was to be afraid, didn't she? She knew what the world was.

"But she never tried to stop you, to keep you from going. She knew you had to leave her to go and tell the people about God. But I wonder what she felt in the lonely night when her son was not in her house."

Agnes lifted her hands and clasped them together. "I am going to be like your mother, as much as I can. I am going to say, as we say in the old country, 'Go with God!' To little Joe. Because, unless I say that, he loves me so, he won't go."

She stood up. She tried to smile through her tears. "And I'm going to finish that black sweater for him to wear in the seminary. Did your mother ever make you something like that to keep you warm? Yes, she did. 'The robe without seams.'"

124

SOUL TEN

The Pharisee

For I have known them all already, known them all:
Have known the evenings, mornings, afternoons,
I have measured out my life with coffee spoons—
  T. S. Eliot: "The Love Song of J. Alfred Prufrock"

Alexander Damon sat down in the comfortable armchair near the window of his room in the city's most modern and most expensive hotel. He was a tall, thin man of considerable elegance and grace of movement, in his middle forties, with brilliant blue eyes, smooth dark hair, and well-bred features. He looked at his watch. It was only half-past four. He had driven five hundred miles today and was proud of it. At this rate he would reach Reno the day after tomorrow—and begin the boring business once again of waiting six weeks for a divorce. He was not a gambler and disliked gambling not on principle but because a man of his particular temperament found no in-

125

terest in gambling. Gambling, even as a recreation, demanded at least a minimum of attention, and when he had leisure it was necessary for him to employ it in a more disastrous way.

Three wives: Sue, Ellen, and Moira. Boring, pointless women. He had liked Moira more than the others, Moira with her red hair and quick but gentle disposition, her light brown eyes and white skin. Within three years, however, he had tired of her as he had tired of his other wives. I must have a calamitous prospensity for picking out the shallowest women, he would say to himself. What liars women are! Each one of them—Sue, Ellen, Moira—gave me the impression that there was something stimulating and alive about them, something exciting, something that would lead somewhere, something of "infinite variety." Something significant. But always, they merely turned out to be the usual dull and desperately boring woman. ". . . The women come and go, talking of Michelangelo."

He looked restlessly through the window. He was very tired. He saw the late autumn crowds moving along the street in the usual bright topaz air of autumn. It was a handsome city, for a huge metropolis, and had, he thought condenscendingly, somewhat of the air of New York. It was clean and tall, faintly Southern in atmosphere, though it was not in the South. Perhaps it was the shine in the sky, the way the light fell on sharp slabs of buildings as on colored marble. For a minute or two the city held his interest. And then the interest was gone, not fading away, but suddenly, blackly gone, like a large light blown out in dark-

126

ness. Following that oblivion of interest came the familiar nausea in the pit of his stomach, and with it the usual black, empty despair, speechless, motionless, sightless. It robbed his whole body of vitality, slackened his muscles, sucked out his life. It was not the active kind of despair that drove a man to suicide, though it was as intense. It was merely a profound inertia and apathy. Sluggishly, as the light outside failed, he turned his head and looked at his suitcase, its fine smooth leather dimly glimmering in the rapid dusk. He glanced at his watch. Five o'clock. He was very particular about time—about the time. That alone, he would tell his doctors impatiently, was proof that he had control. He always waited until half-past five. He put his watch to his ear; it was running. But it was running very slowly. That last half hour was inevitably the worst. It was not that he craved the damned stuff; he hated the taste of it; he thought those who looked at the whiskey in their glass with beaming approval and anticipation to be liars. Who, honestly, could stand the taste of alcohol and enjoy it? The acridness of it, the sting of it, the first sickness of the first drink, the first strong metallic finger laid at the root of the tongue! Who could enjoy that?

The liars pretended that they enjoyed it, but they wanted, as he always wanted, only the effect. If it was taste they wanted, there were better tastes, God knew, even ginger ale or orange juice. They had meager little natures, most people, and so the effect they wanted was meager also. Thank God he had a large appetite for experience of all kind. At least he used to have it.

Here it was again! He stood up and began to walk around the room, prowling. Should he go outside and take a walk and then stop in at some bar? No, the presence of others wearied, angered, or disgusted him. Anger came, especially. There was always some jovial soul who was ready to speak to a man alone, and so inevitably he would get into some argument with the lout. As few people were intelligent, the lout, without fail, would turn out to be one of those whose interests centered in sports, women, local news and scandal, or the nefarious doings of the local politician or school board. Worse still, if the lout was a stranger in the city, on business, he always had a wallet full of photographs of his retarded-looking children and a wife who was composed solely of teeth, fat legs in toreador pants, and pixie hair. (Thank God Moira had had the intelligence not to cut her long red hair. She, at least, looked unlike other women in a country, a world, that was becoming to look more and more faceless all the time.) The lout, after a few drinks, would become maudlin. "Have any children?" he'd say.

Damn Moira. When had he wanted to leave her, divorce her? Six months ago. Why? He could not remember, but it was between one breath and another.

He passed by the dresser, stopped. The usual beguiling dinner menu which always tasted exactly like the food in New York, Philadelphia, London, Cincinnati, Brooklyn, Paris, Chicago, Rome! No variety. Were all the chefs trained in one particular school? Vichyssoise was a blanched, pasty insult to the palate wherever you ate it. The menu could be in French, or Italian or English or German—it never varied. Even cheese, which had once had a sharp and distinctive flavor in its many varieties, had become bland, with an aftertaste of starch. Bland. The whole world was turning into a whitish, bland featurelessness. He was sick of it. He was sick of all of it. He wished some disaster would come to it, some fiery fury—not that he hated the world. He was civilized enough to tolerate it. It was only that he wanted some point to it, some excitement, something which would—— What? He did not know.

There was a pamphlet on the dresser, small but of excellent paper, with a photograph on the cover: "The John Godfrey Memorial Building." Alexander loved buildings of all kinds. This one looked strange. It had the aspect of a small marble Parthenon, though without columns. He turned on a lamp and examined it closer. Really interesting. Flat roof. Whole thing set on a slow rise, surrounded by trees, marble benches, flower beds, winding walks. Too small for a museum, too small for a library or a religious building. What, then?

Listlessly he began to lay it down. What did it matter? He would never see that building; he was not concerned with the mystery of it in this anonymous city. He liked the idea of leaving a mystery, however small and worthless, behind him. It had become a kind of fetish with him over the years. "You and your damned chic! Do you know how boring you are sometimes with your little airs?" Moira had cried. Had he become fed up with her at that very moment?

He looked at his watch. Twenty after five. In

ten minutes he would open his suitcase and take out his bottle of bourbon. Then he would have a quiet hour or two with himself, the darkness and despair slowly seeping out of him. He would call room service then. "I will call room service," he said aloud in a determined voice, as if reminding a heedless companion who would forget to eat if not guided. "At eight o'clock; not later." After all, he had to be on the way by seven in the morning, at the latest.

He had dropped the pamphlet on the dresser. It suddenly became interesting; why leave this insignificant local mystery behind? Moira and her "conceits." Damn Moira. Damn everybody. He opened the pamphlet and sat down, smiling indulgently at both himself and the pamphlet. It would turn out, this building, to be the DAR center or something, or a place for flower arrangements, or a "study group." He put on his black-rimmed glasses and opened the pamphlet. His hand felt heavy yet weightless, and the black despair was taking him more and more.

But the prose in the pamphlet was not ebullient and coquettish, as he had expected. There was a close-up of the arch over the tall bronze doors: "The Man who Listens." Aha. A clergyman, no doubt, or a social psychologist, or a marriage counselor, or a teacher, or some other uplifter or do-gooder. Alexander read. This building had been built ten years ago by an old local lawyer, John Godfrey, in memory of his wife, Stella. A sort of coy Taj Mahal, by God! Doddering old fool. Fountains inside, no doubt, and pretty little green arbors, and the stink of hothouse vegetation. Exotic, top-heavy deadly flowers. Soft lighting. How demure could even an old man get?

"This building," the pamphlet informed him, "was built for the reason that Mr. Godfrey believed that few listened these days to anyone. He believed that it was desperately necessary for men to listen to each other, as they had listened to meistersingers, priests, poets, and philosophers in the past. He believed that time had taken on a kind of 'fragmentation,' and that though there was more leisure than ever before in the world there was less time, less solidity, less meaning, fewer roots, and no real security. Therefore, more despair and loneliness.

"And so he built this 'sanctuary,' as some call it, where someone will listen to anyone who comes. There is no set time. A visitor may take up ten minutes, or an hour, or even two hours. The building is open twenty-four hours a day. It is maintained by the Stella Godfrey Memorial Fund, established by Mr. Godfrey, her husband."

The room darkened. Alexander Damon stared before him, the pamphlet limp in his hands. Half-past five came, then six. Suddenly he started as church bells began to ring, filling all the mild autumn air and penetrating the room. He looked at his watch. Six o'clock! What had he been doing all this time? Not reading, certainly. Had he fallen asleep? Not possible. He was always too tense, and he was more tense than usual because of the long drive today. He threw the pamphlet from him, went to his suitcase, and took out the bottle of whiskey. He went to the telephone to call room service for ice. The pamphlet lay near the chair where he had thrown it, its little white "Parthenon" staring up at him. "The Man who Listens."

"To what?" he asked contemptuously. "To every driveling little housewife, yuk, truck driver, petty doctor, teen-ager, failing lawyer, grocer? The Man who Listens. I'll drink a few to you, sir, and sympathize with you."

Still, he picked up the pamphlet and turned a page. "This pamphlet is left in your room to inform you that someone is waiting to listen to you if you feel the necessity. Hundreds of visitors to our city have visited John Godfrey's memorial to his wife. No one knows who the man is, or, if he is known, no one has told. You are invited, at any hour of the day or night, to enter this building and speak to the Man who Listens."

Alexander always prided himself on the fact that though he was a gentleman, and successful, and an "intellectual," he was always "up" on the latest modern jargon. "What do I have to lose?" he asked himself, and laughed. "Besides, it might be amusing. 'Something to tell the folks at home.'" He was to be the guest of a very witty commentator in three months on a nationally popular television broadcast: "Visit Him Now." Mr. Alexander Damon, famous architect. Raconteur. Personality. Author of the sparkling book, *Why Build?* No one who intended to build a larger, glassier, more steely building than any yet built—whether for business or for living—failed to consult Alexander Damon. Brighter, bigger, better, full of softly controlled and filtered air, colorful steel doors, new "miracle" floors, aluminum, chrome—but not flashy or gaudy. Quiet, modern, efficient.

132

Everything at the touch of a button. Elegant. Sanitary. Even self-cleaning. Smooth as velvet. "Easeful living or working."

"Easeful."

An account of a visit to John Godfrey's coquettish little Taj Mahal would be good fun, and the television audience would enjoy it. There was nothing so enjoyable these days as scintillating malice, elegantly spoken. Devastating. But not for the yuks, who were often bewildered, preferring their humor "straight." But who cared for the yuks? What had a scientist, concerned over the population explosion in the world, said about the terrible danger of an increase, a swarming increase, of yuks? "It would take," the expert had said seriously, "several hydrogen bombs every three years to keep down the engulfing populations." He had meant it quite seriously. If necessary, nations would have to resort to that. "Splendid," said Alexander aloud. And saw Moira's face.

He put the whiskey bottle on the desk. He really must see that Taj Mahal. He phrased sentences in his mind and smiled. Perhaps this city would become so embarrassed over his broadcast that it would pull the infernal, ridiculous thing down and build in its place a fine apartment house with aluminum and stone balconies.

Alexander smiled with pure, delighted hate. He hated everything that was "popular," best-selling, widely accepted, revealing public vulgarity at its worst. He hated the gross businessman, the brash politician, the inelegant, the openly enjoyed. He hated Hollywood and movies (except the esoteric little foreign films), large restaurants teeming

with people and smells, women who were simple
and kind and had no finesse—American women,
for instance—and American automobiles, and "the
American way of life," whatever in the name of
God that was! He loved little slim stream-of-con-
sciousness volumes of poetry which few read, except those like himself. He loved Joyce, because
only a few understood him. He loved "the dance,"
provided it was ballet, Russian or British preferred. (Americans really could not interpret ballet very well.) But, as he was a liberal, he also
loved swarming, after-theater, furiously lighted
large dens where one could buy a proletarian
hamburger (two dollars) and a good, rousing glass
of beer (one dollar) and mingle with "the people."
He loved the people, provided they did not intrude upon him. He could become quite eloquent
on the subject of "the people." Fresh, earthy,
Gothic, he would call them. He never saw "the
people." But, as a liberal, he loved them just the
same. "Virtue resides in the people." The throngs
on the streets of New York were not "the people"
to him or to his kind. They lived somewhere far
in space, or as a symbol.

"You are a pretentious mess," Moira had said
to him. "You are as insulated as a baby in an incu-
bator." Had he begun to despise her then? Stupid
Moira.

He really must go to the Taj Mahal. He forgot
to open the bottle of whiskey. Smiling happily, he
put on his black coat (London-made) and his
black severe hat (London-made). His ridicule of
the Taj Mahal would reach the European corre-
spondents, who would then write articles for their

134

foreign newspapers on the "naïveté and utter un-
sophistication of the American people." "Mr. Alexander Damon, the Architect," one London fea-
ture writer had written, "is one of the few truly
intellectual Americans of today." Alexander loved
to make charming bons mots about Americans,
which were widely quoted in Europe, and especially in Russia.

Alexander was in almost a happy and exhila-
rated mood when he took a taxicab to John Godfrey's little "Parthenon." (It had overtones of
Zen-Buddhism.) He regarded taxi drivers as part
of "the people." Witty, wise, illiterate Socrateses.
He said, "Have you ever been to John Godfrey's
building?"

"Nope," said the driver sullenly. (What could
you expect outside New York? Even the taxi
drivers were stupid.)

"Do you take many people there?"

The driver was silent.

Alexander looked with cool distaste at the interior of the cab. A typical American "job." He
said with his usual sang-froid when he was speaking to a member of "the people," "Why don't you
fellers insist on the European cars? Quicker, more
agile, and not gas-eaters? There's nothing like a
foreign car. I have a small Mercedes-Benz, myself."

"You do, huh?" said the driver. He had a thick
neck, and now it became crimson. He did not
turn. "Look, mister, I got a son and his family in
Detroit. He works in one of them automobile
joints, makin' cars. You're puttin' him out of business, you and your foreign cars! What can they

135

make better'n an American car? You tell me that! If people want little cars, we got the tools in Detroit to make them better than in Europe. You one of the Communists, everythin' better outside this country than in?"

Alexander was startled. But then, he was in the "hinterland," where everyone was one hundred per cent American, no matter where one was born. He knew how to handle "the people." He peered at the driver's certificate. "Now, Bob, you know that Europe does have some talents we don't have, don't you?"

"Sure, I know," said the driver. "We're all Europeans here, ain't we? Your dad or granddad, or maybe even way back—they was Europeans. Think we're all Indians, eh? You're sure mixed up. Mister, you sure are mixed up!"

Alexander did not answer. He felt hot and disgusted. He liked love and humility in "the people," and an eagerness to learn obediently. And an anxiety to be "led" by their natural rulers, the intellectual elite. This driver was definitely not one of "the people."

The driver stopped the cab. "One dollar fifty," he said in a surly voice. "Can't drive the car up there. You gotta walk a little." Alexander got out of the cab. He counted out precisely one dollar and sixty-five cents. The driver looked at the money and snorted, "I shoulda known!" he said, and drove off.

Alexander laughed softly. That idiot was exactly like any New York taxi driver. They wanted nothing but money. That was the grossness of America. He walked up the gently winding red

136

gravel walk; everything was dimly illuminated. Almost European in its effect; no glare. No neon signs. He had expected neon, in various flaming colors, going on and off, in big pink and blue and purple letters: "Come! The Man who Listens!!!" Like a Revivalist temple. It was nothing like that.

The small marble building raised itself purely against the dark sky, shining and simple. Alexander thought, Why, it's very artistic! And very emotional, in a restrained and serene sort of way. The gravel under his feet reminded him of Oslo, of Rome, of Stockholm. He nodded approvingly. No smooth concrete or asphalt. That would be out of character. He detested things out of character. The men who built this place, laid out these gardens, were very sophisticated and knowing. He could not have designed this better himself.

Nor, he thought, could he have imagined anything more restful and beautiful than the waiting room. No money had been spared. Where had that silly old lawyer gotten that money in this city? And the decorator? Very restful. No modern furniture, no amoeba-like, free-form glass tables on one or two scattered legs. But I designed an office like that, thought Alexander Damon. It was photographed for a national magazine. It gave me the horrors. In fact, everything gives me the horrors. He sat down in his coat and hat and looked before him. "The horrors," he said aloud. There was no one there but himself. The proletarian dinner hour. There was a chime.

"For me?" he asked courteously. The chime sounded again. He stood up, smiling in anticipation, and went into a stark-white marble room with blue velvet curtains concealing an alcove, and a marble chair.

He sat down in the marble chair. He looked at the curtains. There was no sound here, no hurrying, no shrill whisper. No sense of amusement. The white walls were without decoration. They beamed at him, illuminated and waiting.

He sat. No one asked him any questions or gave an indication of impatience. He continued to sit and to wait. The room waited with him. What had that pamphlet said? "All the time there is."

"That's the trouble," he said to the curtains. "There's too much time."

He was aghast at this blunder.

"I must be candid," he said in his cool voice. "I'm not here because I have a 'problem.' I am here only as an investigator. I won't tell you my profession or business. That is immaterial."

What was wrong with him? His profession, immaterial! He must call his analyst tonight. When a man thought his work was "immaterial" he was out in the deep end.

"Are you a psychiatrist?" he asked contemptuously, "not that I dislike psychiatrists. We all need help. I have an analyst of my own. If there were more psychiatrists in America we'd all come to understand ourselves more. 'Know thyself,' said Socrates. A very sound idea. My analyst assures me that I know myself completely. But I have the worst possible propensity for selecting wives that are bad for me. He has studied my last wife, Moira, and is convinced, as I am, that she is the most stupid selection of them all. She has no flair, no style, though she had convinced me she had before we were married. A dull, plodding woman, Moira, though she paints. But every woman, I am sure, is dull and plodding. Their biological necessity, their nest-building. But who would have thought it of Moira, the modernistic painter? Everyone lives in deception."

There was no sound, no movement, no rustle of traffic.

"Every psychiatrist, and I am sure you are no exception, wants to know your background, from birth on, your childhood traumas, your parents, your siblings. Your teachers. Your playmates. Your relatives. It is only in that way that they can fix the blame where it belongs, for your misery, your meaningless life."

He leaned forward, flushing. "I'm sorry. That was a slip of my tongue. My life has meaning. The only trouble is that there is no meaning in others. They exist only as impediments, slowing up your flow of ideas, your enthusiasm, your dreams."

No one spoke. "And when that happens there is nothing left, no life, no drama, no significance, no zest, no meaningful end, nothing to strive for, to hope for, to work for. No color, no vitality, no excitement, no passion, no drive—no goal. We kill each other, not with an honest knife or a blow, but through our inertia. That is the real murder. I've been murdered, from my childhood on. By pointless people, by conformists, by repetition. Always repetition."

He smiled slightly at the curtains. "I have read your pamphlet. If one doesn't wish to see the face of the psychiatrist who listens, one doesn't need to press the button. I have no intention of pressing it. I prefer that you hear me in silence and in anonymity."

He said, "I wish to be perfectly candid. I'm here to expose this silly nonsense. I was always an honest person. I intend to speak of this place when I make my appearance on a certain television program called 'Visit Him Now.' Very poignant, isn't it? 'Visit Him Now.' No doubt you are familiar with the program. Very urbane; civilized. One of the few civilized programs on the television circuit. It has a high rating, I'm told, and this surprises me. I was under the impression that the public prefers Western shooting and gangsters and what they call 'situation home dramas.' But Mr. Brewster—Gene, we call him—is very popular, even if he has a late broadcasting. Every intelligent person listens to him. Of course the yuks are in bed at that time."

Alexander waited. He looked coldly at the curtains. "Of course you have seen his programs?"

Why this damned, white, marble silence? Oh, the Man who Listens.

"I'm a listener, myself," said Alexander. "In fact, it seems to me that I've been listening—too much!—all my damned life.

"At any rate, I am going to expose this sentimental slop on that program. I hope you don't mind. After all, when your identity is known you'll have more publicity than you ever had before! Is that your object?"

He shrugged. "Everything is Madison Avenue," he said. "Look, I'm not condemning you. We all live by advertisement, don't we? And I must say that the way you advertise—discreet and artistic

140

—is very well done. I couldn't do better, myself. Of course you know the origin of the word 'broadcasting.' It was done by the Romans, and the Greeks before them, and the Egyptians. 'Public letters.' So even the most stupid would understand when the letters, or the parchment, or the paper, appeared on the walls of the city. Catiline was famous for it. He would make it especially dramatic by pinning the broadcasts to the walls of the temples with a naked dagger. Very startling; caught the attention of the populace at once. It didn't really matter that the daggers could be bought for five hundred a sesterce. Very cheap metal; of no value. But interesting. Very interesting. But even politicians in these days are dull. No bright ideas. They must hire people to give them ideas, who will then broadcast them in the names of the politicians. That is public relations."

He paused. He felt a hungry, sick crawling along his nerves, a desperate aching. "It is not," he said, "that I am an alcoholic. My analyst assured me I am not. It is only that I can't stand——" He stopped. Then he exclaimed, "I can't stand living!"

He rubbed the palms of his hands together, over and over, in the immemorial gesture of despair, and did not know it. "What an idiotic thing to say," he murmured apologetically. "I never blurted out that to my analyst! I'm sure if I had said an imbecile thing like that he'd have recommended shock treatment at once. Manic depression. I'm not in the least 'depressive.' You can take the word of one of your colleagues about that! I am not even manic-depressive-manic. I'm

141

quite normal. If I sometimes drink to excess, who can blame me? No one."

He stood up restlessly. "I'm afraid I'm taking up too much of your time. After all, you don't find many people like myself, do you, in this city? Still, it may be interesting to you to listen to someone who doesn't have bunions, or constipation, or bewildering teen-age children, or a quarrel with a husband or wife—ordinary, foolish problems. One of my friends, who is an advertising manager, told me that the 'problems' of the stupid were big business in America. They created 'wants and needs and demands.' To satisfy the 'problems.' In other words, give a man whose soul is aching a nice sweet strawberry-flavored lollipop. That will do it! Suck like a baby, and smile and gurgle, and then there are no more problems. The soul doesn't ache any more. It settles down to enjoy the momentary syrup. I'm sure you understand that I'm speaking of the soul in a loose sense— the psyche. An aching soul."

He had a sudden intense sensation that someone had moved closer to him and was listening acutely. He shrugged, smiled about the room. He sat down again.

"Do you know what happens to me when I drink too much, as I usually do? You see, I'm being candid, and no alcoholic is candid. When I was in preparatory school we studied Swinburne, that Victorian, gloomy, unsophisticated poet. I remember his *Garden of Proserpine*—when I'm drinking. Only one stanza, I'm pleased to say. May I repeat it?

"I am tired of tears and laughter,
Of men that laugh and weep;
Of what may come hereafter
For men that sow to reap;
I am weary of days and hours,
Blown buds of barren flowers,
Desires and dreams and powers
And everything but sleep.

"I drink," said Alexander Damon, "for sleep. Only for sleep. To forget."

He settled deeply in the chair. He was exhausted, yet he felt released. He said, " 'Blown buds of barren flowers.' All my life was barren. And pointless. And without meaning."

He looked at the curtains again. "I am not whimpering. Everybody's life is like that. Nobody's life ever was fruitful. Not even Christ's. His was the most fruitless of all. Don't you agree? Two thousand years! And there are no real Christians. When you come down to it, there are no religious people anywhere, are there? Can you imagine them in public relations, or business, or anywhere else, for that matter? The very idea is calamitous. I met a Jewish writer the other day, a young man. A Talmudist, he called himself. He was actually writing a book about his 'God.' I told him he'd never get a publisher for such a naïve idea. He said, 'I certainly will. We need a new affirmation, every generation, of the presence of God in our lives.' Everyone at the table laughed. I'm afraid that I laughed the hardest of all. Moira—she is my present wife—was very indignant. She told me I'd been drinking too much. But all my wives have said that, though they understood I am not an alcoholic. They make, as the proletariat say, a federal case of it."

The wild hunger moved through every organ of his body, demanding, screaming. He moistened his lips. He would leave almost immediately. It was late, very late. But he could begin his slow, steadfast drinking as soon as he got back to his hotel. Be quiet, he told his urgent body. His thirsty, hungering body that would never be satisfied or contented. That was always waiting for something.

The white light and the silent walls waited.

"My father," said Alexander Damon, quietly mopping his face and hands, "was a very successful lawyer in New York. Unfortunately, he died when I was only fourteen. I missed a father's influence. My mother was one of those Victorian ladies with a high sense of rectitude and duty and responsibility. The minister was always at our house. My father used to make fun of him when he left, he was such a simple soul, very naïve and earnestly full of faith. 'Louise,' Father would say to my mother, 'how can you endure that droning nonsense? After all, you are an intelligent person for a woman. We aren't living in the Dark Ages any longer, you know.' But my mother would say, 'Don't be silly, Edgar. If you'd listen to Mr. Thayer you'd find some direction, some purpose, some meaning in your life. You would know why you had been born.' I remember my father laughing. He was a very distinguished man, really, and civilized and adult. He would kiss my mother and say, 'You're my meaning in life.' She'd become very disagreeable to him then and push him away and

144

warn him, 'Alex is listening. I don't want him to be as frivolous as you.'

"You can see now what a wretched influence my mother had on my life. If she'd let us alone—my father and me—we'd have come to understand each other, I suppose. Not that he was particularly interested in me; he was interested in enjoying himself and being successful, and we had what they called 'fine wine cellars' in those days.

"But I've gone over all this with my analyst; I could repeat the whole story by heart. Which I am doing, I am afraid. When my father died—— I forgot to tell you—he killed himself. He hung himself, without warning, without even leaving a note, in his library one night. One of the servants found him the next morning."

Alexander was sweating profusely. He took off his coat; it seemed to hamper him and grasp him, like clutching arms. He tore it from his body and threw it from him.

"My analyst," he said in a faint, weakened voice, "told me that he suspected that it was my mother's frigidity that drove my father to his death. I don't quite believe that. We found out later that he had quite a number of women who were consoling him. But of course he had no consolation at home, where everything was geared to finding out why you were born, what you were to do here, and to prepare for what, as our minister said, was 'our life hereafter.' In that gloomy atmosphere—can you blame my father for killing himself?"

He waited for an answer. But none came. He looked at the walls. They had an air of listening, of weighing. He shook his head impatiently.

145

"I'm sorry that I said 'gloomy atmosphere.' It wasn't really. My mother was an amusing and pretty woman. She had a peaceful air about her; she was very popular in New York. Strange that I should have given you the wrong impression that she was a severe and stern sort of woman. She wasn't. She just seemed to have a meaning in her life. In all justice—I must remember to make a note of that when I next talk to my analyst—I'm afraid I misled him. I told him that my mother was a sort of tall Queen Mary, all propriety and uprightness. At least I think I told him that. But no, now that I think of it, he suggested it himself! Apparently he has numbered slots where he inserts people with a click. I let him do that about my mother. What did it matter, anyway? It may have been misleading—I don't know. After all, I was my own problem, not my mother's. It is easier sometimes to let people think that what they believe is the truth.

"My mother died shortly after I was graduated. She had been sick for some time, though I never heard her complain. Just before she died she said to me, 'Alex, there is a meaning why you were born. You must try to find it, not just in your work, but in yourself. Your father never found that meaning. God help him.'

"I had never forgiven her for my father's death. I think perhaps that I never forgave him, either! He loved no one except my mother. Of course he was interested in me, but my mother was first. He was a man of wide interests. When you consider my mother, who, though popular and pretty and home-loving and devoted—she wanted several

146

children—was a somewhat shallow woman, it would make anyone wonder why my father thought she was earth and high heaven. And why, thinking that, he killed himself."

Alexander Damon stood up. "I know why he killed himself. He found no meaning in life. None at all. And neither do I." He rubbed his hands over and over. "What meaning is there, for anyone?

"Let me tell you about my stupid wives, who all resembled my mother in one way or another. (My analyst has been very interested in that.) At first they seemed sparkling and interesting to me. They offered a sense of excitement, of something about to happen. But invariably, after a few years, they became dull to me, and pointless.

"Perhaps it was my work, too, that accentuated it all. I'd see my finished—structure—and feel flat and empty as death. Then another would begin. All those buildings. Repetition. Everything was repetition until I'd feel myself going mad inside. Once, when I was younger, I thought that hell must be like that. Repetition. Working, planning, struggling, completion. Then begin again. Repetition. If the repetition had had any meaningfulness, I'd have been contented. But it didn't. For what is a man born? To throw up more and more buildings, more and more offices, more and more apartment houses? For what? Tell me, in God's name, for what?"

He began to pace with agitation up and down the room. "Like bees. Like ants. Surely a man is more than a bee or an ant! Isn't he? Surely what he does will make a mark on the world? But only six years ago I saw one of New York's most famous

147

and beautiful buildings torn down—to make room for one of my icy glass-and-aluminum structures. I thought of the architect who had designed that building, and how he had cared for it, and how he had watched it go up day by day. And then it was torn down. No one even remembers his name. No one cares that he ever lived. It will be that way with me too.

"Listen! All my wives wanted children! For what? To eat, to sleep, to grow, to go to school, to be graduated—to do what? 'In the grave there is no remembrance,' I once read in the Bible. Why should a man repeat himself in his children? Why bring them into this horror of realization that you have no meaning in your life, that the world has no meaning, that all is repetition, a treadmill, a squirrel cage? No matter what you do! Nothing has any lasting meaning, significance, worth."

He stopped and looked at the curtains and did not know that he was crying.

"Can you understand that? Can you live with that, knowing that you were born for nothing, live for nothing, die for nothing? Why not put an end to it, as my father did, or forget your meaninglessness in drinking?

"You listen to the noise of the world, and the hurrying and scurrying, and the voices, and the slamming of doors, and you watch the people coming and going, as if what they did was relevant. Then it all takes on a quality of nightmare, of hell. There's no escape, except in drinking. I can understand why people take drugs too. It's the despair of the thing, the hopelessness. Oh, it's all right when you are young! You are full of ginger;

148

you are going to accomplish something. Accomplish what? When you become successful you've reached the end of the road. After that—you only repeat yourself.

"I've tried to tell Moira that. (She resembles my mother even more than my first wives did.) And she says, 'Why, you work, of course, not just for your own fulfillment. You work for God. You put God in your work; you try to help Him find the pattern in what you do and what He wants you to do, even if it is only raising potatoes or buildings. It is all of one pattern.'

"You can see how utterly absurd she is. Just like my other wives. 'Do you think this world is all there is?' she says. 'This is only the beginning of your work. How you do it here will result in what you will do after you die. You're just like a child in the first grade. You think the first grade is all there is, and there's no higher grade after it. But you—you're flunking even the first grade.'"

Alexander moved closer to the curtain, almost within touching distance.

"And now you see why I must divorce Moira, too, and why I drink.

"Oh, God! What meaning is there in life? Do you find a meaning in yours, listening to all this babbling? You listen! For what purpose? What did you find of meaning in yours, in the world, or any world hereafter, if there is any?"

His hand involuntarily reached out and touched the button.

The curtains fled aside, and he saw the light and who stood in it, listening. He stepped back. He

149

looked away. He wiped his face. He looked again and stood looking and thinking for a long time.

"Well, yes," he said slowly. "I see what you mean and what Moira means. You've worked a long time, haven't you? Repetition. Endless years of it. Repetition. But eventually—yes, I suppose so. What you do does have meaning."

He sat down in the marble chair, his elbow on the arm, his chin in his hand. He was no longer exhausted and driven, or hungry or desperate, or full of craving. He continued to contemplate the man before him, his face moved and listening.

"Yes," he said. "I do see what you mean. And now I know it's my fault that my life has no zest, no significance, no value, and why I married over and over looking for something I lacked in myself.

"Men like me, millions of men like me everywhere, have made the world faceless, because we have no features of our own, no real potency, but only pretensions which we call flair and style, and attitudes instead of movement. How did we come to be born, so many of us? Did an ugly, industrial, utilitarian age breed us, so that there is no variety in us, no pillared glory, no power, no real poetry, no color? Or did we make this barren age and all its glittering horrors, and ease, and too much idle, unfulfilled time? We are surrounded by the hugest of machines, which do all our work, and they've castrated us. We are without virility in our custom-made clothing, with our correct manners, our glassy houses which reflect back our smooth faces.

"Could it be that communism itself is the barbarian's repudiation of us, though he clumsily envies us? And tries, God help him, to imitate us? We are the men of death, though we don't make bombs, and deplore the making of them. If we write, we are concerned with form and not substance. If we produce plays, they are of mechanical violence, which does not resemble the emotions of men at all. If we are diplomats, we are not even expert and imaginative liars. We are cliché-makers. Phrase-turners, without sense or magnitude. If we 'study' man, as modern philosophers or executives or leaders, we regard him as a 'unit' of so many man-hours, or energy, or as a consumer, a belly without a mind.

"We are men who are sick. Not only factory workers have grown empty on assembly lines because there was no occasion for pride and individuality in their lives. Men like me have made assembly lines of the whole world—everything clicking along smoothly, never out of order, evenly spaced, with a bigger and better event, law, invention or amusement, or novelty popping up immediately after the one before, bland and polished, mechanically efficient and inhuman, easier, more sterile, more lifeless than the last. Even our crises are the crises of the machine. All that is needed is a little more oil, a few more dollars, a turn of the screw, an adjustment of the gears, a few more sparkling bolts, a new surface tension, a newly invented belt that will move things faster. If the barbarian howls at us, he has reason to howl. We give him the horrors, too. What we do can't satisfy a man's emotions or his human needs.

"Look at the buildings I design! They mirror me and my kind. Set on steel piles, glittering like mad

151

with acres of glass, the windows outlined in metal guaranteed never to rust, never to mellow, never to be burnished by weather and use. There is no honest authority in them, the authority of basic wood and stone and brick, the power of the authority of natural things. They are mirages of today, gone in a shatter tomorrow, for they are not set on earth. No soaring splendor, no grace, no emotion, no eloquence, no lifting of the eye—only blank straight lines and gleaming facelessness.

"We've enclosed the wild frontiers and made them safe, and we've neatly enfolded their mountains in cellophane and have neatly cut down their forests and have set up neat lawns. That is what the Hottentot wants, we assure everyone earnestly. We never know that he wants, more than anything else, to be treated as a man, a soul. He doesn't want our germless, frozen food, our impotent way of life, our meaningless way of life, our deadly 'know-how.' He doesn't want our collectivized death, our helpless unproductive leisure, our organized fun, our desperate play, our refrigerators, and our lethal machines. He has his own meaning, which we deny, because we have no meaning ourselves."

He leaned his head against the cushions. "But you had a meaning, for you loved, and love, man as he is and as he can be—a joyous, free, and valuable soul. The point now is—can you find it in you to love me if I become a man again and not a posture? Can I ask you to help me find the meaning of why I am here and what I must do? Will you give me muscles instead of flair, and bowels instead of style? Will you give me faith instead of

152

fashionable platitudes, and truth instead of lofty lies? I'm not a young man, and I've been weakened by my 'good taste.' If I'm to have flesh and blood again, and decency instead of careful manners, then I'll need all the courage you can give me. Above all, could you make me love my fellow man instead of devising ways to 'help' him become what I am, all for his own good, of course!"

He stood up, pale but with excitement. He felt young and potent again, and vigorous. "Yes, you can. And will. I can see it in your face. You've worked a long time and you are still working, so that alone, if nothing else, gives all of us a reason for being. You wouldn't have been born, and you wouldn't have lived, unless there was a profound meaning in it for all of us. Even men like me. You must have met them often in your life. And you meet them every day. Do you pity us a little for our stupidity?"

He paused. "You don't know how I despise myself now. I'm going to call Moira when I get back to the hotel and ask her to forgive me and tell her I'm coming home. Do you know that she outraged me when she suggested children? That is why I ran from her, to divorce her. I didn't want deathly replicas of myself! Instinctively I knew what a poseur I was, and how parched inside, and how thirsty and hungry."

He moved toward the door. He did not have to remember now that he must move with grace and style. He paused at the door and said: "The ancient Greeks poured out wine in a libation to God. Would you mind very much if I poured out my whiskey in a libation?"

153

SOUL ELEVEN

The Teacher

*And who is there to harm you, if you are
zealous for what is good? But even if you
suffer anything for justice' sake, blessed
are you. So have no fear of their fear,
and do not be troubled.*

I Peter 3:13—14

The man who sat in the white room with its
blue curtains and marble chair was young, but he
appeared old, for his color was grayish and weary,
his features pinched, his eyes wizened in his tired
face. He had a long thin nose with a sharp point,
an intelligent and sensitive expression, though it
was bitter now, and an intense and embittered
mouth. Everything about him was neat and
brushed and careful, even if his clothing was
cheap, even if his shoes had not cost more than
ten dollars. His fine hands were carefully kept,
and they moved restlessly on the arms of the
chair.

He looked at the curtains somberly. "I am not

going to give you my name," he said. "After all,
I need my salary and I don't want whispers to
travel back to the school board about my 'complaints.' Oh yes, I'm a teacher. A teacher must
never complain; he must always be dedicated to
'the children' and his 'sacred calling.' Yes, I heard
the president of the PTA say it was that—a
'sacred' calling. She was wearing a spring hat that
cost, at the very least, half of my month's salary.
She beamed at us, all radiance and pink dimples,
and congratulated us on having been 'called.' We
smiled back at her in a sickly way; her husband's
income, per month, is more than any of our yearly
salaries. I wonder what she is 'dedicated' to and
what her 'calling' is. She thinks that because she
gave birth to three staring and impudent children,
each a separate curse to his teachers, she has done
the noblest thing of all and we should be happy
to give our lives to her offspring.

"She was very eloquent, and she made little
ballet gestures with her hands and rolled her eyes,
and her voice became lyrical. 'A teacher,' she
warbled—how I hate these warbling, professional
mothers!—'cares nothing for money, and isn't that
wonderful in a materialistic age?' He or she has
given his or her life to the holy 'children.' I looked
at Marcia, sitting opposite me, and thought of her
salary and her invalid mother and how I had just
co-signed a loan for her so she could pay the doctor's bills. Marcia, who, like myself, must find another job in the summer, instead of studying or
resting and refreshing herself on a little holiday
so that she could be not only a strong teacher in
September but a full human being. That is part of

the horror of it all: we aren't full human beings. We were never permitted to be. 'Dedicated.' Why does everybody believe that a teacher should have no life of his own, no pleasure, no joy, no money, no laughter, and occasionally no innocent sin? Who are they, these professional mothers and fatuous fathers, to believe that their children are worth our death in life? Or anyone's life, if it comes to that? Or even their own? The majority of people only take up room in the world, without contributing a thing to it but endless replicas of themselves who must be 'educated.' "

The room was very quiet, very still. The man sighed, looked about him. "You don't know," he said, "how wonderful it is to be in a place that is as silent and peaceful as this! No children, no school board, no principals, no PTA, no shrill voices and pounding feet, no worry, no anxiety. Above all, no voices and no bells.

"Only recently I overheard a man say to another, "It's very funny, but the teachers are always complaining about their low salaries. But I've noticed they leave very fat estates, most of them. Did you see where old Miss Thompson died the other day? She was all of eighty. She left nearly two hundred thousand dollars. Not bad. Not bad at all.'

"I wanted to tell the fool," said the teacher, his voice rising, "that old Miss Thompson had been able to save a large part of her salary before high taxes came on the scene. And in an age when a schoolteacher's salary was substantial compared with an unskilled laborer's and prices were low. Moreover, many teachers had been left respect-

157

able estates by parents. Moreover, many of them remained unmarried and had small expenses. Unmarried. Now we must remain unmarried because we can't afford to marry! Marcia——"

His features drew together in a spasm.

"The only time we see anything beautiful is when we are in our schools—all glass and landscaping and fine hot and cold running swimming pools and pretty furniture and colored walls and lavish gyms and auditoriums that resemble expensive theaters. Then we go home to our drab rooms and look at the old furniture handed down to us by our mothers, or at the miserable sticks of a furnished, cheap apartment. Yet we teachers are the ones who are scolded in the press and at public meetings for 'palatial schools' and 'high budgets' and extravagance! This always happens when we timidly ask for a raise in salary so we can live too. We are blamed for the high estimates of new schools or expansions of old ones.

"None of the scolders, of course, ever blames himself for the gigantic and luxurious school plants. They want the very best, and the most expensive and luxurious, for 'the children.' They demand these things; the children 'deserve' them. I should like to know what law, spiritual or national, declares that people 'deserve' anything simply because they've been born! I was taught as a child that you must justify your existence in this world. I've had kids whimper in my class that they didn't 'ask to be born.' Well, neither did I, and neither did my parents, or their parents before them, or anyone else in the world! But once here we have duties before rights, and responsibilities

158

before 'demands.' Try to tell that to your class! The principal will ask for your suspension or resignation at once. The professional mothers will be all shrieking mouths and baleful eyes and angry gestures."

The teacher sighed, a faint sigh that spoke of exhaustion and hopelessness.

"The kids don't need luxurious school palaces. My generation didn't. They need only sound buildings; no luxuries. They don't need 'supervised' play. Why can't people let kids alone? They've become 'projects' now, of idle mothers who in other generations were too busy caring for their homes and cooking and baking and washing and sewing and scrubbing floors and ironing and window-cleaning and baby-tending. There is nothing so dangerous to a whole nation than a tribe of idle women busying themselves with 'projects' of one sort or another. I'd like to hang the men who invented automatic washing machines and other gadgets! Now the majority of people don't have homes; they have 'housing' for electrical equipment which gives them more time—more time for what? Mischief. No wonder we have the problem of juvenile delinquency."

The teacher rubbed his lined forehead. "I could talk all day about this," he said apologetically. "The teacher's problems are the problems of a whole nation. I do want to thank you for listening to me. People never listen to a teacher. They think we're prosy, proper, and stiff, almost as bad as the clergy. They've forced that archetype on us. We're flesh and blood; we hate the pattern they demand we fit.

159

"I was speaking to you about the school palaces. A school is a place of learning, not of 'fun' and recreation, not a place of baby-sitters. A school is an institution where children should be taught as widely as possible, and drilled and disciplined, and informed about their present and future public duties, to their family, their Creator, and their nation. I could spend another full day telling you of the silly and embarrassing 'courses' which are now part of the school curriculum, which were demanded by parents and not by teachers. Each facet of a teacher's life would fill a whole book. And each facet is expensive, and the taxpayers scream—yet it is the taxpayers who demand all this nonsense and all this lavishness. When they look at their tax bills, they next look at the salaries teachers receive and talk about five hours' work a day and 'holidays' and 'long summer vacations' and why are teachers so greedy? Why do they want more money? Where is the old-fashioned teacher who was 'dedicated' and never thought about money at all?

"Yes, where is the old-fashioned teacher who was regarded with awe and respect by his students, and with even more respect by his students' parents? What happened to an age when children understood they came to school to learn, to be grateful for the chance to learn, and to listen with eager interest? What happened to an age when parents kept their hands off the schools and attended to their own business—which was earning a living by sound labor and caring for their families and taking them to church? I think I have at

160

least one answer to that: too many people have too much money, too much time, too much 'fun.'"

He sighed again. "If all this money, leisure, and fun had resulted in a spiritually stronger people, a nobler people, a people with higher principles and strength of character, a more free and intelligent people, a more responsible people, a people more aware of what there is to learn in the world, a people who desired more libraries and a continuing education after they had long left school, it would be worth it. It would even be worth the miserable salaries paid schoolteachers; we'd be happy, have a high feeling of self-esteem and satisfaction; we'd know we had accomplished something worthwhile. We'd feel, then, that our demanded 'dedication' was dedication indeed, given with all our hearts and all our souls. If a man has any rights at all, it is the right of pride in his occupation.

"But all the money and leisure and fun have been disastrous to us as a nation. They've sent us searching, not for learning and wisdom, but for trivialities, newer amusements, newer mischief, cheaper and more vulgar entertainment, more ornate cars, more toys to fill idle, restless hands. Where is the American character now, the character that opened frontiers in the wilderness, that sailed on dark seas, that established free schools and churches, that voted for men of integrity and not men with four-cornered smiles full of glaring teeth, that considered morality the very foundation of a people and God its keystone? Where are the Americans now of courage and faith and prin-

161

ciple and understanding? They are a dead race. They're laughed at in books and articles as 'Victorians' and 'puritans.' You see, they never had much money and they knew nothing of jet planes and fun. They only knew how to build a nation, free under God, and how to form a Constitution that is the noblest document ever written by man —under God."

The teacher rested his worn cheek on his palm. "Because of the kind of people we have now we shall lose that nation, conceived in liberty and faith. Because we teachers are not permitted any longer to teach the children what they should be taught, they'll become increasingly weak, undisciplined, fierce, bored, unprincipled and dutiless —and uneducated. The children aren't more stupid than their grandparents, even if some teachers bitterly say they are. It is only that they are ignorant, and are kept ignorant, by the insistence of their parents that their brains not be taxed in schools, that they not be disciplined, that they be amused in the classroom and not taught, that school be only a glorified, warm, luxurious play pen. While Mama busies herself about her 'projects' and bridge games.

"Mama loves the word 'trauma.' She's picked up a great deal of psychiatric jargon in her careless reading. I wonder if she ever thinks of the incurable 'trauma' she is inflicting on her children by making life too pleasant and comfortable for them? I wonder if she ever thinks of the 'trauma' she inflicts on the teachers of her children by denying them the right of pride in their occupation and a decent recompense as some of the more important people in her children's lives?

"She's taken our ancient pride from us, the pride of Socrates and Plato and Aristotle, and the whole grandeur of the teaching profession, from the very beginning when teachers were also priests and philosophers. To Mama, we are baby-sitters, paid to amuse her children and 'care' for them. If she despises what she has made of us, does she ever wonder how much we despise our-selves for letting her do this to our spirits?"

The teacher looked with haggard eyes at the curtain. His lips were dry. He moistened them. He leaned forward a little.

"Were you ever a teacher?" he asked, coughing apologetically, then hating himself for that apol-ogetic cough which was now part of a teacher's mannerisms. He waited. The light in the room seemed warmer, gentler, like an assent. "Oh?" he murmured. "Then you were, or are, a teacher! Then you know." For a moment he was appre-hensive. "I wonder if you can see through those curtains. I'd—I'd prefer it if you could not. I wouldn't want the board——

"I'm sorry," said the teacher. There was a dry smarting along his eyelids. "I shouldn't have said that."

Something tight in him began to relax. He coughed, wiped his lips. He was trembling a little. "I don't know when I've talked so much, and in this way, before, except when I'm with Marcia. You see, Marcia and I want to be married."

He rubbed his dry hands over his dry face. He

mumbled. "Even my bones are tired. I go to bed tired and wake up tired. My life is one drab gray tiredness. I can't eat without feeling the grit of tiredness in my food. The uselessness——"

He said, "Marcia and I grew up together, and that's a miracle now, considering what the social scientists call a 'mobile population.' Approvingly. As if the mere moving of legs and bodies and cars and trains and planes and buses were a virtue in itself. Mobility is assumed to be 'dynamism.' Then the desperate pacing of lions in a zoo is dynamism too. The desperate pacing of creatures who want to be free—free of what? I don't know! Perhaps of comfort and leisure and entertainment and 'fun.' Perhaps they want to find some solid worth in their lives, and they go looking for it restlessly and never find it. They only exchange places and habitations, and they're all the same. So they move again. Mobile. I'd prefer to call it desperation.

"As a teacher yourself, you'll understand this. No doubt you encounter it every day. I wonder if I know you."

Again the warm and beaming assent reached out to him with love. He coughed.

"Marcia and I went to school together in old Number Ten. We saw each other in class; we had to run—and I do mean run—home after school to help our mothers. Marcia had two brothers and one sister. They're all married now. They have 'responsibilities' to their families and so can't contribute to their old mother's support. Marcia, they say resentfully, isn't married, and as a teacher she'll probably never marry, so it is her 'responsibility' to support their mother. It's very strange that people who are not responsible themselves always demand responsibility in others—especially if it involves their wallets.

"Marcia was always a gentle, quiet girl and, like myself, she always wanted to be a teacher. We used to talk about it whenever we had a moment to talk, in the hallways, just before the bells rang, at Sunday school. And so we studied very hard. We were, in the true meaning of the word, dedicated young people. We couldn't think of anything nobler and finer than taking up where our hard-working and dedicated teachers had to leave off, in death and old age. We loved and reverenced our teachers. We knew what they were. Why, our teachers were the same kind of people as our pastors!

"We would often talk of Our Lord as The Teacher. When we were at State Teachers College we'd walk on the campus and discuss Him. We knew that the word 'rabbi' meant teacher, and He was called 'rabbi' by His disciples. What greater calling, then, was there beyond teaching, except the priesthood and the ministry? In fact, teachers were the laymen of Holy Orders. We wore vestments on our spirits.

"We didn't think of salaries—then. Because we had the pride of our profession, the nobility of it. That was above money."

The teacher laughed gently, sadly. "I am thirty-eight," he said. "Marcia is thirty-seven. We've been teaching many years, if you want to call it 'teaching.' At first it was exhilarating. It was exciting, satisfying, fulfilling.

"Then one day when Marcia was teaching history—her subject—she happened to mention that if one looked acutely at history one saw the hand of God in the rise and fall of nations. A nation flourished, said Marcia, when it obeyed the immutable Law of God, and it declined when it disobeyed. There was a terrible inevitability in it all.

"What happened to Marcia, then, was also terrible. A mob of parents stormed into the school loudly denouncing Marcia as a violator of the 'principle of separation of Church and State.' Marcia is such a gentle soul. She could only stand in confused silence in the principal's office while the professional mothers scolded her. Didn't she know that the Constitution expressly forbids the establishing of a State religion? Wasn't she modern? Hadn't she learned yet that no prayers or mention of God was permitted in the public schools? 'Separation of Church and State.'

"Then Marcia said, 'But God is the State.' She was suspended immediately. The principal was a kindly, religious soul. But there were the parents. And something more sinister behind the parents. Why, she and I were taught the Lord's Prayer in our public schools, and the Ten Commandments, and were told our duty to God. I never heard any Catholic, Protestant, or Jewish mother protest then. It is possible, of course, that parents in our youth were more concerned about the souls of their children than the milk they drank and the hot free lunches they had and the playgrounds and the mental health, as they now call it. (What is 'mental health' but harmony between a man and his God?)

"Marcia was heartbroken. She is too gentle to fight. She had no money with which to fight. I had five hundred dollars. We brought up the whole matter in court. It was finally decided—the judge looked tired and embarrassed, himself—that Marcia should be restored to her position but that she must never violate the principle of 'separation of Church and State' again.

"I've studied that Amendment to the Constitution. It speaks only of the fact that the government must never set up any particular religion as the State religion, such as they have in Britain and the Scandinavian countries. No particular religion must be recognized as the one and only religion.

"What did Marcia's speaking of God in history have to do with any established religion? The Old Testament speaks of God as the foundation of nations. So does the New Testament. 'A people without a vision will perish.' They have removed the 'vision' from our people, the vision of God in the affairs of men. Who are 'they'? I don't know. I only know they're there. I only know that any teacher who mentions God is under danger of discharge. Who are 'they'?"

He leaned forward eagerly. "Don't you think, for our children's sake, that we should find out and expose them? Are they politicians? Evil people? Stupid people? I don't know." His eagerness expired. "I am only a teacher, God help me."

The light became brighter, closer, as if a colleague had moved nearer to him in sympathy and profound understanding. "Yes, you do understand," he murmured.

After a while he said faintly, "I tried at first.

167

At first there was no pressure on the teachers. We taught our subjects and did the very best we could. If one child suddenly looked at us with bright comprehension and enlightenment and with the joy of discovery, it filled our whole day with warm satisfaction. My subject, by the way, is mathematics, the 'Apollonian art.' Quite often, as I explained and mentioned the 'art,' the whole class would come alert. Mathematics wasn't something dry and dead. It wasn't just an abstraction. It was a great and exciting mystery. The whole universe is governed by the law of mathematics. The children would understand then. Everything, from the feeble movement of an amoeba to the rush of the farthest and most tremendous constellation, was governed by the basic law of mathematics. Without mathematics, the encompassing art and law of mathematics, the universe would become chaos and cease to exist.

"I think," said the teacher, "that one of the most beautiful days of my life was when one of my pupils gave me a poem he'd written about mathematics. Not a good poem by poetical standards. But a fervent poem of what mathematics meant to him, not as a future CPA, but as a soul.

"I haven't," said the teacher, "had a pupil like that for the past eight years. And what I must teach now mustn't tax 'the child.' They come to me, in the junior year at high school, without as much knowledge as we had in the seventh grade of grammar school. They lounge around in their seats, chewing gum, winking at each other, exchanging notes, suddenly laughing boisterously, yawning, dozing, primping, combing their hair, putting on lipstick, chewing candy, suddenly and senselessly giggling. Four of my girl students, this year alone—and they only sixteen—have had to leave school for reasons of pregnancy."

Again he scrubbed his face with his dry hands. "Who are these young people? Who has been destroying them systematically? Their parents, their teachers, their schools? Who has been denying them life and joy and excitement? I don't know. I only know I am tired. I am exhausted by trying to maintain discipline in my classes. Trying to maintain order in my classes takes up all my time. Not teaching. Just hopeless attempts at control. The lurching youths—they lurch out of their seats and start for the door with wild, uncontrolled, and hating faces. I say, 'Where are you going?' And they answer, 'None of your goddamn business.'

"I complain to the principal. He says, 'It is the parents' fault.' The parents say, 'It is the teachers' fault.'"

The teacher stood up. He cried loudly, "It is the fault of all of us! This dreadful decay of the human spirit, the human nobility, the human reason! It is America's fault, trivial, fun-loving, laughing, moneyful, amusement-seeking, circus-wanting, demanding, whining, dancing, greedy! A people without a vision! A people which must die!"

He sat down, as if struck. "Because they have too much money. Because they have no duties, no responsibilities. Because everything comes to them without effort. If other people despise us, it is our own fault. We are ancient Rome."

He sat in silence. The light became colder, and there was a question in it.

"A big, fat, and profitless people. 'Wind without rain is profitless.' "

He looked at his hands clenched together, the fingers whitened by intense pressure. He studied them a long time.

"I was afraid," he whispered. "I was afraid for my job. A few thousand dollars a year. But now I am done with it all. I've been offered a position in an accountant's office. Twice as much as I receive now. No children, no ugly, huge, fat children, no screaming shrill parents, no frightened principals, no exigent school boards. No school palaces like hothouses. A good salary, without struggle, without despair. And Marcia and I can be married at last."

He looked at the still curtains, which seemed to wait. The question was all about him, urgent.

"What did you say?" he said.

He looked about him helplessly. "What can I do?" he muttered. "Teaching is—was—all my life. But no one wants to be taught. I'm tired. I've given up. The fat, rosy, stupid faces! The big fat legs! The empty eyes! The big tooth-filled grinning mouths! Their huge porcelain teeth: they are more important to them than knowledge, than their immortal souls. I'm not my students' guide any longer; they drag me along in their senseless lurching as a man is dragged along by an elephant."

The light became colder, fainter.

"When did I begin to give up?" he pleaded. "When Marcia was suspended? When the parents hounded me? When the principal murmured to

170

me that 'we must go along with the times'? When no one wanted what I had to give?"

He looked anxiously and with despair at the curtains. "You are a teacher! You taught all your life, didn't you? Are you still teaching—teaching the stupid multitudes, over and over? Why?"

He jumped to his feet. "I don't care any longer! I've lost my spirit, too. I'm quitting. I'm not going to struggle to teach the Apollonian art to morons, or try to teach it. Why should I inspire them? Why should I struggle against the system? Are they my children? Tell me, are they my children?"

He had had no intention of pressing the button, but now his despairing extremity interfered with his prudence. He ran to the curtains and pressed the button.

The curtains rolled apart, as if weary. And then he saw the light and who stood in the light.

He stood there for a long time. He cried a little. He blew his nose and cried again. "Pardon me," he said. "I haven't cried for a long time. I've been too afraid."

He looked at the Man who Listens, and his whole face trembled.

"Yes," he said, "you were, and are, a teacher. You've never stopped teaching and trying to teach, have you? You never gave up. Did you ever encounter parents such as I encounter, and authorities? Of course you did. It didn't matter to you, did it? The eating, restless, pushing multitudes—you still taught them, didn't you? When they laughed at you and lurched away from you and cursed you, you still taught them. When the

171

higher authorities denounced you, you still taught. You labored, as I did, in a wilderness.

"Because you had Authority."

He looked humbly at the man in the light.

"And I have authority, above parents, above school boards who are afraid of their own positions. A teacher always has authority to teach the truth. If only one—— How many did you have all your life? Very few. If only one looks at you with sudden understanding, it is enough, isn't it? It is more than enough.

"How tired you must have been! Are you tired now? No, I don't think so. One out of multitudes is enough for you. One eye suddenly brightening, one face suddenly becoming alert, one hand suddenly writing down what you said—it was enough, it is more than enough. It is the whole world. And what a class you had—have! Compared with mine, it was almost hopeless. It is almost hopeless.

"But if you could—can—still teach, then so can I. I can refresh myself every day, thinking of you. I can go on, because you went on, and still go on."

He went to the man, very slowly. He touched his hand. "Teacher," he said, "let me teach again. And Marcia. We can marry; it's just that we were afraid. And now I can say, 'I can do all things in Him who strengthens me.'

"I will, with your help, reteach the ancient values and the ancient principles. I will be a teacher again. We still have the ancient Authority and grandeur. If we abdicated them, it was our own fault. We must take them up again. Against the whole world."

SOUL TWELVE

The Doctor

. . . and brought to him all the sick . . .
Matthew 14:35

Dr. Felix Arnstein smiled at his patient. "You could have called anyone locally, Jim," he said. "I've told you; it's your gall bladder. And now this time are you going to let me make arrangements for taking the damn thing out when we get home?"

"Now, now, Felix," said the yellowish fat man with the eyes like varnished raisins. "I've been reading all about it. There's this diet."

"I gave you a diet ten years ago," said Felix Arnstein. "Remember? If you'd kept to it, or even tried it out once in a while, the thing wouldn't have blown up this way. Now the bladder is full of stones; we showed them to you on the X rays."

"Diet!" snorted Jim Merwin, winking at his slender, pretty wife, who seemed younger than her forty-five years. "If a man can't eat what he wants——!"

"Some can. Some can't," said Felix, trying to remain amiable. (He wondered if Miss Lillis had been able to soothe his patients in his home city who had had appointments with him today, or if they had immediately flounced off to consult another man. That was the devil, being a general practitioner. He ought to have gone back to the hospital for another two years and then he could now call himself an internist.) "I know," he continued, "that some men can eat their bellyfuls of fish and others will have an attack of giant hives if even the smallest slip of clam appears in their soup. You're one of the boys who ought to have started dieting in your teens. You didn't. And now you're over fifty and have a bag of stones that would choke an elephant. What do you say about having it removed next week when you get home? It doesn't make medical history any more when a gall bladder is taken out; it's routine."

"Nah," said Jim Merwin. This time he winked at Felix. He was a winking man, by nature and deliberation. It gave him a reputation for being big and generous and good-natured and brought him prosperous business. "I don't have the time, fella. I'm not like you medical guys, always able to run to Jamaica or Florida or Sorrento. I got to work. I got to make money. I've got five kids, ain't I?" He was a university graduate; it made him one-of-the-boys to use illiterate expressions.

Felix Arnstein was a small, slender man with an unexpectedly plump face. He had a very delicate fair complexion, expressive blue eyes, and

174

thin fair hair. He had been trained, by necessity, to keep an amiable expression on his face. But sometimes, as of now, it was almost impossible. Jim Merwin, with his chain of sports-equipment shops, was at least a millionaire. He belonged to all the country clubs which were firmly closed to Felix; he had a house at Cape Cod, as well as his fine house in their mutual distant home city, and he visited Florida and other choice spots several times every winter. But that, of course, was business, and tax-exempt, including Lucy Merwin's expenses. She had once been his stenographer; she took "notes" on their excursions. She had stenography notebooks to prove it.

Felix was tired. Lucy had called him in panic, long-distance, at four o'clock this morning. Jim had been taken sick with one of his "attacks" while attending a convention in this strange city. "Really terrible this time, Felix," she had pleaded, weeping. "No, your tablets don't help! . . . What? . . . Oh, Felix! You know Jim wouldn't have anyone but you! And in a different city, and a hotel, at that! He wouldn't trust anybody but you! Look, I've already called the airport, Felix. There's a plane at five-thirty. You can just make it if you hurry. You can be here at seven. Just pick up the tickets at the airport. Felix, you've got to come!" She sobbed. "I think it's a heart attack this time, or maybe that gall bladder has ruptured, as you said it might. Or something. . . . No! He's too sick to get up and fly home just now. He's all doped up, though it doesn't stop the pain much."

So Felix Arnstein had wearily dragged himself

out of bed. He had hardly warmed it; he had been out on an emergency call until less than four hours ago. His patient, a close friend, had died of a heart attack only half an hour after Felix's arrival. It had been a bad blow, a shock. He said to his wife, Gay, as she looked at him with sleepy concern, "Go back to sleep, honey. I must go out. I'll leave a note for you on the breakfast table." He did not tell her he was leaving town.

The Jim Merwins of this world were the backbone of a general practitioner's life. They paid large bills and did not complain. It gave them a sort of éclat to receive such bills, even from a general practitioner. "Give me a general doc every time," they would say, and they would wink if they were winking men like Jim Merwin. "Not these specialists who're always out golfing or on vacations and never at home on the weekends. What them specialists know, fellers like Felix Arnstein's already forgotten."

Maybe so, maybe so, Felix would think to himself a trifle sourly. But the specialists were cleverer men than he, and so they'd arranged to be born of wealthier parents who could afford to send them to medical school and give them a large allowance besides. Or the specialists had not married in poverty as he had married. They had waited until they were at least partially established. But he was already thirty-one when he completed his internship; there had been three years when he had had to stop everything to work to pay his way. Three years between his university degree and the medical school: Gay would have waited, but she had already waited for him for over ten years, and he loved her and needed her. She had continued to work in the largest department store for two years after they were married, until their son, Jerome, had notified them of his coming. Felix then had an income almost as large as a mechanic's, after expenses. He was sharing an office with another doctor on the third floor of a made-over old house in a very unfashionable neighborhood. They also shared one part-time secretary-receptionist, two filing cases, one telephone, and a handsome set of medical books bought secondhand—and unread—from a specialist. "He never opened the damned things from the day he got them from his parents when he set up shop," said Dr. Robert Sherman to his colleague. "But he didn't need to; he just walked into a fine big office next to his dad's, with a secretary in silk stockings and a peekaboo blouse and a receptionist who looked like a model. That's all. Just took over his dad's rich practice. He had it made."

If I'd just stayed in the hospital for another two years, Felix would think, I'd have had it made too. But I couldn't. Gay and I had waited too long as it was.

Jerome had brought his "luck" with him. At least his coming had forced his parents to search for a little larger apartment, though more expensive and in a better neighborhood. Felix was retiring, but he had an air of integrity, and Gay was charming, as bright and vivacious as a bird, with auburn hair and shining blue eyes. They soon attracted the attention of their neighbors in the apartment house. Many of them were elderly people with no children, and some were childless

177

widows. Gay's obviously pregnant state had drawn the solicitude of the ladies in the self-operating elevators. She was also the youngest woman in the building, and her trusting little smile and eager ways excited maternal feelings in the older, lonelier women. The ladies visited her, clucking, warning, advising. One was the widow of a physician, who had left her comfortably wealthy. Of course she took an interest not only in Gay but in Felix. She gave a cocktail party for them a week before Jerome was born, and all the guests liked the young couple. The next step came when some called Felix in emergencies when their own doctors were sick or otherwise unavailable. The following step was when they decided to stay with Felix.

Jerome was a handsome little fellow with his mother's hair and eyes, his father's reserved but engaging ways. He became the pet of the whole apartment house, from the janitor to the owner, who lived on the top floor. Felix's fortunes began to look up definitely. He and Gay talked of a "little home somewhere, for Jerome's sake, with grass and trees." (They did not talk of more children; they could not afford them.)

Then the war came, and Felix had to go. As he was not a specialist, he never rose above the rank of lieutenant. He did not see Gay and Jerome again for four years. Four terrible years. He saved what he could; he knew Gay saved all she could from her allotment. What he did not know was that Gay had gone back to work, leaving Jerome in the wise old care of the physician's widow. He did not know until Gay, laughing through her tears after their first embrace when he came home, showed him a bankbook with five thousand dollars in it. "Our down payment," she said. "See, it's in another bank. I saved two thousand from your pay too."

Jerome was five years old. They bought a pretty little suburban house for not more than twice its actual worth; inflation had begun. Dr. Sherman, who had not been drafted, moved out of the office. Felix had it for himself now. He had eight thousand dollars in the bank, after the house was bought, a large mortgage, a second-hand car; half his former patients returned to him. He and Gay had never had a week's holiday in their married life or even before that.

Gay had an elderly great-uncle, a sullen, irascible old man with bunions, a hearing aid, and a high suspicion of everyone but Gay. He was obviously not a man of material substance. After he had had a heart attack, he wanted, he said plaintively, to move into the old folks' home, to forget and be forgotten. A widower with no children, he had been living alone for forty years in a side-street hotel, in one room. He had once been a diamond cutter, and Gay could not recall ever having seen him in a new suit or wearing a new hat. She had been kind to him for years, for no reason except that she was naturally kind. She insisted that he move into her house, "and Felix will be there all the time—at least some of the time—to watch over you." Felix did not think highly of the idea. Old Harry Stern had never been one of his favorite people, but Gay, who had worked so hard for this house, deserved to have

179

her uncle here if she wished. So old Harry Stern moved in, with his endless complaints, his prayer shawls, his skullcaps, his peevish comments on Gay's cooking, his shouts at Jerome, his insistence on ancient ritual, his heavy colds, his fiendishly stinking cheap cigars, and his habit of bursting into tears for his dead wife, whom he had treated very unkindly when she had been alive.

He died suddenly while Felix was struggling to reestablish his practice. A lawyer called, with a will, after Felix and Gay had buried the old man with all the ritual they knew he had wanted. Old Harry Stern had been living on an annuity which he had shrewdly bought forty years ago and which had paid him one hundred dollars a month for life. He had left ten thousand dollars in cash to Gay.

Felix judiciously restrained his jubilation in respect for the dead. He found himself suddenly very fond of sly old Harry. He made a substantial payment on the mortgage, which reduced monthly interest and payments. Then he rented an office— a small one—in a good medical section of the city, in a new splendid building all white brick, chrome, and self-opening doors and switchboards and parking lots and big windows. "I think," he said cautiously to his wife, "that we're finally on the way."

He, and only he, was the general practitioner in the building. Worse, even most of the specialists were younger than he. They did not despise him; secretly they had let him have the office in their jointly owned building for much less than they could have rented it to a bright young specialist

180

with sound parental money behind him. General practitioners referred patients to specialists, especially if the specialists were handy, on the same floor or the next, and especially if the specialists were kind and displayed fellowship and had G. P.'s to dinner occasionally and introduced them "around." "We are certainly on the way," Felix said to his wife when he paid off the mortgage entirely. He now had at least eighteen men like Jim Merwin as patients, and as they usually over-ate or overworked or abused their bodies in countless other ways and firmly believed in regular "check-ups" and all the latest "shots," Felix, who would by nature have detested them, spoke of them as "our bank accounts."

Jerome was seventeen and in a good private school when he had informed his father that he wished to be a doctor. He was already eight inches taller than Felix, and an excellent student. "That's no news to me," said Felix, smiling at his son tenderly. "I've watched you for years reading my medical books. What kind of a specialist do you want to be?" he added jovially.

"I don't want to be a specialist, Dad," said Jerome, who was as reticent as his father. "I want to be a general practitioner. Like you."

"Good God! Why?"

"Because I want to be the kind of man you are."

"I? What in the name of hell do you mean by that stupid statement?"

Jerome had blushed. He was naturally inarticulate. "Well," he said uncomfortably, "I just think that this country needs fewer specialists and more G.P.'s. That's all." He took a deep breath and

181

plunged on, awkwardly, "You can't divide up the human body into so many compartments! If you're sick in one part, you're sick all over. Besides— well, I think of a G.P. as a 'healer.' A helper, if you know what I mean. A friend. A specialist's all steel and chrome and impersonal. You see—well, it's this way: I like people."

"You do, eh?" said Felix a little grimly, thinking of the Jim Merwins. "I don't."

"Yes, you do," said Jerome, smiling at him with Gay's own smile.

It was all nonsense; it was all stupid. He'd expected better than this for Jerome. But the boy, in his way, was as stubborn as himself. Felix threatened not to send him to medical school. Jerome only smiled. "Do you want a life like mine?" cried Felix. "Never knowing if you can get a full night's sleep? At the beck and call of everybody, at any hour of the day or night? Delivering a baby for about fifty dollars? Those who can afford more go to an obstetrician. Wangling and waiting for years to get a little spot on the hospital staff? You don't know the snobbery in the medical department, my boy. The specialists despise you, though they keep their doors open for your patients. The nurses even despise you. The staff officers despise you. You can never belong even to the better Jewish clubs; you can't afford them, anyway. Do you know what my income is, even now, after all these years, after expenses? Twelve thousand dollars a year! And I'm lucky to get that. And you want to be a man like me!"

"Yes," said Jerome.

"You have no ambition. Why, that little squirt

182

of a proctologist down the hall from me clears over twice what I do in a year, and he's only thirty-five. I'm fifty. When he's my age he'll have a suite of rooms, assistants, and be a rich man."

Jerome only smiled.

Jerome was in a good university now, with an excellent medical school, and he was nineteen. He and his father had no more arguments. Felix hoped and prayed that the boy's teachers would be able to persuade him where he had failed. Gay said, "If Jerome is half as good as you, dear, and has your integrity and gets half the love you do from your patients, I'll be very happy."

"Love!" said Felix. "From the Jim Merwins?"

"They're not the only ones, dear."

"Sure. The others don't pay their bills, or they take years to do it. A doctor's always the last to get paid." He touched her hand. "I bought you that mink coat eight years ago, and it wasn't good quality to begin with."

But the Lucy Merwins changed their minks at least every other year. They had their own bright convertibles. Gay drove an ancient secondhand car, a cheap one even when new. Lucy Merwin had diamonds. Gay had only, even now, the one-carat engagement ring Felix had given her and which had taken him over four years to pay for in full. They spent two weeks every winter in a motel near Miami Beach, and two weeks in the summer at a little cottage "on the lake" which had no utilities. When they had paid their real estate taxes and the school taxes, the twelve thousand dollars a year had shrunk to less than ten. They lived frugally; Gay did all the housework herself. They saved to send Jerome through medical school. They had two annuities on which they were paying, and a life insurance policy for twenty-five thousand dollars. And Felix was fifty-two. He needed some new equipment for his office. He was also saving for an X-ray machine. This would annoy some of the specialists, but he had become desperate on reaching the age he now was. "There's no place in America any longer for G.P.'s," he would say to Gay. "No one wants, or needs, personal attention."

"Oh yes, that's exactly what they do want!" cried Gay, whose auburn hair was very gray now. "Didn't you know that?"

She added, "The poor people. And I don't mean financially poor, either."

Today, in this strange city, in this opulent hotel, Felix suddenly thought of what Gay had said. "The poor people." He looked at fat, winking, yellowish Jim Merwin and at his wife, Lucy, who was only three years younger than Gay but appeared to be at least twelve years younger, with her touched-up hair, her smooth face, her soft white hands, her slender figure.

They had engaged a splendid room for "our doc" in this same hotel; in fact, next door. "Nothing too good for you, old Felix," said Jim Merwin, who was a year older than Felix. "Why don't you stay over a couple of days more, and then we'll all go back together?"

"No, thanks," said Felix. "I have a big list of appointments tomorrow. I'm taking the midnight plane back."

It was a beautiful spring day. "Now that I've

184

gotten you quieted down and assured you that you aren't going to die immediately, I think I'll take a walk," said Felix. "Anything worthwhile to see locally, besides the usual things?"

"Nope. Except that maybe you want to see that funny thing they got here. Show him that pamphlet, Luce. Crazy thing." Felix put on his glasses and studied John Godfrey's pamphlet. The Man who Listens. "That's interesting," said Felix. "Who goes there?"

"Oh," said Lucy, "one of the local girls was telling me about it. People in trouble who want someone to listen to them. Isn't that the craziest? Someone to listen! They need a psychiatrist, that's what. Who else wants to listen?"

Felix took off his glasses and absently laid them down. He kept the pamphlet in his hand. He thought of Jerome, for whom he had had such large ambitions. Who could he tell of Jerome? The specialists he knew? Gay, who was contented? He put the pamphlet in his pocket. "I'll be back in an hour or so," he said.

He forgot the pamphlet before he was in the hotel lobby. He thought he would buy a newspaper, then find a park nearby, if there was one, and sit in the sun and read. The sun was very warm. He felt for his glasses and remembered he had left them in Jim's room. He went to the elevator and got off on the right floor and went down the richly carpeted hall to Jim's suite. The transom was open. Then he heard Jim say with contempt, "Felix? Don't worry about him none! Not that you do! We shouldn't't've called him; that was your idea. Oh, shut up; all right, it was my idea! With

185

all that damn pain. You can bet he'll send me a bill as long as your arm! Always trust a Jew doctor to do that. 'To the bank, bank, bank!' That's all they think of."

"Oh, now," laughed Lucy, with that sweet, joyous, cruel laugh of women who are amused at the spoken deprecation of others. "You think of money too, darling."

"Sure, but not the way Jews do. Hoarding it. Bet he could buy and sell me. Look at this car of his; at least four years old, and not a big job, either. Gay's got that old ragged fur for years; you'd think he'd be ashamed to let her be seen in it. And a house you could put in one corner of ours. Saves every cent. He was practicing and making big money when I was still a clerk in one of the sports shops I own now. Don't you worry any about a Jew. Look what it cost me to bring him here, and the hotel room, and the bill. He'll make me sting; you can bet on that. Get me a drink; double."

Felix backed slowly away from the door, his face white, the muscles about his mouth rigid and hard. He, a mild and gentle man, was trembling with hate and rage and humiliation. He'd never permit Jim Merwin to enter his office again.

Yes, he would. He needed the Jim Merwins. Because he was a general practitioner, of no status.

He was sick when he reached the lobby again. He looked at the newspaper in his hand. He could not read it without glasses, he thought numbly. And he could not go into that suite—yet. Not yet, if he wanted to keep the Jim Merwins. He couldn't

186

trust himself. Not yet. "Damn him," he said aloud, thinking of all his work, all Gay's work. And then he thought of Jerome, who would be a general practitioner. He put his hands helplessly in his pockets, and one of them encountered the pamphlet. The Man who Listens. "Hell," he said. But he went out and found a cab.

The flowering shrubs and trees about the white building were just bursting into spring bloom, pink, red, magenta, bright yellow, brilliant white, purple, rose, fuchsia. Tulips and daffodils and hyacinths stood in the warm brown earth, row upon row of them. The red gravel paths sparkled in the fine sun. Felix slowly walked up one of the paths, looking at the square white structure against the intensely blue sky. He saw a bench on which an old man was sitting, his hands on his cane. The old man was smiling at a squirrel. Felix hesitated, then stopped. He said, "I wonder if you could tell me something. Who is the Man who Listens—up there?"

The old man looked at him tranquilly. "I don't know. No one knows. He only listens. Some people think he's a doctor, or a teacher, or a social worker, or a priest. Half the people who talk to him never want to see him; half do. You can choose for yourself."

"Did you ever go?" asked Felix.

"Yes, I did. I talked for a long time. But I didn't press the button near the curtains. I want to have my own picture of him. I was going to kill myself," said the old man with calm simplicity. "But after I talked to him, I didn't."

187

"That's interesting," said Felix in the pleasant voice that inspired trust. "Would you mind telling me what he said to you?"

The old man looked thoughtful. He took off his old hat and rubbed his pale bald head with the palm of his hand. "I don't know," he said. "I don't remember that he said a thing. Perhaps he did; perhaps he didn't. Frankly, I don't know, and that's all I can tell you. I only know that I had peace for the first time in seventy-five years. And that's a long time to live in hell, isn't it?"

He looked at Felix's white, strained face and the pain in his blue eyes. He said kindly, "Why don't you go and talk to him yourself? I think you need to."

Felix colored and set his shoulders stiffly. He almost turned away. Then he glanced at the building again. He frowned. Well, it would do no harm to tell someone, anonymous, who would never see him, of the Jim Merwins. The damn Jim Merwins.

He entered the sitting room and saw two people waiting in silence, a young woman, a youth. He was a doctor, and through their silence he saw the stony shine of despair on their still faces, the hollows of suffering. A young woman, as thin as a corpse. A young man Jerome's age. It was terrible for anyone to suffer; it was even more terrible when the young suffered. He wondered who they were. With a practiced eye he evaluated their clothing. The girl was expensively dressed. The boy wore poor shoes and a worn suit. They did not glance at the newcomer; they were absorbed in a timeless agony of their own. Felix suddenly thought: The poor people!

188

Impatiently he put the words out of his mind. He saw the slit where a brass plate above it invited visitors to drop a note about their problems. No offering was asked. A psychiatrist or a doctor— certainly. Who else? He sat down, feeling foolish, and waited. An old woman crept into the room, timidly. Obviously a cleaning woman, from her scoured hands and clothing and the painful way she walked. Yes, even more terrible than the young who suffered was the suffering of the lonely aged who had no one, who must work until they dropped dead. He smiled encouragingly at the old woman and stood up and helped her to a chair. Her feet were swollen; edema. Heart? The pallor of death was on her cheeks; the shadow of death was in her eyes. The poor people. Damn, thought Felix. He saw the old hands, scarred, broken almost to bleeding, the nails corroded. She saw him looking; she lifted her white head and stared at him with pride, rejecting his awful pity. The old, familiar, tearing pity that had torn at him when he had closed dead and hopeless eyes in miserable rooms, when he had to tell a mother that her child was dying or a husband that his wife was breathing her last breath, when he comforted a stricken wife whose husband would never speak to her again! Somehow these things always happened after midnight, when the specialists were cozily asleep and uncaring. Or in Bermuda, or Paris, or London, or in South America. Felix thought of the tired priests and ministers and rabbis who had stood with him in those anguished moments, and how they had looked at him as at a colleague, knowing his pity and sorrow. He had felt a strange

189

and poignant fellowship with them, these shabby men in shabby rooms.

A bell chimed softly. The young woman and youth had disappeared. Felix hesitated. The old woman said curtly, "It's your turn."

"I'll wait; you go first," he said, looking at her feet again.

"No. That wouldn't be fair. You're supposed to take your turn," said the old woman firmly. She panted a little, and he heard it and frowned.

Felix went into the white room with the marble chair and the closed blue curtains. He examined everything with the objective curiosity of a physician. He went to the spot where visitors dropped their notes. He smiled a little, skeptically. There was a steel box set in the wall. So "they" read the notes, then gave advice. There was a slanting cover that concealed the top and he opened it. He smelled the acridness of burning paper. Then he saw that the slit outside admitted the notes and they were burned at once at the bottom of the little shaft. He could see a faint flicker of flame far at the bottom and, caught at the side on a little roughness of the metal, the wavering flutter of a ten-dollar bill. Its end was already charred.

So no one read the notes; they were invited, he could understand, so that the visitors could first acquire confidence in expressing themselves, thus clarifying their minds. "Very sensible," murmured Felix. "Psychologically sound."

He walked reluctantly to the chair, then leaned on its back, facing the curtains. He was very curious again. "I like to talk to some people," he said. "But I'd prefer not to see you, under the circum-

190

stances. By the way, there's an old dying woman waiting outside. She probably needs to talk to you more than I do. I think I'll call her in." He went to the door through which he had entered. It could not be opened except on the farther side. He went to the curtains and read the little brass plate sunk in the marble wall. "Well, I hope they thank you," he said.

The room waited. It had a calmness as of absolute eternity, where time did not exist. Felix thought of his everlastingly crowded waiting room; the walls inside were lined, too, and sometimes patients had to wait outside in the hall. The specialists would often pass in the hall and would look expectantly at the faces. A kidney case here, an arthritic patient there; obviously this was a heart case, another as obviously cancer, or this or that. Old Felix would refer this one or that one; it had been an excellent idea to have an old G.P. in this building. He never asked or hinted for a cut, either. Yes, an excellent idea.

Felix could see his waiting room sharply and clearly, the frightened faces of the patients, the dun clothing, the shoddy shoes, the bandannas of some of the poorer women, the children whose faces were twisted with apprehension. And then, when he appeared, the sudden lightening, the hope, the diffident smiles. Well, that was all very nice! But the thin sheaf of checks at the end of the month wasn't so heartening, as his secretary pointed out; he was lucky to get a check for every six bills; he was lucky, sometimes, ever to get anything at all. He turned bills over to the collection agency only when he was positive that the patients

191

were trying to cheat him or when they had the ability to pay at least in small installments. He was a fool. He was fifty-two and, outside of the score or so of the Jim Merwins, he'd never be able to attract the "right" kind of paying patient, who could sponsor those who could not pay.

He found himself sitting in the chair. He faced the curtains. "I suppose you're a doctor," he said. "Well, meet a fellow sufferer. I'm a G.P. Are you?"

He did not hear a sound, a voice, or a rustle, or a movement. Yet all at once he was certain he had heard a murmur of affirmation somewhere. He looked about sharply. He'd been imagining things! Your mind could play tricks on you in such a quiet place, where there was no time, no intrusion, nothing but yourself facing—who?

"I heard you are here twenty-four hours a day," he said with his faint, skeptical smile. "Well, I'm like that too. On call twenty-four hours a day. I'm lucky if I'm able to get five hours' sleep a night, a few nights a week. Don't you get tired too?"

Again he thought he heard a murmur, but this was a negative one. He rubbed his ears until they were pink. "You don't?" he said incredulously. "When do you sleep?" The white walls and ceilings smiled at him. He sat upright. "Don't you have parents? Brothers? Sisters? Children?"

The gentle warmth flowed about him, assenting. He forgot to wait for a voice. He did not know how it was, but he was content with the sensation of listening, of assent or dissent. He had not thought of his old grandfather for years, in his

192

skullcap, sitting near the kitchen stove in his mother's house, warming his hands in the winter and rocking in the comfortable chair she had always kept for him. His grandfather had rarely spoken; he had only listened, and very often he had smiled. It was enough; he understood, and answered, without words.

"You remind me of my grandfather," Felix said suddenly. "Are you old? Very old?"

Was that assent, or dissent, or both? Felix sat back in the chair. He said nothing. He thought of Gay and Jerome and the little worldly evidences of success he possessed and of the Jim Merwins. Time passed; or, rather, it seemed not to be at all. Felix started, came to himself. "I suppose," he said, "I should tell you my troubles."

Then—he must be losing his mind!—he was positive that someone had been listening to his thoughts all this time and that the man behind the curtain knew everything about him. This unnerved Felix a little. A skeptic, he had smiled at extra-sensory perception, though he had admitted that there might be "something to it, something that will be explained easily enough sometime." Was the man who was listening gifted with ESP? All at once Felix was certain of it. He was more than ever unnerved. He cleared his throat. He had had to learn, while still a child at school, to conceal emotions that could become vehement. People disliked vehemence or anything else that threatened their superficial lives or disturbed their determined "happiness." They were particularly offended by people in trouble, or at least by those who revealed in expression, abstraction, or gesture that they were in trouble. Everything must be "happiness."

"A damn-fool phrase," said Felix aloud. " 'Happiness.' That's for babies. I wonder when we'll grow up as a nation and learn there's no 'happiness'? You should see my waiting room, or the waiting room of any doctor, or the wards in the hospitals! Yet even the patients, when leaving, will put on a smirk as if to show the displeased world that they are 'happy,' too, even if death is in their bodies. So they'll be accepted by the 'happiness cultists' and not be rejected as unpleasant reminders that there's pain in the world, and death and funerals."

He shifted, hotly vexed, in his chair. "I spent four years in Europe," he said. "Yes, there was a war on—another damn-fool phrase. 'A war on.' As if there isn't all the time, somewhere. But, discounting the war, the people seemed more adult, in some way. No one expected anyone to be 'happy, happy, happy.' If you were, then you were to be congratulated. But no one demanded it as a rite you must perform in public, as a social duty. No one thought you were inferior or degraded if you were in misery, as they do in America. What the hell is all this 'happiness' bit, anyway?"

He looked at the curtains. "But that isn't what I came to tell you. It's just something that's been like a flea irritating my mind all the time."

He was a nervous man but always concealed his nervousness except in his constant cigarette-smoking. He felt for his cigarette case. Then the desire passed and he withdrew his hand from his pocket. The tension in his neck and shoulder muscles was ebbing away; it was a strange sensation, this ease, one he hadn't felt for a long time.

He said abruptly, "I've wanted 'happiness' for my son, Jerome. I've wanted an easier life for him, not like mine. I've wanted him to have success, so that he can——"

He stared at the curtains. "Why, damn it, so he may be accepted by the Jim Merwins of the world and join their clubs and not be outside the pale! So he can play golf with them, and bet with them, and be invited to their houses, and have as good a car as they have, and a house at least as fine as theirs, and marry some nice girl of good family who has money! A social success! Not to be outside the pale!"

He felt sick with his embarrassment and shame. But he made his voice challenging. "Do you know what that means—being without the pale? Do you know what it means, being a Jew? I do!"

The room appeared to enfold him with sadness a comprehension, and yet with hope. "You're a Jew!" he exclaimed incredulously. "A Jew? A Jewish doctor?"

He stopped, straining toward the curtains. Then he sighed. "If you are and you have a son, you'll understand why I wanted more for Jerome than I had for myself. Oh, Gay gets impatient with me. She says, 'What does that matter? Pale, nothing. Everybody's outside of some pale. If they only admit one or two Jews to Jim Merwin's clubs, and they Supreme Court judges or something, they also have a quota on Catholics. A Catholic member has to die before another is admitted, and they have to be top-drawer. Just to associate with the

195

Jim Merwins! The Italians and the Poles are out-side some invisible pale, and so are millions of others, through lack of education or money or background or family. Why, some Jews put other Jews outside a pale of their own! It's a nasty human custom.' "

Felix laughed shortly. "I suppose, in a way, that Gay's right. But I don't want Jerome to encounter any more pales than he has to. I want him to be hap——" He stopped, and his fair skin became brightly pink. "Oh, damn," he murmured sheep-ishly.

Then he was defiant again. "All right, so I'm stupid. Let's forget what I said. I've been wander-ing. I don't, I think, want Jerome to have enough money so he can associate with the Jim Merwins. At least I don't now. But I do want him to be a specialist so he'll have an easier life than mine, a more secure life, and not be a grubber like me, with my door and my telephone open twenty-four hours a day. For the sick."

Had the room become slightly cooler, more withdrawn, more thoughtful? He could sense it. He stroked his eyebrows in agitation. "Perhaps," he said, "I don't mean it quite that way. After all, I'm a physician, and the sick are my charges. Yes, my charges. It's funny, but I don't know if I've consciously thought of them like that before."

Then after a little he brightened. "Well, yes, I have. Underneath, I mean. I've been mixed up, I think. That's what comes of being a father. At one time all physicians were priests, thousands of years ago, and they didn't marry and they didn't have children. They dedicated their lives to healing the sick and comforting them and giving them courage to face death. Can you understand an attitude like that? I think I can. Now."

He was silent for a long time, thinking. His thoughts flowed quickly, bringing thousands of pictures before him. The strain left his face. He began to smile.

"I've just thought of something. When Gay inherited that ten thousand dollars from old Harry Stern, she said to me, 'Now you can go back for a few years' more study. If you want to. To become a specialist. If you want to.' And she looked at me with her pretty eyes and waited."

Felix sat up straight, excited. "Do you know what I said? 'Oh, it doesn't matter.' I thought I was thinking that we'd better use the money to pay off the mortgage or something. But I wasn't! Away back in my mind was the thought that I just wanted to be a G.P., with my door and my telephone open twenty-four hours a day for people who knew that specialists had certain hours, and appointments rigidly scheduled, and a telephone-answering service which they didn't bother to check if they had a dinner appointment or a golf date, or a weekend coming up at someone's country home.

"As if," said Felix with contempt, "people can schedule when to be sick or dying or injured, or when to have a baby! I know one obstetrician who actually does schedule the babies! If he wants a winter holiday, he takes his patients to the hospital and induces birth. Sometimes it's all right.

197

And sometimes it isn't! But even the women who lose their babies swear by him. He has charm. I don't."

He brooded on that. Then he said, "But I have something else. My patients trust me. When they call their priest or minister or rabbi, they call me too. Even when they know I can't help them any longer. Now that's something, isn't it?"

His tired face was bright and excited. He forgot to control his emotions. He jumped up and walked rapidly up and down the room, gesticulating, murmuring to himself.

"People are people. They can pretend to be civilized and brave and sophisticated, but when it comes to death they are all the same. When they take off their clothes and put on the white shirts I have for them, before examination, they're all the same. The same human faces, the same emotions, the same fears, the same hopes, the same loves and hates. They are only men. Even," he said, "the Jim Merwins."

He stopped. All his hatred for Jim Merwin was gone. Why, the poor, fat, suffering, cowardly bastard, he thought fondly. He's scared to death of an operation. He thinks he might die. Then what about his money and his clubs and nice smooth Lucy? He knows she'll marry again before he's cold. And those kids of his! He doesn't know, nor Lucy, either, that the shine in his eyes, his pampered eighteen-year-old daughter, is coming to me to be cured of syphilis. His innocent little ewe lamb. It would kill them both to know, and so I haven't told them. I've just given the sneaking little bitch a few hard lectures which her parents should have given her years ago, and put the fear of God in her. That's what a doctor is for. That's what a G.P. is for. If I'd been a specialist—— Why, a specialist would have sent her bills her allowance couldn't cover, and so Jim would know. I charge her five dollars a shot, which is one fourth her weekly allowance. She'll be cured soon, and she's a different girl now. Thanks to me.

He looked at the curtains, and again he had the thought that he had been heard.

"I'm thinking," he said, "of all the people who might die because they can't afford specialists. I don't mean the poverty-stricken, who get the same treatment free from specialists that the rich get. I mean the lower middle class, the people I have. They can pay so much, and they know it. So without the G.P. they'd get no treatment at all, and they'd go on suffering the rest of their lives. Or they'd die."

He smiled at the curtains. "Do you know the most wonderful thing my son ever said to me— that anyone ever said to me? 'I want to be a man like you.' Now what greater satisfaction can a man have than that? A man like me. I'm going to write Jerome a letter tonight! I'm going to tell him I'm proud of him because he wants to heal the sick, whether he gets paid or not, whether or not he'll ever get rich. He won't. But that doesn't matter, does it?"

He took out his handkerchief and wiped his eyes. "For why was a man born, anyway, except to help his fellow man, to heal him, to comfort him?"

He went closer to the curtains. He looked at the

button. He hesitated. Then he pushed the button quickly. The curtains rolled apart.

He saw the light and who stood in it.

His face worked strongly. He said, "Yes. You healed the sick, didn't you? And you were outside the pale, weren't you? I—Gay and I—we belong to a book club. We've just read a book about you and what you did.

"You never wanted to be accepted or be a social success. If I remember right, the poor and the sick came to you in droves, and you never turned them away because they had no money. You never had a fine house, or servants, or good clothing. That didn't matter. You were a doctor. I suppose you still are.

"That awful thing on your head—— Do you know something? Every real doctor wears it around his heart."

SOUL THIRTEEN

The Unhonored

Peace be unto you.   John 20:21, 26

Mrs. Ami Logan watched Felix Arnstein go
into the room beyond. She, too, had a practiced
eye. Some kind of businessman, she thought, or
maybe a lawyer or a doctor. Don't make too much
money; you can see that. Good clothes, but I've
seen better. That suit wasn't so new, either. But he
had nice ways. Not the kind of "nice" ways some
folks had, being pretty sweet about "the poor
working people" and all the time they didn't give
a darn about "the poor working people." It just
sounded nice to them and their friends coming in
for cocktail parties. She'd heard more talk about
the "rights" of the working people for the past
twenty years than she'd ever heard before, and
it didn't mean a thing. Not a thing. Funny. The
ladies who employed her would talk for hours—
just hours—to their cocktail friends about prog-

ress and Labor. You could hear their high voices, talking, talking, getting excited; you could listen from the kitchen, where you'd be setting out the plates of ham and cheese and all kinds of fancy meats that wouldn't set well on your stomach, and awful salads with things in them, though you knew they cost a lot of money. And all kinds of little foreign cakes, and ices. Not that you'd get even a snitch of it; the ladies of the house were sharp about that. Watching every mouthful.

And then when your feet wouldn't be feeling nothing any more they'd come into the kitchen with shiny eyes after all their talk, and then their eyes wouldn't be shiny no more. They'd say, real sharp, "Let me see. What time did you come, Ami? Does that really make nine hours? Oh no! It's just eight hours and forty minutes! Ami! Now, let me see; where's that pad and pencil? I'll figure it out, and the carfare."

They did, too. To the last cent. If they could break a cent in half with their teeth, they'd do it. They looked like they wanted to do it. And they'd never think of driving you to your bus stop, a mile away, sometimes at night.

But that man who just went in. He hadn't looked at her like she was Labor. He'd looked at her like she was a human being; he'd looked at her feet. Well, that had made her mad, a little. After all, when you're on your feet sometimes twelve hours a day your feet'd get like cushions and ache like sin. Besides, he was young; he didn't know what it was to be seventy-one—and no place to lie your head, soon. Still, he'd been real nice, getting her a chair and wanting her to go in first.

202

She didn't want his pity, though! She didn't want
no darn person's pity. She'd worked all her life,
and she could go on working. If she still could
have a place to lie her head. And be independent.

She'd been independent all her life. Why, she'd
been out working after school since she was nine
years old, washing dishes in the neighborhood
when some woman was sick in bed or just had a
baby, and cleaning windows and shoveling snow
and churning ice cream and taking care of little
kids, and sweeping porches and cellars, and putting out the ashes. Hundreds of things. Ami tossed
her head. It hadn't hurt her none, no sir. It was
being lazy that hurt people, and having things
easy and never getting their hands dirty. Why,
give her a good broom any time and not one of
those electric brooms like they called them! They
just didn't seem to get the rugs as clean. And the
vacuum cleaners. Sure, they was easy; nobody
took up their wall-to-walls any more; nobody ever
beat carpets and hung them out in the air.

She could smile a little now. It was spring outside, and she recalled the forgotten drums of
spring in the city, the slap-slap-slap of carpet-
beaters everywhere, the carpets hanging on the
line. It was part of spring. Just like the smell of
tomato catsup and grape jam cooking was the
smell of fall coming from the houses. It was the
sounds and the smells that made people remember. Peaceful. People had a lot of peace in the old
days. They worked harder. But they had a lot of
peace. It was a long time from sunup to sundown,
a long, quiet, happy time. Sometimes, in the summer, a breeze would come up and you'd hear all

them Chinese glass things singing on the porches
in the lovely quiet, especially on Sundays after
church. And then the look of the white linen cloths
on rocking chairs on the porches, with the little
tatting on the edges. And somebody singing a
hymn in the back yard. They had flowers and
grass and trees in the back yards then. Now they
had asphalt and garages. And everybody getting
into cars after dinner and running up and down
the streets, staring at the other cars or rushing
down to the lake, where they'd sit and stare some
more, and the kids would throw all kinds of trash
around on the beach or the grass and whine,
whine, whine! In the old days the mothers and
fathers would sleep after hot noon Sunday dinners, and the kids would sit on the steps of the
porches and talk, and maybe, if somebody wasn't
looking, they'd throw rubber balls at each other
—the boys—but the little girls would just sit all
nice and stiff and starched, with the lace gimps
on their dresses, and their sashes and hair ribbons and their black patent-leather slippers, and
they'd hold their dolls and maybe comb the dolls'
hair.

Then around four the parents would wake up
and come out all fresh and pink, and they and
the kids would take a long walk to the park and
sit under trees and eat ice cream cones and listen
to the band, or maybe they'd go visit relatives and
drink tea or coffee and eat a good, rich, homemade
five-layer chocolate cake on other porches. Ami
could hear the soft glittering rustle of the trees
in the warm sun of many years ago, the clump-
clump of a horse's hoofs on the cobbles, the dis-

tant, sleepy rattle of a streetcar, a child's clear
and contented laugh, the Sunday murmur of a
mother's voice, and church bells. Even the poor
didn't worry much in those days. There was something to live for; it was so sweet and pleasant. She
had been one of the little girls on the hot splin-
tered porch steps, and so she knew. Her mother
would put up her hair on Saturday night, after
the bath in the washtub; she had pretty brown
hair, but very straight, and Mama would roll her
hair on long rags so that in the morning she'd
have smooth and glassy tubes hanging around her
face. Mama and Pa had been very poor, but somehow it hadn't seemed poor. Somehow. It was so
peaceful. And people had pride and gumption.

There was always an old grandmother or aunt
in the houses too. They got the tenderest pieces
of the Sunday chicken or the roast beef because
of their teeth. She could see her own grandmother,
in the gray-print calico and her fresh white apron.
Granny could make the best cookies for kids and
tell the best stories. And Mama and Pa treated
her like a princess, too. Or a queen. Once, for
Christmas, they'd paid three dollars for one of
them big old Spanish combs with all color beads
at the top, and Granny had put it in the thin white
bun of her hair and it had stood up, real pretty,
over her head. She, Ami, would never forget that
comb. Granny had left it to her; it was in her
trinket box. She'd take it out and look at it, and
sometimes she'd put it in her own hair, just for
fun. It was like a little crown. That's what Mama
and Pa had thought of it, too: a little crown for
Granny. Kids who didn't have old grannies and

205

grandpas in the house were jealous of those who did. It was something to have them. Peaceful.

She could hear Granny sing right now:

"Rock of Ages, cleft for me!"

Rock of Ages. But there wasn't no rock of ages for anybody any more, anywhere. Now it was all plastic and ranch houses and stuff that wasn't made of good cotton, linen, wool, and silk. Even the carpets were what they called "miracle fibers." She hated them. Well, all this stuff was just like people now. What did they call it? Synthetics? Yes, well. People were synthetics now too. And no peace. Never any peace, never any long warm Sundays, or white winters, or Christmases with real trees, and real candles on them, and red popcorn strings, and peppermint-candy canes, and those wonderful, wonderful glass ornaments that came from Germany, angels, to hang on the trees, and little bags of candy, and helping their mothers make the mincemeat. Chop, chop. Cracking the nuts, washing and steaming the raisins, cutting up the citron, stirring the sugar with good butter that tasted like butter, sifting the flour—all in hot steamy kitchens with the wood stove and the sound of sleigh bells outside. So peaceful. No wars, no hurry, no telephones splitting the air, no radios screaming, no nylon sheets, no movies. Just people in their houses, loving each other and making every holiday something to remember all your life, even if you didn't have a lot of money in your pocket. It was love. There just didn't seem to be any love left now. Just that sex they was all talking about these days, even the kids!

Synthetics. That's what they all was these days, their houses, their cars, their children, their amusements. And, above all, themselves. No wonder you didn't see happy people no more these days. They just weren't *real!* That was it, they just weren't *real!*

There wasn't even God—much. Not God like He used to be. Every house had a sign in it: "In God we trust," or "God bless our home," or "Jesus, be with us." You'd just look at the signs, and you knew God wasn't far off; He was right here, at the table where the papas said the grace, even though it was just corned beef and cabbage on the table. God was right here when it was very cold in your bedroom but snug under the feather beds, with the big bright stars showing even through the frost on your windows. He was right here when you got up in the morning; He was with you all day long, too, at school and when you worked. Why, sometimes, if you listened real close, you could hear Him breathing! You could hear Him singing in the trees, or in the high winds at midnight in the winter, when everything was so white and the moon was shining. People thought of Him all day long. He was just part of their lives. Where was He now? Who'd driven Him away? The radios blasting all the time, or the TV sets, or the cocktail parties, or the shows? No. It wasn't that. People had just driven Him away. They didn't want Him around. And that's why there wasn't no peace any longer. That's why parents weren't honored

207

any more but just thought of as nuisances that you
hid away or thought were "problems." That's what
they called them in the newspaper columns:
"problems." Granny wasn't no "problem." She
was Granny. A queen.

One of these days, thought Ami Logan, taking
off her misted glasses to wipe them, people would
begin to think that God was a "problem" too. Or
maybe they'd already come to that. They didn't
talk about Him easy in the houses any more. In
fact, they didn't talk about Him at all! But how
could synthetics talk about God? God was real,
and they weren't.

It was terrible that they'd driven Him away.
That left nothing for the kids and the grannies and
the grandpas. That left nothing at all for anybody.

It was funny. Pa worked in a machine shop.
They didn't call him Labor, then. He was a man.
He wasn't Labor. He was a person. Independent.
He'd have his beer on the porch at night, and his
neighbors would come and they'd talk politics and
get real excited. And sometimes swear. Who were
the Presidents then? She didn't remember. Presidents come and then they go. Nobody remembered
them, except when they did some kind of harm,
and then the people cursed them. But it was a kind
of happy cursing. Washington was a long way off.
Now it was kind of everywhere. Who wanted it?
It was like something looking over your shoulder
all the time and breathing down your neck. Making you hurry, hurry, hurry. "Growth." For what?
And Washington wanted your money; she had to
pay out taxes on what she earned by her hard
work. For what? Who wanted your money and

made Washington scream for it like it was a pack of policemen? It didn't make sense. What a person earned was always his own, earned with the sweat of his brow, like the Bible said. Now, it looked like, it wasn't yours. It was somebody else's. Why? Did they earn it on their knees in somebody's kitchen or doing somebody's laundry? No sir. They didn't. But they wanted your money all the same, even if they hadn't earned it themselves. She wondered what Pa would say about all this. He'd say, "The country's gone to the dogs, for sure. And maybe we'd better roll up our sleeves and get it back for ourselves." Yes, that's what Pa would say. And all the men like him. They talked all the time about the Revolution and the Boston Tea Party. Maybe what the country needed was another Tea Party.

But what could you expect from a people that wasn't real no more, people who was only synthetics, with no idea of duty and work and God? And no notion of earning their own way and asking nobody for a cent that wasn't theirs?

Oh, they said all these drugs and things kept people alive longer these days. What for? Just to be "problems"? Not to be honored when they was old? Just to be thrown out like a dying cat or dog? That's what came of people driving God out. It wasn't how long you lived that counted. It was how you lived. But people sure set a lot of store on how long you lived, like living was all there was. Just living in a world that didn't have no peace and no God.

That was a nice little man who'd just gone in there. An hour ago? He had problems too. He looked kind of white, like he was sick. He was sorry for me. I didn't tell him I was sorry for him too! Dear God, I'm just sorry for everybody.

> Rock of ages, cleft for me,
> Let me hide myself in Thee!

But, thought Ami Logan, I ain't got anyplace to hide any more. It's all open, everywhere. No shelter. Like you lived in a desert. "The Shadow of a Rock in a weary land." Funny she should remember that just now. A weary land. That's what it was, everywhere, a weary land, in spite of all the new cars and the rushing around and the fun and parties and the washing machines and people talking about going to the moon. What was it they was running away from, that they wanted to go to the moon? Themselves? That's what comes of having no peace and no God. That was what was making her feel so old, and she only seventy-one, and Granny was real chipper and did a lot of work when she was eighty-five and went to church every Sunday and the Ladies' Aid every Wednesday night, walking miles. Granny had lived to be ninety. She'd have lived longer if she hadn't fallen down the porch steps and broke her hip. It was a terrible time then. Mama and Pa almost lost their minds, worrying about her. Who worried about people any longer? Except themselves? Who cared about their parents? They were "problems."

The chimes sounded for her. She started. She was all alone. She pushed herself heavily to her swollen feet and legs. She walked slowly to the door; her legs felt like logs. She opened the door and went into the quiet, white marble room with the blue curtains.

She stood near the closed door for some moments. No one suggested that she sit down. No one suggested that she do anything. It was peaceful in here. The Man who Listens. He was waiting so quietly for her. He had all the time there was. All the time there was, like when she was a kid on a warm Sunday afternoon, with the church bells ringing and the Chinese glass things on the porch tinkling.

She sat down in the marble chair, putting her large raffia bag next to her swollen knee. She folded her bloated and scoured hands on her lap. She said roughly, "You a minister, mister? That's what I heard."

The warm white light gently enfolded her. So peaceful!

"I can't complain," she said proudly. "I've worked most of my life, ever since I was nine. I'm not coming here for pity. It's just I'm a 'problem.' That's what the newspapers call me, and my children." She paused. "My children." She sat up in the chair. "It's funny, but nobody thought anyone else was a problem when I was a kid. But you don't know anything about me, do you?"

The room waited, tenderly enfolding her. 'I'm a mother," she said.

The light became even more gentle. "I wonder," she said, "if you've got a mother living who's a problem to you." She waited. "Did your mother work for you, hope for you, maybe, and worry about you? Did she make your clothes and everything? And cook for you? Did she pray for you

211

when you was out? Did she wake up in the morning, thinking about you, and if she'd done the best for you? Did she make you go to school and tell you about God?"

The room's light appeared to hover about her. She looked at it. She was not a tearful woman, but now there were tears in her eyes. "She did? Well, then, maybe you can help me. I never asked help of nobody before. I just feel I kind of need it now." She added hurriedly. "Not that I'm asking for money! No, it's not that."

She scrubbed at her eyes with her broken knuckles. "It's something else that kind of eats at me. It's not having any place to lie my head. Now."

She looked at the wet tears on her knuckles and grunted. "Haven't cried since Chris was eight and had diphtheria and I thought he was dying. Maybe I'm getting old, after all. Maybe they're right. Mister, did you tell your mother to go into a home? Or maybe I should call you 'Reverend.' That's what they called ministers when I was a child. Reverend. Reverend, did you ever want to send your mother to a home? Give her to somebody else to take care of?"

The light, the white walls, the closed curtains were so peaceful. She felt a listening, a deep tenderness. But she could hear no sound. She sat and thought, and she thought of her childhood and her grandmother and her parents. Especially her grandmother. She started.

"What did you say?" she said anxiously. "Oh, I guess you didn't say anything. But I thought you

212

said something about your grandmother. I must be getting old, thinking I heard something."

She paused. "I called my granny 'Granny Ann.' She was old, but she was young to me. Granny Ann. Mama worked around the neighborhood. Pa worked twelve hours a day. Granny Ann used to tell me stories, mostly Bible stories. Maybe you never had a granny you knew?"

She bent forward, puzzled. "Seems like I heard you say yes. You see how old I am? Thinking I hear things? Excuse me, Reverend."

She sat back in the chair. It was very comfortable. A person could sleep in this chair; the edge didn't eat into the backs of her calves. Her heavy, tired body relaxed.

"They say you listen. That's fine. I want somebody to listen. Nobody ever listens. It's hurry, hurry, hurry. Make the bus in the morning, make the bus at night. Get in the store before it closes. Run home and get your dinner. I hear this TV program. 'Be alert,' it said. 'If you're nine or ninety, be alert.' What for? Nobody asked you to be 'alert' when I was young. You just did the best you could on your own time. They didn't want you jumping around and grinning and being all agog. What's the matter with people now? They don't seem to get anything done as well as we did it when I was a child. They just fly at things, then fly away, then fly at something else. Like they had a fever or was out of their minds. Moving their legs real fast. And everything just plastic around them. Nothing real. No homes, no places to rest, no quiet. Just plastic. You know what I mean?"

213

The room seemed to give her a sad affirmation. She let her weary legs spread out before her. She looked at them. "It's kind of nice, knowing someone's listening. Like they did when I was a little girl. Always time to listen to anything, anybody. All the time there was, though they worked twice as long as they do now. Sometimes the days run out of your fingers like water. They're not there. Ain't that the silliest thing to say? I heard that's the way it is when you're old. But it wasn't that way with Granny Ann, and she was ninety when she died. The days were just—solid—to her. They had hours in them and lots of time to read and sing and have picnics and go walking and talk about God. Lots of long hours, lots of long days and nights. Peaceful."

She forced herself to sit up. "But that ain't why I came here, to talk about that. You see, I was seventeen when I got married. His name was Eli Logan. It's from the Bible. Nobody names any kid from the Bible any more. Come to think of it, my name's not in the Bible, neither. Mama was kind of romantic. She named me Ami. She said it meant love. The teachers put it down as Amy. What does it matter? But still, I like to think of my name as Ami. I write it that way. I make them make out my checks as Ami. It kind of means something to me. I just can't explain."

The silent white room with its soft light appeared to be full of understanding. "Is that name French, or does it mean anything?" She asked. She tried to listen for an answer. Then she smiled. She had been answered. She was certain of that, even though she had heard no voice.

"My husband. He was twenty when we got married. He was a man, not like these little boys who're twenty and think they're kids. Eli was a big, grown man. And I was seventeen and a big, grown woman. Pa was dead then. I'd been working all my life, like Mama. Papa and Mama had a house; it'd cost two thousand dollars, and there was a mortgage on it. Eli and me got married, and Eli moved in, and there was Mama. Eli didn't have no parents; they died when he was fourteen, fifteen. He was glad to have Mama as his own mother. 'We're a family,' he said to me, and he kissed Mama first when we was married."

She sobbed suddenly, great racking sobs. But she was smiling. "We was a family, Mama, Eli, and me. Eli worked in the brewery; he was real good; he got fifteen dollars a week, and that was a lot of money then. A lot of money. And there's another thing. Money don't seem to have any feeling these days, neither. Like it was synthetic too. Why, we lived high on Eli's fifteen dollars a week! We paid on the mortgage, too. And then when Chris was born we'd paid off all the mortgage. Eli burned it right in front of me, in a china bowl, with Chris on my arm, and the other two kids jumped and jumped, and their eyes were like stars. Kids knew things those days." She paused. "But they've forgotten now."

She examined her broken hands. But she was not thinking of them.

"We had three kids. One was when I was eighteen; that was Katherine. The next when I was twenty; that was Arnold; it was a stylish name then. Then Chris come when I was twenty-one. We was a real family then, Mama, Eli, the kids, and me. Mama took in sewing, or she'd go out sewing. And then Eli got a raise, to twenty dollars a week. We felt rich. Real rich. Not the way people do today. Money was something then. Every dollar counted. Five cents a loaf of bread, though I made the bread most of the time. Six cents a quart of milk, but you could go about a mile and get a quart for three cents. I did. Why, we had a good, big table for six dollars a week, and all of us! Mama and I made the kids their clothes, and it cost hardly nothing for yard goods. We made Eli's shirts and all our things, and the blankets too. We got the wool goods and put hems on them; blanket stitch. We made the quilts. And the curtains. There was the time when Chris was five, and we treated ourselves for Christmas. Curtains all through the house, new, velveteen, crimson. It didn't cost us more than twelve dollars for the goods, and Mama and I made the curtains and hung them, and the kids cheered. They was just as happy as we were. Lovely, lovely curtains, full and rich. It was our Christmas present to each other. Of course we had stockings for the kids, too, with an orange or a tangerine, and a bag of candy, and little paper parasols, and a candy cane, and a jack-in-the-box, and some jacks, and a red ball, and a penny wrapped in gold paper, and maybe a little doll for Katherine, and some licorice drops, and nuts and an apple. It was a wonderful Christmas. The best Christmas I'd ever had.

"It's funny how my children've forgotten how wonderful it was. And the goose. I bought a goose for sixty cents, nice and fat, and I rendered the fat and we had goose grease all winter to cook with or rub on the kids' chests when they got colds. Oh, sure, they'd get sick, but they got over it fast. Mumps, chicken pox, measles. It didn't mean anything. Not the big fuss they make now, like everything's going to be fatal.

"Wonderful Christmas. Mama made her bread sauce for the goose, with onions. And mashed potatoes, and squash, and cranberries. And her own mincemeat. I just loved to see the kids helping her make it, like when I was a child. Then on Christmas Eve we sang carols, and then in the morning we went to church, and our faces were all stung and red with the cold, and we hurried home to a nice hot kitchen and all the good food waiting. And Eli said grace at the table, and he said, 'Please be with us all our lives, dear Heavenly Father, for the sake of Thy Son, Our Lord, Jesus Christ.'"

Ami Logan's face was still and dreaming and reflected the pure white light in the room. It was a young face now, without seams or drabness, the face of a young and happy woman. Then it changed.

"That was our last Christmas all together. Mama died in February. She just died in her sleep, smiling. She hadn't even been sick. She was forty-four years old. Why, she was even younger than Mrs. Brewster I work for! But Mrs. Brewster seems older, even though she has her hair done every five days and her skin's smooth as silk and she's got a figure like a girl of fifteen. And all those clothes! Even her slips cost more than our Christmas curtains did. But, somehow, she seems older. Maybe it's all that bridge and community activities and cocktail parties and being 'alert.' She's real old, Mrs. Brewster. She makes me think of a poor little girl when I was a little girl myself. The little girl wasn't all there; that's what they called it then. She could walk and talk a little, but she made you think she was an old woman, though she just babbled kind of senseless and ran all the time. You never saw her walk. She just ran, bumping into things and falling down. And she'd giggle for hours at a time, laughing all the time, not meaning anything. She died when she was six. I can't think of her without shivering; she's just like Mrs. Brewster."

Ami Logan shivered. "It ain't that Mrs. Brewster's feeble-minded like that little girl. It's just that she makes me think of her, and I don't know why.

"Well. You see how old people's minds wander? I hope you're still listening.

"It didn't seem the same without Mama in the house, the grandma. There was just that empty place. The kids missed her. She always had a story to tell them after prayers at bedtime. And cookies. Just like Granny Ann. They kept crying for her. It made me ache, and it made Eli ache too. We sure had something to cry about! In March, Eli was coming home from work, and he slipped in front of a streetcar and it cut off his legs, and he died. Right there on the street. It was March nineteen."

She put her scarred hands over her face and cried. "Seems like it was yesterday, and I was all of twenty-five then. Mama. Then Eli. The streetcar

218

company said it wasn't their fault. Eli shouldn't've run on all that ice in front of it just when it was starting up. But they was real nice. They came and offered me five hundred dollars. And I said, 'No sir. I don't take charity. If Eli was wrong, he was wrong, even if he was in a hurry. Me and the kids, we'll get along all right. We're not the kind of people who take something for nothing.' When I got Eli's insurance—it was three thousand dollars—I paid for his funeral. It was one hundred dollars. And I got him a nice headstone, too, out in Calvary Park, and it's big and good, even after all these years. Granite. You can hardly read the name now, but it's in my heart, and what do you need a name on gravestones for? When it's in your heart?"

She sat up resolutely and looked at the curtains. "Does a name on a headstone matter? Why, Reverend, they won't even look at your headstone when you die! But the people who remember you —they'll remember you all their lives. You'll never be dead to them, just like Mama and Eli and Granny Ann and Papa will never be dead to me. You'll be with the folks who love and remember you, until the day you die, and maybe even afterwards. Don't you believe that?"

The room gave her a warm and gentle assent. She nodded, satisfied.

"Well, I had that insurance money and Mama's house. It's a good house even now, though it's old. It was built when people really built houses and cared how they built them, too. Brick; not that veneer brick. But real brick, two brick walls close to each other. Brick between the rooms, too,

219

though the walls're plastered and they've got paper on them. Warm as toast in winter. Cool as can be in summer. The windows are little, but they never need any work but washing. And the doors are like—well, like doors should be. Thick and strong, never warp. Good, heavy oak wood. And you never hear a squeak in the floors. They was laid right, and I keep them shining like mirrors, waxed and polished. Maybe the closets are little, but people didn't think of lots of clothes all the time the way they do now. I put in a new coal furnace twenty years ago," Ami Logan added proudly. "Warm as can be, and no dirt, either."

She lifted her head higher. "We used to have a nice lawn, too, with trees right out to the sidewalk. Then they said they had to widen the street for the cars. They cut down the trees and ran the asphalt almost right up to the steps of the porch. So people in cars can get home quicker, just to have their drinks and then eat dinners that don't taste like much, and then go out bowling or look at TV or maybe play cards or run around the neighborhood in their cars. Looking and running. That's all they do now. And it don't seem to give them anything. They got faces like starving people. And they cut down the trees for them! Just so they can run home to do nothing, then run out to do nothing faster. You know something. Nobody around today's worth a tree. Not any tree. If a dead tree made them happier, it would be all right. But it don't. They don't even notice anything, not even that they're alive. Or supposed to be. I don't know.

"They say," said Ami Logan, "that you're get-

ting old when you think the old days were best.
Maybe so. But my son Chris has got one of them
ranch houses—look like big old sheds or big
chicken coops—and it's only five years old, built it
himself, and he has to put a lot of new shingles on
the roof every spring. But my house has thick
slate, and it's never leaked once. And the floors
in his house squeak; nothing substantial under
them like a big old cellar where you can put apple
barrels and put down your own pickles and jams.
Why, he spends more a year keeping up that big
chicken coop than I spent since Eli was killed!
All the rooms running into each other, too, so you
can't get away from anybody when you're blue or
want to read or just be alone, thinking. They've
got dividers, they call them, wooden boxes full of
crawling green plants, so Chris's wife, she says,
can see everybody at once and see what they're
doing! Isn't that terrible, I ask you? No one can
get away or shut a door. Her name's Eva; she's
real thin and quick and you can hear her voice all
over the house; she calls it being together, or
something like that. No place to go to be alone
and maybe pray a little. Why do they always want
to huddle up together like scared sheep?

"Maybe," said Ami Logan, "it's because they *are*
scared sheep. And no wonder, with nothing real
around them. Why, the walls in that house are all
shiny; thought it was wood at first, but it's only
plastic, painted kind of to look like wood. If you
can't afford wood, I said, don't put up any imitations, and Eva gives that high old little smile
of hers and says, 'Why, Mother Logan, this cost
a lot more than wood!' Don't make any sense to

221

me. Imitations costing more than the real thing! Maybe that's the way with everything. Imitations costing too much.

"Even Chris's job don't sound good and solid to me. Public relations for the big ice cream company here. You know it? Barton's. If an ice cream is good, what do you need going around talking to people about it for? They'll buy it. I'm not sure what public relations is. Anyway, he gets seven thousand dollars a year. Almost four times what our house cost us! And he can't save a cent, not a cent, and I always save something, myself, even if it's only two dollars a week. Can't save anything on seven thousand dollars! Well, he says, there's the house mortgage and the two kids and the taxes. And the dancing school for the girl and lot of things the boy belongs to. And those taxes. 'For government services,' says Chris to me, like I was a fool. 'What services?' I ask him. 'I don't want no government services. It's all right to have a big army and such, with Russia, but how did Russia get to be so strong, anyway?' (A lady I know said we did it, with our money. Is that a government service?) I don't want nothing from any government but just to have it keep right away from me, except city government where you got to have police and firemen and schoolteachers and schools, and such. 'With everybody having needs and wants and demands,' says Chris, looking older at fifty than my grandfather looked at seventy, 'you've got to pay for it through taxes.'

"Well, sir, I don't have no needs and wants and demands. I just want people not interfering with my business. That's not much to want, is it? Well,

222

anyway, Chris don't only not have any savings; he's in debt all the time. It's that sleazy money that don't buy nothing hardly any more. No yellow bills, no bills saying repayable in gold or silver, no gold money. Just some bank will pay you one hundred cents. The stuff doesn't have a feel to it, if you know what I mean, no more than the other synthetics. It gives me the creeps sometimes, looking at the world we got now."

She laughed wearily, coughed somewhat hard, then laughed again.

"And there's Arnold; he's fifty-one. We used to call them bookkeepers when I was young, but now they call themselves CPA's. He don't get as much as Chris, but he's got only one boy. A kind of nice boy, that Robert. Sensible boy. He reminds me of Eli; got the same kind of brown square face and big hands and comes in to see me sometimes on Sundays. Twenty years old. Working his way through the university."

Ami Logan paused to reflect, and she smiled, and her seamed face shone a little. "He's the only one on my side. His ma ain't like Eva. She belongs to clubs; she leaves people alone in a different way than I mean. She don't hardly notice Arnold and Robert. All the clubs are uplift kind of things; she's on boards. Maybe she ought to stay home and uplift around the house, such as uplifting the rugs once in a while and uplifting the bedspreads to get at the thick dust, or making her own jams and jellies and uplifting them on shelves. But real stylish; she calls herself Elise, but her name's really Elsie; knew her before she married Arnold, and her family. She always was a girl to be poking her nose in other people's business, even when she was a kid. But tight! Anyway, they don't owe any money and probably got a lot saved, because Arnold's tight too. They live in a big-front apartment house with the tiniest little rooms you ever saw. Like boxes. Arnold does the bookkeeping for the owner and so gets his rent for nothing or almost nothing. Well that's thrift, but they could have a house somewhere like mine. No, they ain't thrifty, they live like dogs. Cheapest food you ever ate; why, we was real poor, dirt poor, when I was a little girl, but my ma'd be ashamed to put the kind of food on the table that Elsie puts. It don't have any taste at all. But it's all vitamins, Elsie tells me. Salads.

"And now there's Katherine. She's fifty-three and don't have any children at all. And she's a widow. Katherine's kind of squeezed-mouth. She never did say what her husband left, but she's got a good fur coat and a car of her own and lives in a better place than Arnold, and she takes trips. She's been a widow for fifteen years, and her husband was in real estate. She sold Chris the lot where he built his house, and it wasn't no bargain, no sir!"

Ami Logan sighed and shook her head drearily. "You have your children and you raise them, and you don't know a thing about them. No. I sometimes say, 'Chris, you remember that Christmas we all made things for each other because we couldn't afford to buy anything? And what fun it was, making the things?' And he looks at me real cold and says, 'No, Ma, and it's a sign of growing old when you remember like that.'

224

"Well, maybe. But a person has to have some pleasure in her life, don't she? I raised those children of mine; I put the rest of the insurance money in the bank, and I went to work wherever I could find it. Cooking. Practical nursing. Sewing. Cleaning. Washing. Waiting on store sometimes on Saturdays. I didn't mind what it was, so long as it was honest and we had our house, even if it's small, and it was snug, and I had my children. And after Eli'd been dead three of four years I began to sing again, knowing I had my children and my house and was strong and healthy and able to work. What more does anyone want?

"And that's where the whole trouble is."

Ami Logan rubbed the palms of her callused hands on the soft velvet that covered the arms of the chair. She stroked it absently, then with attention. "Now this," she said with admiration, "is real silk velvet! Just beautiful. It gives a person a good feeling when she finds something real.

"Well, Reverend, I'm taking up a lot of your time, and I hope you don't mind too much. I'll make it shorter. I've got six thousand dollars in the bank, and my house. And I'm seventy-one years old. I didn't feel so well last winter, so I went to my doctor—he's an old man, too—and he said, 'Ami, you've got a bad heart condition. You've got to stop working. Look at your feet and legs! You've worn them out, just like you've worn your heart out raising your children and working all your life.' And I says, 'And you're all worn out, too, and what does it matter?'

"He agrees with that, but he's known me since Eli was killed, and he calls up Chris and tells him.

225

And they all come down on me. Katherine says she's been ashamed all these years with me being a cleaning woman and everything else. She would have given me money to stay at home, Katherine says, if she'd been able to afford it. And Chris says he's ashamed, too, and has a lot of debts and can't seem to get nowhere, and Arnold says I'm embarrassing Elsie."

Ami Logan sat up very high in the chair, and her cheeks flushed. "Ashamed of their ma working! As if working was something to be ashamed of! Why, they're the ones should be ashamed! I was shamed for them. And I said, 'What makes you all so fussy about me, when you wasn't before?' And Chris says the doctor says they should or he'd go to some authorities, and it would be terrible. Well, I'm mad at that doctor, and I look at my children and try to think they're worried about me, and then I began to cry. I said, 'All right. I'll rent this house and I'll move with you. Which one first?'

"Well, Reverend," said Ami in a low and trembling voice, "they looked at each other, and then they wouldn't look at me. Then Katherine said, 'Oh, Ma, you know how busy we all are, and we've all got responsibilities of our own. Even me. The boys have children and wives. But look, Ma dear, and don't get that tight look on your face. I can sell this house right away for you. I ought to get at least seven thousand dollars for it. There's a gas station that wants it, a corner lot.'

"And I said, 'You mean pull down my pa's house, and my house, and the house you was all born in and your own pa paid for?' I couldn't believe it.

"Then Arnold says, 'Let's not be sentimental.' Anything anyone wants that Arnold doesn't is sentimental or stupid or ridiculous. He says that with my six thousand dollars in the bank and the seven thousand dollars for the house I can go into the Methodist Home in Valley Hill. Elsie's on the board. Nice place out in the country, they said, with other old folks like myself, and companionship. And food, and share a room with some clean old lady, and they have a lot of fun out there, and games, and go for rides.

"I get real sick, thinking even now of what they said. Thirteen thousand dollars—that's what I'd have. But no place to lie my head, no place of my own. And no privacy. People like Elsie always poking, poking, at you. No place to hide, to get away from people. Only chatter, and marching through halls, and sitting in parlors, and waiting for death to come and tap you on the shoulder. Just waiting for death. That's all.

"I just can't face it, Reverend. I want to go on working until I die, free in my own house, free to shut my own door, free to go to bed and then get up and work, or maybe stay home a day when the weather's nice.

"But the worst of it is, my children don't 'honor' me like I did my parents and they did their own parents. I'm just a problem to them, a shame. Their houses don't have a room in it for me. Their children don't want me, except Robert. They want me to get out of their minds and stop shaming

227

them or something and go to a kind of charity home. Me, in a charity home! Oh, I'd be paying in thirteen thousand dollars, but the sleazy way money is now, that don't mean anything these days.

"It's not having a place of my own to lie my head down, and not having my children honor me. That's the very, very worst. Maybe I didn't do right. I don't know. I did my best, but maybe it wasn't good enough. But I just don't see what else I could have done. Can you? I didn't know I shamed them, but I guess that's why they told everybody, when I was in their houses, which wasn't often, that I was a nurse."

Her voice had risen to the crest of shaking despair, and she pushed herself painfully to her feet. She wobbled across the marble floor and earnestly faced the curtains. There was a sudden huge and sinking pain in her chest. She ignored it.

"There ain't anyone in the whole world that cares about me," she mourned. "And I didn't know that until just a little while ago." She clasped her hands together. "What can I do, Reverend?"

She looked anxiously at the button and peered forward to read the plate near it through her blurred glasses. She bit her lips. Then she put her hand out and touched the button.

The curtains moved aside quietly, soundlessly, and the light flowed out to hold her. She looked at the man who stood in the light. She lifted her clasped hands to her lips and pressed them deeply. "Oh," she murmured. "Oh. Yes. I should have known." She caught her breath. The pain was crushing, smothering.

She moved back slowly, clumsily, felt for the chair, and sat down and faced the man. They looked at each other a long time.

"I remember," she whispered, and she smiled even while she cried. "You didn't have no place to lie your head either, did you? No place of your own. Not when you were a grown man and out working. For people like me. You didn't forget me. And I never forgot you, not one day in my life. Not one day in my life! You were the best I had, and I still have you.

"I'm just thinking," she said in a dreaming voice, and her smile was young as well as mournful. "You must think about this world we got now the way I do. It was peaceful when you were a child, wasn't it, at home with your mother, and helping her? You and I—we've got a lot in common."

Her eyes closed. She dropped into a slight doze for a few moments, then awoke without a start. "Why, thank you," she whispered. "Or maybe it's a dream. I dreamt that you spoke to me and that I heard your voice. It was just like I thought it would be. Peaceful. 'The peace beyond understanding.'

"I shouldn't've been so hard on my children. They've got this awful world to live in, perhaps for a long time yet. Maybe it gives them the creeps, too, looking at it and wondering how it got this way. Maybe they're scared about their children too. Maybe they know their children won't

229

honor them, either. Nobody ever honors anyone or anything now. Why, the poor world. And my poor children too. They don't have a place, themselves, to lie their heads, a place to call their own. No matter how hard they'll ever work, they'll never have a real place. I had. And I'm grateful. Yes, I'm grateful. I'm even grateful for all the hard work I did, and glad I could do it. It was a different world—I don't suppose it'll ever come back. My poor children. They don't have you, as I did. They don't even want you. That's the real bad part, not wanting you."

She dozed again. The man moved toward her and held out his hand, and she took it and said, "Yes—oh yes."

Ami Logan was the first person ever to die in the white marble room. When she was found she was smiling, and her face was full of joy.

She had left her money and her house to her grandson, Robert Logan. When he heard, he thought: Don't worry, Granny. I remember all the things you told me on those Sundays about the peaceful world you lived in. I'm going to keep on remembering. Someday I'm going to do something about it. For you.

SOUL FOURTEEN

The Judge

Woe unto you, Scribes and Pharisees,
Hypocrites! because you pay tithes on
mint and anise and cummin, and have left
undone the weightier matters of the Law,
right judgment and mercy and faith.
These things you ought to have done,
while not leaving the others undone.
Blind guides, who strain out the gnat
but swallow the camel!

Matthew 23:23–24

It was a very wet, cold, and rainy night, the wind driving and whirling sheets of water against windows and doors and all who walked on the streets. Great bellowing gusts roared out of the black sky, thundering at eaves and drumming on walls. The sidewalks ran like streams. The man who climbed the rise to the stark-white building shuddered, pulled down his hat, and tried to hold his coat about him. He cursed under his breath. He had never known his wife, Helen, to be hysterical before, not even when one of the boys had been struck by a car when he was a child. But now she was frantic, and no matter how he explained or reprimanded, the more frantic she became and

231

the heavier she sobbed and cried. One would think John Hathaway was her brother and Alice Hathaway her niece. It was not only bewildering, it was infuriating. Worse, it was dangerous to his own prestige and threatened his convictions. " 'Judge not, lest ye be judged,' " Helen had wept, startling her husband to anger and embarrassment. For he was a judge with a reputation for absolute objectivity and respect for the Law.

Then, to his angry repudiation, she had urged him to talk about the matter with the Man who Listens. At first he had not thought her serious, but only unstrung. When his daughter, Ruth, joined in her pleading, he did not speak to either of them for days. But when Helen began to show alarming symptoms of the return of her nervous breakdown he had furiously consented "at least to talk to that damned, maudlin fool on the hill. If only to shut you up," he added with unusual savagery. What did his family know of the pressure on him, particularly in the Hathaway case, the uneasy, wordless pressure?

The damned, insistent pressure of being a judge. The misunderstanding. The hatred. What did laymen know of the Law, written precisely, meaning only what it said and no more? Oh, there were judges who interpreted the Law in a lazy fashion and so set criminals loose on the community again to plunder, murder, and steal. The frowsy judges were the real criminals, elected by people no less venal than themselves. Even worse than the judges were the juries. Anglo-Saxon jurisprudence was an excellent thing, provided one really had "juries of one's peers." Peers! Cattle!

232

The gravel, running with water, churned under the judge's impatient feet. He almost forgot where he was going. If anything could have prejudiced him in favor of John Ellis Hathaway, it would have been the jury, selected after dreary days of challenging by the defendant's lawyers and the district attorney. Was this jury the "peer" of Hathaway, who was not only a prominent businessman but a distinguished scholar as well, a man of an old and excellent family which had given judges, clergymen, two governors, and three senators to the nation, and, during President Hayes's term, a Cabinet officer? The jury was composed of little shopkeepers, three mechanics, two opened-mouthed young housewives who thought they resembled the current movie queen, a man who owned two battered trucks, a service-station operator. And what not. These were the "peers" of Hathaway! He, the judge, had frequently caught the small and venomous smiles the jury had directed at the defendant, smiles full of envy and mean, hateful triumph that such a man was at their ultimate mercy. Yes, the jury alone would have prejudiced the judge in favor of Mr. Hathaway.

"God damn," said the judge simply, and stopped. He was standing before the double bronze doors of the white building with its arch letters that proclaimed that within it waited the Man who Listens. The wind threw itself upon him, almost flung him down, though he was a tall and sinewy man of about fifty, accustomed to weather and hunting and fishing and camping. A diffused light streamed gently down over the bronze doors. "No," said

233

the judge. But his hand reached out and turned the knob. He peered carefully inside. If a single person was within he would have to retreat, for fear of gossip that his honor, Judge Meredith Hazlitt, had actually come to this place for consultation. And what the newspapers could do to that fact during this sensational trial! Tomorrow he was to charge the jury, and it was already midnight.

He moved quickly into the empty waiting room. He closed the doors even more quickly behind him. He stood in the center of the room, his sharp hazel eyes scrutinizing everything, his sharp nostrils a little distended, his thick black brows drawn together. His father had known old John Godfrey well and admiringly. Yet this was a silly, sentimental place to come, and a dangerous one for a man like himself. However, he was rarely photographed. His face had appeared in the newspapers once eight years ago. He did not believe that judges should be well known to the populace. For that reason he belonged to only one or two clubs and attended them infrequently. Once his wife had told him that he was really out of place in America; his real milieu was England, where judges kept themselves apart and lived in their high-wigged dignity under the Crown. He had often wondered why he had been elected in the first place, for he was not popular and had few friends. He scoffed when his wife and two sons and daughter assured him affectionately that it was because of his integrity. Could such people as average jurymen be impressed by integrity? Nonsense. They preferred only some vague and medieval abstraction called "security" and their daily beer and their television sets and their small, furtive sins. Judge Hazlitt, from his childhood, had looked upon the world of men and had not found it good or righteous.

He looked at the oaken door. Now, what if the Man who Listens was a judge, himself, or a lawyer? A nice contretemps! In spite of all the repeated assurances he had overheard that no confidence was ever betrayed, the judge, in reality, trusted no one except his immediate family. He thought of Helen irascibly; there were times when Helen could be a little stupid in spite of her fine mind. He turned on his heel to leave, when he heard the soft chime. He looked over his shoulder at the door. Well, he had never broken a promise yet. But he would be very careful. He laughed shortly to himself and went into the white room.

He had seen photographs of the interior, so he was not surprised at the cool and silent light on the marble walls and floor. He looked at the blue curtains, then walked quietly to them. He tried to move them apart; they were like iron, for all their surface softness. Could anyone see through them? He pressed his nose almost onto the velvet fabric but could see nothing. If this gets out, then I'm finished, he thought. He went to the marble chair and sat down, staring threateningly at the curtained alcove.

"Are you a judge?" he asked in his strong and resonant voice.

No one answered him. "Silence," he said wryly, "is frequently an affirmation. Do I know you?"

But no one answered him. He held his dripping

hat on his knees. He had walked the two miles here in the rain, taking even the precaution of not using his car. (Helen would be upset when he returned, soaking to the skin. In view of everything, she deserved that anxiety.)

"I am a judge," he said. "I have heard that sometimes you speak—or is that correct? I'm not certain. Sometimes people see you and sometimes not. You can be assured, my dear colleague, that I'll not press that famous button beside the curtains."

Then he remembered that no one really knew who the man was and that it was rumored that he was not only a judge, but a psychiatrist, a teacher, a social worker, a clergyman. Even a doctor, someone had said. Of one thing he could be sure; the man hidden there was not one of the jury in the Hathaway case!

He was always a tense man, alert and coldly quick, owing to his nature and his physique and his secretly violent temperament. Yet he found himself relaxing as he always did after a fast walk. The chill was leaving his flesh; he was becoming comfortably warm. A peculiar thing was occurring, too, something which the judge had never experienced before: a sensation of kind confidence and patient waiting and brotherhood. It all appeared to emanate from the presence behind the curtain. Suddenly he was certain that he would never be betrayed, and this certainty startled him and he sat upright. He had been a constrained child, youth, and adult, confiding rarely in anyone, not even his parents and his wife.

He heard himself, to his astonishment, speaking

aloud: "It's not as if anyone has ever betrayed me in an important matter. No. But I've seen others betrayed. However, that should not have affected me, should it? And I did not know the circumstances of the betrayals." He stopped and thought of his involuntary words and was more astonished than ever. He had actually confessed that he had sometimes not known "the circumstances"! A hot sense of humiliation came to him.

The room waited, and the man behind the curtains. The judge frowned. A judge, he thought, must always be aware of circumstances, even in his private life, and make allowances for them. Could it be that he very seldom did? But the Law did not; that is, the Law when properly administered to the letter.

"The Law, to me," said the judge, "is a sacred thing. It is the accumulated wisdom of the centuries. Of course there have been evil laws; I can think of some amendments to the Constitution itself which are, or have been before repeal, actually evil and disastrous to the nation. I can think, at this very moment, of one amendment which should be repealed at once if we are to survive as a people. But too many hundreds of thousands of maggoty bureaucrats have a vested interest in it, and until the people are determined to shake it from the Constitution the bureaucrats will continue to fatten on it—to our terrible peril."

The judge cleared his throat. "But, on the whole, the Law is the strength of a people. It is their assurance that we are ruled by Law and not by men—though I've read informed and cogent opinions lately that we are beginning to be ruled by

237

men rather than by Law, and that always leads to despotism. Am I boring you?" he asked suddenly.

He was not a man of particular imagination, but he almost believed that he had heard a negative murmur. Or had it been a sigh, or the rustle of a late-autumn tree?

"That is why I, in my capacity as judge, adhere to the Law absolutely, as it is written, and never diverge from it. The newspapers have frequently implied that I'm merciless, which I am not. I did not write the Law, but it is my duty to uphold it."

He hesitated and listened for the slightest sound. There was none. It was as if he were sealed in some white and shining tomb.

"I'd not be here except for my wife," he said grudgingly after a few moments. "Helen is in many ways a very remarkable woman, extremely intelligent and logical and poised. She knows it is her duty as my wife not to discuss my cases with me, nor even to mention them. We've been married for twenty-six years. I had just been admitted to the Bar when we were married. My father was a wealthy lawyer. Helen and I did not need to wait until I was established. We were married a week after she was graduated from college."

His harsh face softened as he remembered the young Helen, only twenty, in the white bridal dress she had made herself. Her old fool of a father had lost all his inherited money and had compounded that folly by shooting himself. There had been just enough money left for Helen to complete her last year at college, and she had continued bravely and steadfastly in the face of all the ma-

licious gossip. Even when her mother, a feeble
soul, had died that March twenty-six years ago,
Helen had not been swerved or overcome. She
had enormous courage as well as gentleness, en-
durance as well as sweetness. He had loved Helen
from the time he had first known her, when she
was only seventeen. She had not been a pretty
girl; her great dark eyes had been her one attrac-
tion, and probably her expression, which com-
bined fortitude with womanliness. But she had
been rather small, a trifle stocky. It was strange
that she had had so many suitors, for young men
were notoriously fascinated by beauty alone.
Girls, too, had been devoted to her.

"I think," said the judge meditatively, "that it
was Helen's character. And I also think that it
was really because of Helen that I was elected, and
not from any value in myself!" He gave his short
laugh again. "Everyone," he added, "loves Helen.
She's a very wise woman, and very kind and discreet. That is why I cannot understand——"

He paused. "But I didn't come here to talk about
my family. By the way, I have two sons, both at
Harvard. Good boys, with Helen's eyes. And a
daughter." He paused again, and now his mouth
became soft and grave. "Ruth is twenty-three. I
don't mind saying that she is my favorite child.
But fathers usually prefer their daughters, I've
discovered."

He looked at the curtains expectantly. They did
not stir. It was now long after midnight. Was it
possible that there was no one there at all, though
it was said that the man waited all night? Non-

sense. Relays, no doubt. The judge smiled. Even a judge could not be on duty all the time, though God knew that the world needed them!

"Ruth," he said, forgetting that he had not come here to talk about his family. (He never talked about them to anyone, and he did not stop to wonder why he was doing it now.) "Ruth is all right again. She had married a scoundrel, one of the young Shelton boys. Good family. Not much money, but sound. Robert was the only rascal among them. A liar. A thief. Excellent university training, but a lazy bastard. I didn't know all this when Ruth told us, when she was twenty, that she wanted to marry him. I knew old Bob, his father. One of my best friends. Too bad he's dead. I wasn't too impressed by Robert, and I was disappointed in Ruth. He was too airy, too charming —that's a hell of a characteristic for a man to have, isn't it, unless he's a confidence man or a salesman or a politician? He is in politics now, by the way, and no doubt," said the judge bitterly, "he'll go far. I'd not be surprised if he became governor later on, or a senator. The people love charm these days and prefer a big smile and a big handshake to honor and intelligence. No wonder the country——" He stopped, shook his head.

He continued in a hard voice: "When old Bob died he left each of his three sons ten thousand dollars apiece. That is all the money he had, and he was a widower. The two older boys put it into their profession, or business, and are doing well and married excellently. Robert told me he still had the ten thousand dollars—safely invested. What reason did I have to disbelieve him? None.

We gave Ruth eight thousand dollars when she married Robert, and I bought their house for them. Helen furnished it. Everything was radiant and happy and young," said the judge in a louder and bitterer tone. "Robert was already vaguely connected with politics; he had, he said, a salary of about nine thousand dollars a year.

"He had nothing. He'd married my Ruth for her background and the money she would inherit someday—my pretty Ruth. When he discovered that I was not going to continue Ruth's large allowance or subsidize him, then the marriage ended. It had ended a long time before Helen and I knew about it. We did notice that Ruth was becoming pale and thin and too quiet; she was always a lively girl. We thought perhaps that she was pregnant at first. It was only by degrees that I found out that he'd squandered his father's ten thousand dollars even before he had married Ruth. He confiscated Ruth's money. It was two years before I discovered that he'd put a mortgage on the house I had bought for them. I found that out the day Ruth went to the hospital. She was sick a long time. Nervous and physical collapse, the doctors said. And no wonder! She had continued to love that swine up to that very day. It was a dreadful time, I assure you. We thought we'd lose Ruth; she didn't put up much of a fight to live. We finally had to call in a psychiatrist. Then we brought Ruth home. Then Helen became sick; a nervous breakdown from worry. I'll never forget that year until the day I die. The marriage, of course, was over, though I'm not a man who believes in divorce or countenances it. Ruth re-

241

ceived an annulment. There was considerable of a scandal after that. Robert had to file a bankruptcy petition. He had nothing at all. He had spent everything he had, what Ruth had, and the mortgage money—where, how, we never did know. I could have had the bastard thrown into jail!" exclaimed the judge, his tight face red with renewed rage. His hands clenched on the arms of the chair.

"But that would have hurt Ruth even more. There was enough damn talk. I believe in letting it die out. Ruth had loved him; he'd never loved her; that was the worst part. And now he's in politics!

"Well," said the judge in a spent voice, "that's all. Ruth is taking an interest in life again. She's going out, and sometimes we even hear her laugh. After all, she's only twenty-three."

The room waited. "All the time in the world." Where had he heard that about this place? The man who listened had "all the time in the world." I haven't, thought the judge grimly. It's nearly one now.

He said to the still curtains, "I don't know why I've told you all this. It isn't like me at all. In fact, I haven't talked so much before about poor Ruth even to Helen. I didn't come here like a maudlin fool to tell you about my affairs. Of what interest could they be to you? I come to tell you about a man, a defendant, in my court, who is being tried for murder. Perhaps you've read about the Hathaway case? Do you know anything about it at all?"

It was strange that the silent room appeared to

242

have answered him in the affirmative. The judge sighed.

"I've known John Hathaway for years. A man my own age. His father was a professor at Yale many years ago until he died. John and I had little in common. He was a little too remote and scholarly for me, though he is an excellent businessman. We don't see much of each other, though his wife and mine are old friends. A cold and formal stick of a man. Not one you could imagine ever committing a deliberately planned murder. Under any circumstances. Even under those circumstances."

The judge stopped speaking. His face became set and frozen. He contemplated the curtains for a long and silent time.

He said, "Circumstances similar to mine—and Ruth's. He had only one child, a daughter, about Ruth's age. Alice. A quiet girl; I remember her as a child when she came to see Ruth. Not pretty, like Ruth. Tall, thin, a little awkward, but intellectual, like her father. She married well too. I never did care for the Eldridge family, but that's of no consequence. They have all those lumber mills near the river. Alice married Dick Eldridge, a competent enough young man, considerably older than Ruth, but morose and sullen. I'd sometimes see him at the club. They say he was his father's right hand in the business. A bad-tempered face; once, when he was playing golf and lost, he hit Jack Moley over the head with an iron. He was almost expelled for that, but the family influence and money kept him in after all. I voted for his expulsion myself.

"But that's neither here nor there. Two months ago, however, John Hathaway calmly loaded a gun he had bought, drove over to his daughter's apartment. He knew she wasn't there; in fact, she was with her mother. I'll come back to that in a moment. But calmly he went into the apartment and found Dick Eldridge sullenly reading, and without a word he shot and killed him. He then immediately called the police and gave himself up."

The judge found himself sweating. He pulled out his damp handkerchief and wiped his face. With amazement he looked at his hands. They were trembling. He cleared his throat several times before he could speak again.

"It's first-degree murder, of course. He could simply have persuaded his daughter to leave Eldridge and come home; he could have settled things the way I did. But there's something else, though it's no excuse, under the Law, in spite of what the defense attorneys try to tell me. They met with me in my chambers, with the prosecuting attorney, for a confidence they didn't want to make public. Yet.

"It seems that Alice and Eldridge hadn't been married three months when he began to abuse her. I can say that for Robert Shelton—he was too easygoing and even too good-natured ever to have abused Ruth. Why that stupid girl, Alice, didn't leave him, I don't know. Probably loved him in spite of everything. Women can be ridiculous about these things; there are times I can't understand even Helen and Ruth.

"In any event, the defense attorneys told me,

244

Alice became pregnant four months before the murder. Eldridge, they said, became violent over it. He wanted no children; he hated children; he detested them. He forced Alice to have an abortion; that was about five weeks before the murder. A horrible thing, I admit, but I don't agree with the attorneys that abortion is exactly in the same class as a man taking a gun and killing another man in cold blood. An adult. Of course someone bungled; the—devils—often do, you know. And Alice almost lost her life. She was in the hospital for a month; septicemia. Dreadful, yes. Then she went home to her parents, still sick. In fact, the girl is sick even now. The attorneys, who are noted for being melodramatic, showed me photographs of the girl in her bed. She looked like a corpse. Poor girl.

"I can understand, in a way," said the judge after a few moments. "Hathaway lost his head, even though he had carefully planned the murder. He admitted verifying Eldridge's presence in the apartment. He had taken his daughter's key to let himself in quietly and give Eldridge no time to defend himself. He did not plead self-defense. In his statement before the trial he said he intended to kill his son-in-law. It was verified, by the way, that not only had Alice had that abortion but at the time of her admission to the hospital she was covered with bruises. Unfortunate. Terrible. However, even that does not justify cold-blooded murder. The Law is explicit on that. Self-defense, defending another in mortal, imminent danger, defense of property: these are admissible as defenses in cases of murder. In the majority of the cases the defendant goes free, or, at the worst, he receives a year or two in prison for manslaughter, third degree, or the sentence is suspended.

"Hathaway can claim none of the circumstances. His daughter is a young woman Ruth's age, but she certainly wasn't dragged to the abortionist; if she went unwillingly, she did go on her own two legs. True, she's still very sick and broken. Unfortunate, yes. She could have left Eldridge as Ruth finally left Shelton. She could have gotten a divorce. But the defense attorneys say that she loved that wretch, in spite of everything, until the abortion.

"I just don't understand women, of course. And I don't understand why Hathaway wasn't sensible enough just to take back his daughter and help her divorce her husband and let it go at that. He didn't have to kill Eldridge."

The judge shook his head over and over. "I made that clear to the defense attorneys. I suggested that they bring the abuse and abortion matters into court, but I also assured them that these in themselves are not an excuse for first-degree murder. Later Hathaway, when consulted, explicitly forbade it, and I don't blame him. After all, the girl has her life to live.

"Tomorrow I must charge the jury. I must inform them fully of the Law. Deliberate, planned, cold-blooded homicide, as admitted by John Hathaway, is first-degree murder. That is the Law. You can't get around it. That is the Law. Grudge killings are no excuse; there are no extenuating circumstances. Hathaway, if the jury brings in a first-degree murder verdict, will probably be executed. He doesn't seem to care, by the way. He merely sits with his attorneys, looking as remote and cool as ever, and that sort of thing doesn't prejudice juries in your favor. In fact, that's a hanging jury if I ever saw one.

"I'm sorry for Hathaway. But there is the Law. Damn it, why wasn't he at least in possession of enough self-control as I was? And I'm like him in a way. Ruth, with our help, Helen's and mine, was extricated from the mess she was in."

The judge paused. "I've told you that Hathaway's wife is an old friend of Helen's. Naturally, when I knew the case was to come before me— no one had any doubt but that I would adhere to the letter of the Law—I told Helen she could not meet Margaret Hathaway any longer for their weekly lunches. She understood. At first. Then Margaret did really an unpardonable thing under the circumstances. She hysterically called Helen one night and told her of the abuse and the abortion and begged Helen to try to influence me in behalf of her husband. Of course the poor woman is half out of her mind now, with her sick daughter and her indicted husband, but still she should have been more discreet.

"And Helen," said the judge angrily, "should be more discreet too. She knows that she is never to speak of my cases to me or discuss them. Yet now, for over a week, she has been crying desperately for me to help Hathaway. When I say 'desperately,' I mean exactly that, and I've never seen

247

Helen in such a condition before except for the time Ruth had her nervous and physical collapse and almost died——"

Very slowly the judge's hard-set face whitened, until his lips were dead white and the very tip of his nose. Very slowly he sat up rigidly in the marble chair. His very breath seemed to stop.

He spoke whisperingly, "I'm by nature a violent man—Helen knows that. I have self-control, but only God knows what effort I have to use to exercise it. I've wanted to kill—once or twice in my life. But I didn't, of course."

His throat suddenly became stiff and dry and he could not swallow.

Then he croaked: "Ruth!"

He remembered his daughter's illness. He remembered that he had become wildly impatient with her doctors. They had been evasive; he could not get them to tell him exactly what was wrong with his daughter. "Nervous and physical collapse." The doctors were old friends. They would hide——

"Ruth!" said the judge again.

Ruth had almost died. People don't die of nervous and physical collapses in the modern world, with doctors all about them. They don't have the stresses. Particularly Ruth. She had been hurt by her marriage, but one doesn't die of such a hurt today. "Men have died, and worms have eaten them—but not for love." No. And the fever! The burning, raging fever the girl had suffered for weeks. Infection. The half delirium, the mutterings, the murmurs, the tossing in bed. The anti-

248

biotics! He had forgotten them. They had given Ruth antibiotics. Septicemia. The weeks of recovery, the feeble walking, the expressions of pain, the sudden silent weeping, the shaking of Ruth's head when questioned, her muteness. She would not talk to her father.

She and Helen had never told him. They knew he was a coldly violent man when aroused. They knew he might have killed.

The judge stood up. straight and rigorous, and his face was terrible.

He looked at the curtain. "I'd have killed him," he said. "I hope to God I never see him again. I might not be able to control myself. Ruth!"

He caught the back of the marble chair to steady himself. "The Law," he said dully.

A man who committed a deliberate, cold-blooded murder was usually a criminal. If he was not a criminal, then he was temporarily insane, driven to an act against all his civilized and intelligent impulses. A man like Hathaway was not a criminal. He had been impelled by a force stronger than all his training, an outrage that was beyond his ability to withstand. He had killed because of one murder which had been done, and abortion really was murder, after all. He killed to avenge that murder and his daughter's suffering. Reduced to his basic human essentials, he had murdered. In vengeance for the innocent, one who had been destroyed and another who had almost been destroyed.

The judge found himself walking unsteadily to the curtains. He thrust out his hand to the button.

249

He whispered, "You must tell me what to do. There is the Law——"

The curtains rolled away.

The judge fell back as swiftly when he saw the light and who stood in the light. And then he stood for a long time looking into the eyes turned gently upon him.

He said at last, "Yes, I remember. It was the letter of the Law that killed, wasn't it? It's been a long time since I first heard that. And it is the spirit of it that saves. I'd forgotten. I was like those Pharisees. A violated law was a violated law. There was no appeal from it. No mercy. I remember now what you said."

He sat down in the chair because he was trembling. "I've been a bad judge," he continued. "I have followed the letter of the Law and so charged all those other juries. Thank God many of them disregarded me. Thank God.

"I will demand that Margaret Hathaway come into court and tell the story of Alice to the jury. The jury are simple people. I'm sorry I thought so little of them. They loathe the murder of the innocent. There are three young women there who are mothers. I will overrule any protest of the prosecution. Margaret—and I feel it—wants to come and tell what led up to the murder. Her husband's life is at stake. And Alice—she would not want her father to die merely to save her 'name.' No wonder the child is so sick and will not get well! Stupid Hathaway, who is as stupid as I'd have been—if I had known the same circumstances before!

"If necessary, and the jury wants it, we'll go to Alice. She will tell. Yes, she will tell."

He stood up, still white, but resolute. "The simplicity of the people is much wiser than any philosophy, their sympathies quick and certain, their pity instantaneous. Yes. The jury and I—we will save John Hathaway together."

He smiled a little. "I must go home to Helen now. It was she who begged me to talk to you. She knew. Didn't she tell me that Ruth did not begin to get well until she came here too? I wonder if she saw your face. The mercy of your face."

251

SOUL FIFTEEN

The Destroyer, and
THE MAN WHO LISTENS

Turning and turning in the widening gyre
The falcon cannot hear the falconer;
Things fall apart; the centre cannot hold:
Mere anarchy is loosed upon the world,
The blood-dimmed tide is loosed, and everywhere
The ceremony of innocence is drowned;
The best lack all conviction, while the worst
Are full of passionate intensity.

　　　　　　W. B. Yeats: "The Second Coming"

Dr. Atino Kadimo looked through the window of the jet plane and saw the Rockies far below —the Continental Divide. To conventional planes, even now, the Rockies were not something to pass over lightly, with a mere, abstracted glance. The captains and the co-pilots were very alert at this time because of the enormous updrafts and downdrafts. But it was quite different in a jet plane, Dr. Kadimo noticed with great interest. He was fifty-nine years old, yet he had not lost his sense of profound wonder, his awesome wonder, at everything. The Rockies, he saw, seemed a mere long rib of anthills, topped with infinitesimal dabs of snow, apparently the size of his palm. The great red buttes which had fascinated him when he had driven by them years ago appeared now to be but crimson wedges scattered on a smear of yellowish earth; they were hardly, from this perspective, more than an inch high.

For two hours now he had floated almost soundlessly over the brown, yellow, red, and tan-colored earth. Everything was diminished, flat, formless. Even an occasional small city was a mere twinkle. Rivers had disappeared or were mere wandering cracks. Roads, of course, could not be discerned at all. Man had diminished everything, removed the contour, swell, valley, rise, and fall of everything. There was something terrible in this diminishing, this reducing of mountain, hill, stream, city, and field to a flat and sterile monotony. Some nations had tried to accomplish this flattening and sterility among men, notably in Nazi Germany and Communist Russia, and there was a strong and deadly movement under way in America today to diminish man, to remove his contours of individuality, his variety of coloring, to make him, as they were doing to his earth, a frightful anonymity, with all his fruitful rivers of the mind vanished, his soul not distinguishable from his body, his passions one with the yellowish desert, his aspirations merely ant heaps, his spirit an irrelevant crack that led nowhere and died against a wall of stone, the bright cities of his mind hardly a faint flash in the eternal wilderness.

Where were the forests now, from this high perspective in the plane, or in the psyche of man, the green and living forests, full of strange paths and unexpected vistas, sudden bright pools in the glades, a startled and ecstatic cry, mysterious innocent jubilation, song, untrodden revelation? Dr. Kadimo could see no forests through his small and insulated window, not even a blur of green; all was sear, level, the color of dead dunes that looked on a lifeless sea.

In leaving the earth, thought the doctor, man has really left himself.

The stewardess, smiling, came with a tray on which stood glasses of champagne. The doctor took a glass, smiled at her gently, and sipped the wine. Why, excellent! Sparkling on the tongue! Grapes touched with fire and ice! He could see the vineyards of Europe; he could feel the fat warm bunches of grapes in his hand, opaline, white, faintly pink, swelling with hot juice. He sat back in his extremely comfortable seat and smiled almost with happiness. Man, who could create the golden fire in this glass, had not been diminished —yet. His soul had not been flattened—yet. Somewhere in the world, even in the concrete cities as well as in the vineyards and the forests and the fields, there lived men of passion, joy, prayer. Noble anger.

These men must be saved. Now the clenching fingers of chronic agony began to relax a little about the doctor's heart. Something came clear and sharp to him, like the shatter of a trumpet on a battlement, like a call on a lonely ocean, like the ember of a camping place on a desert. They did not live in America alone, these men; they lived on the islands, in Europe, even in Russia, and in the farthest desperate outposts of the world, guarding their precious passions, their dreams, their poetry of being, their souls which sometimes could, for a rare instant or two, encompass God. They guarded these things dearly, as a jeweler guards his treasures, as a lion guards his mate, as the vessel guards the Host. They had altars in their hearts, even if all altars were forbidden; they had sanctuaries of the spirit into which no destruction could crash its fist. It was for these men everywhere, Dr. Kadimo knew between one sip of champagne and another, that he must find a way to save and preserve what they sheltered so jealously and with such reverence. He did not know how. He only knew that he must.

One of the young stewardesses hesitated by his seat, another tray in her hand. She had been trained to regard her passengers not just as passengers but as human beings, subject to pain, fear, eccentricities, and even to dangerous gestures. Dr. Atino Kadimo; that was his name. He had boarded the plane in Los Angeles. He had looked sick and gray in Los Angeles, though he had smiled courteously and had given his name in meticulous syllables with a faint accent and had moved like a young man. She remembered that he was extremely tall, his height accentuated by his thinness. But he had very large blues eyes, absent yet penetrating, as if he were thinking of something else but leaving a soldier on guard to challenge, if necessary, or to alert him. He had seated himself and had not spoken to his companion on the other side of the table between the seats. He had spent most of his time looking down through the window. It must be his first flight in a jet. She could tell them.

And while he had looked he had become sicker, grayer, older. She had given him champagne, and he had thanked her. Most of the others rarely did, especially the silly, arrogant ones from Hollywood, who kept staring about them sharply and getting up and pacing the aisle, wanting to be recognized by the less important, demanding with insolent eyes that they be recognized. Some of the stupid gave them their insistently demanded accolade, with whispers of excitement, and they were pleased and immediately scorned their admirers as if they were impudent bumpkins. The more sophisticated or important pretended not to see them. This made them pettish with the stewardesses. The actresses were more pettish than the men, if possible.

The doctor had fallen asleep. His face looked younger, refreshed, more relaxed. A change had come over him. This made the stewardess hesitate with her tray for him. A nice filet mignon with mushrooms, a Vichyssoise, a good salad. But he was asleep. For some reason she did not want to awaken him, though in less than one hour and a half the plane would land in Chicago. You were supposed to nudge passengers gently awake if they slept when a meal was ready. "I'll take it," said the man across the table from the doctor. "The old guy looks like he needs his sleep." The stewardess gave him the tray. He immediately began to gobble voluptuously, with intense concentration, as if this were to be his last meal on earth. Why did so many people eat like that? It made a person ashamed for them, someway. It wasn't that they were enjoying the good food and

257

relishing every mouthful. It was as if they were hungry, which they weren't. The man who was eating was very fat; he even bulged out of the large seat. "You meet all kinds," murmured the stewardess to her sister stewardess. "I think," she said, "that I'll let that doctor sleep forty-five minutes before we land and then give him his lunch."

"Do you think he's sick?" asked the other stewardess anxiously. She was a very conscientious girl. "Maybe he needs oxygen."

"Well, he looked sick when he got aboard, but now he doesn't. I'll let him sleep a little longer. He seems to need it; it's as if he hasn't slept for a long time."

Dr. Kadimo was dreaming. He was a boy again in his eastern European country. His father was a lawyer; he was also the mayor of the small town; he was also the friend of the local priest, and together they solved the problems of the distressed. The room was all wood, even the ceiling. It was white and roaring winter outside. A bear rug, the color of cream, was spread before the fireplace, and a kettle began to sing over the fire. An oil lamp gleamed softly here and there; leather chairs or chairs of polished wood were scattered over the shining floors. An icon stood over the stone fireplace. The Corpus, made of bronze, glimmered like old gold. A dog whined sleepily near the fire. Odors of thick rich soup came from the kitchen. The wind thundered at the tight little windows, the strong oaken doors. The copper kettle was boiling now; its thin high song sounded over the wind. The dog moved restlessly, lifting his long nose toward the kitchen. The frost made the trees

258

crack outside; they snapped like pistol shots. Darkness pressed against the windows, a darkness like an impenetrable weight, like an ominous presence, like a powerful threat. The room was an outpost in the winter and the dark.

The boy, Atino, was sitting respectfully away from the fire at a broad and polished table, working over his books. He was twelve years old. He was growing drowsy; the fire crackled and he could feel its floods of warmth and could see its curtains of flame rushing up the chimney, which hummed with the wind. He could smell the fine fat smells from the kitchen, cabbage soup and roasting pork and the aromatic, spicy perfume of cooking apples. There was a scent of coffee in the air too. His father and the priest were drinking it before the fire. The priest had pushed his tall hat, like a black tube, off his forehead; the shawl, attached to the rear of the hat, draped over his neck and shoulders. He had lifted the skirts of his clerical robes so that he could warm his old sturdy legs in their long black woolen stockings. He had climbed through snow, and now the room took on another odor, of drying wool, of damp leather and felt. He was not a tall man, but he was a big one in girth, a man with authority as well as kindness, a man of God. Atino, shaking the drowse from his eyes, looked at Father Alexis Rozniak with deep respect. He could rumble pleasantly and thoughtfully, as he was doing now. He could also shout, and everything thundered about him then. He could grow angry, and his hand was hard. When he chanted in the church it seemed the very plaster angels listened; the rich and reverent re-

259

sponse soared among the pillars and against the Byzantine roof with its gold leaf and its faces of the saints. The candles would flicker with the very power of that great chanting, and the cold winter sun slanted through high colored glass windows in beams of many hues. The priest was the heart of the town, durable, eternal, ageless, even though his beard was gray, the eyelids over the fine black eyes wrinkled like old silk.

The priest and the mayor, Atino's father, were talking very seriously now, and when men talked seriously, Atino had observed, it was usually of a dull matter. Their voices were low. Perhaps it was the quality of the tone of their voices that made the boy suddenly strain to listen. "Believe me, dear Jozef," said the priest, "I am not needlessly alarming you. There is a stench in the air, an effluvium of violence and terror. I am a man of the country; you know how it is when we smell the wind, sniffing it deeply into our nostrils. Long before the storm breaks or the first flash of lightning is in the sky, or the first sound of wind in the trees, or the first mutter of thunder, a countryman knows what is approaching. Is it not so? Yes. And before the first long snow begins, a countryman can smell it, pure and dry and clean as starch. And so you must go with your family to America. At once. You are a man of substance, an accomplished man, a teacher, a man of law. They will admit you. But do not wait! It is almost upon us."

It was late February 1914. Jozef Kadimo smiled, tapped his pipe with a finger, smoked, became serious again. Atino sat up alertly. America? So far away, so mysterious, unknown? Why should they go to America? The men before the fire dropped their voices and moved their heads closer together, looking each other's eyes. Atino yawned. He started dimly awake when he heard the sweet singing of his father's violin. Jozef was standing on the bear rug, his eyes half closed, his plump lips smiling, and he was playing. Ah, Chopin. The Polonaise. It was his father's favorite selection. He could make his violin cry with resolution, dance deliriously, deepen to drums, march, weep, laugh, portend. He could hear it now, like a passionate voice calling to him, and he started awake in the jet plane with the sound in his ears.

The plane was rushing into darkness against the sun, but against the purple horizon Dr. Kadimo, blinking, could see the lighter purple of the curve of the earth, tinged with dim fire. The beautiful, beautiful earth! The stewardess came to him, but he shook his head and said, "Coffee, please. Just coffee." He sipped the coffee. The jet engines shrilled faintly, but above them the doctor could hear his father's violin singing, urgent, like a chanted prayer. He put his lean fingers over his eyes and rubbed them and sighed. The resolution rose like a pillar of indomitable stone in his heart. He did not know—yet. But with God's help he would know what he must do and what he must say.

The mighty plane heaved and dropped, and the stewardesses hurried down the aisle to be sure that their charges had fastened their seat belts. "So soon?" murmured the doctor to the girl. She was such a pretty young thing, with a fresh face like a warm summer pear. "There's a snowstorm over Chicago," she said reassuringly. "Bad weather and a little bumpy, perhaps. We'll be there in about thirty-five minutes."

The lights in the plane went on as they were gulped into the darkness. A terrible thing, this speed, thought Dr. Kadimo. I left California in a full hot day, and in just this little while I am in darkness, and it is winter in Chicago. What frightful forces men can now control! But they cannot control the most frightful things of all: their own hearts. They can speed with the sun, but they cannot speed mercy, or justice, or peace, for these are not in them. They can ban the midnight, but not the malignancy of their minds. They can illuminate the heavens, but not their spirits. They can climb the loftiest stratosphere and eye the moon, but they cannot climb the dunghill of their sins and their crimes against each other. They can divide and fission and fuse the atom—how dreadful!—but they cannot part themselves from the terror that lives in them; they cannot fuse God to their souls. "Man is inclined to evil," said the Church, "and to darkness rather than to light." But the Western ethic of the Reformation and of Rousseau declared that man was naturally good and was distorted and debased only by the institutions about him. What folly! He, and he alone, created his institutions, was then imprisoned by them. Tortured and murdered by them. He had made a hell of the green garden of the world. He had filled it with devils like himself. And now——

But still, at the desperate outposts of this staring horror which man had made of his planet, the

262

desperate outposts in the night, stood some men of goodness and charity, men who made wine and music, who worshiped secretly, who loved, who would even die to defend that which was sacred, When all the world had stood sheepishly silent before the massacre of Hungary and not a statesman had lifted his voice in a shout of rage and wrath, some very young Russian soldiers in their tanks had refused to fire upon men and women and little children in Budapest. Those young boys, who had been taught the litany of Lucifer all their lives, who had known nothing but fury and madness! Yet these few, these clumsy youths, had preferred to be shot than to do a monstrous thing. I salute you, said the doctor in his soul. For you, I will find a way. Even hell could not prevail against your sudden holy compassion, could not consume it in fire; knowing nothing of goodness, you re-created it in your hearts. I salute you, brave children. God be with you.

The stewardess brought Dr. Kadimo his coat. She was the conscientious girl. She worried because the coat was so light. The storm in Chicago was tremendous, with a huge blizzard and freezing winds. She said to the doctor, "Why, the temperature is close to zero outside, Dr. Kadimo. And this coat——"

"I've lived in California and in the desert a long time," said the doctor, touched at this gentle solicitude, which had come spontaneously and without a hope of money. "A very long time. When I visited the East before, it was usually summer. Please don't worry. I know what winter is. See, I have a sweater, which I have just put on." He

263

wanted to kiss her cheek, as he had kissed the cheek of his dead young daughter, Stella, who had died of poliomyelitis when she had been as young as this child. Stella had always been so concerned about him after they had been left alone following the death of her mother. He was no longer grieved over Stella. She had died in youth and innocence, before man had increased his madness a thousandfold. She had died the day before the atomic bombs had been dropped on the defenseless cities of Japan. God forgive me, thought Dr. Kadimo as the stewardess helped him pull on his coat. If You can, Lord, forgive me. If You cannot, then let me, out of my most awful guilt, undo what I have done or make it impossible again.

The snow and the wind tore at his clothing. He carried little baggage. He bent his head and rushed into the brilliant airport, where anxious throngs teemed at the airline desks, only to learn that almost all planes East and West had been canceled. He went to his own airline desk. "Dr. Kadimo?" said the harassed agent. "I'm sorry, but your plane to Washington has been canceled. But one plane is leaving for —— in about half an hour. That will take you half your way; we can book you through from there to Washington, though the plane doesn't leave from —— until tomorrow morning. There is a good hotel right at the airport, though, where you could stay overnight."

"And I can't stay in Chicago overnight and then take my scheduled plane for Washington?"

"You'll be taking a chance, sir. The weather reports are that this storm is just beginning. It's expected to be worse tomorrow. This is a bad time of the year."

Dr. Kadimo shivered with cold. His gray face was pinched with it. He was also very tired. Perhaps it would be best to stay in Chicago and wait, even two days if necessary. He could call Washington tomorrow. He wanted only to find a warm hotel room, to take off his clothing, eat a light supper with wine, and go to bed. His whole body ached with the desire for rest. "I think——" he said, and stopped, startled.

The clerk looked at him expectantly. "Yes, sir?"

The strangest urgency had come to the doctor. He regarded it with surprise. The urgency demanded that he take the soon-leaving plane for ——, a city he did not know. He would be in a plane again for at least an hour. He shook his head.

"Sir?" said the clerk.

The urgency was like a strong voice in him. He said quickly, "I think I'll go to ——. I've never been there." The clerk nodded approvingly and made out the new ticket. The doctor said to himself, I'm a fool. Why did I do that? If I could have gone to a hotel here, I could have rested and thought and tried to see what I must do. Now I'll be completely exhausted. He wanted to lift his hand and stop the busy clerk, but his hand felt numb and weak.

And then he remembered an extraordinary thing. When he was twelve, before his family had brought him to America, he had gone walking with his dog. The snows were deep and heavy, but he had snowshoes, and the dog loved the snow.

265

They had gone into the shining marble silence together, he whistling, the dog barking. The house stood on the edge of the small town, and so there were fields and woods about. Atino slogged toward the forest. All at once the dog stopped and whined. "Come on, old fellow," said the boy. But the dog whined. The boy shrugged and started for the forest without the animal. Then the dog, as if possessed, ran after him, seized his coat, and held on. His eyes gleamed up at his young master desperately. His back arched in his struggles to stop Atino. He growled madly in his throat.

"Very well," said Atino impatiently. "We'll go back. You are cold, eh?"

The dog was a small one but resolute. He raced before Atino, as if pleading for him to hurry, and so Atino, to humor him, hurried. They had just reached the path to the house when Atino looked back at the forest. A great gray shape, haggard with starvation, stood like death at the very border of the woods, fangs glittering visibly even at that distance. A wolf.

"A wolf. Yes," said the doctor.

"What, sir?" asked the clerk, startled.

"Nothing. I was just remembering something. What is my gate to the plane to ——?"

I'm superstitious, thought the doctor, hurrying to the gate. What has this delay, this new plane to ——, got to do with that wolf of my childhood? Surely I have not been delayed and rerouted for any significant reason! I am a scientist and I deal with facts, not gauzy mysticism. There are a dozen men, my companions on the plane, going to ——

with me, on their way to Washington. What delayed, rerouted them? Nothing.

But his ancient blood was placated. He took the plane and did not ask himself anything again. He dozed restlessly on the journey. He had to be awakened to disembark. The hotel was comfortable, the food good, the wine excellent. He fell into bed, tried to think. But a warm cloud came over his mind and he slept suddenly.

He awakened, rested. But his fearful problem was still with him, unresolved. And the storm had leaped to this city. The sky was dark and close; the snow blew past the windows in long white curtains torn by the savage wind. He called the airport. All planes had been canceled. They would keep in touch with him, however. And so he missed his plane again to Washington.

Now he called the officer he knew in the Pentagon. "You should have stayed in Chicago," said the officer, his irritation sounding through his deep respect. "The storm stopped there about dawn. We were expecting you at two this afternoon. Now you are stuck, you say."

"Yes. It's very bad here. I'm sorry to inconvenience all of you." He was disgusted with himself. "Perhaps I can get a train tonight for Washington. I've already made inquiries, and they tell me there is not even a seat. Very busy in Washington, eh? But there may be a train cancellation. I'll call you if there is."

"All these important people waiting for you," said the officer reproachfully.

"I know. I know. I will do my best. It was foolish

267

for me to come here. But it was advised. Sorry."

Yes, he should have stayed in Chicago. He'd have been on the way to Washington by now. He thought of the clerk without favor. Yet he had no answer to his problem. If he had arrived at the Pentagon he would have arrived in confusion and darkness of mind. At least he could think here in this warm and quiet room.

The room did not answer his question. He prayed, but there was some obstacle in his mind. It came to him as a surprise that he hadn't prayed for a long time and he had not gone to church for years. When had he made his last confession? Before the death of Stella. Before the bombs had been dropped on Japan. Why had he not gone to confession? Because he was guilty of death and terror and ruin. He knew it in his heart. He also knew now that he had been dreadfully betrayed, himself. He had talked with a certain general later. But though he could have felt less guilty then, he did not. He had been violated. Nevertheless, he was guilty. For a week or two he almost lost his mind in his despair and rage. It was no use for his associates to assure him that even without him this thing would have happened. He had had a part in it, though he had been betrayed.

"If you'd withdrawn, they'd have called you a traitor," said an associate.

"Better to be called a traitor than to know you are a murderer," said the doctor.

"But the Japs were our enemies."

"Do you think that they alone were to blame? No, we all were."

The associate, a close friend, had not repeated

this. He too was feeling guilty and sick and terrified.

The room was quiet and hushed about him. The storm roared on outside. He tried to read a book he had brought, but could not. He began to wander aimlessly up and down the room.

He had always thought with precision. A scientist had no other choice, by nature, by profession. He began to think of himself and his fellows. At one time in the world's history, and in the lifetime of many old men even now, scientists were above governments. They worked in their own version of ivory towers—the laboratory, the observatory. They had a very simple, even naïve, code; they searched for truth, for the nature of the universe, for the nature of man. Politics was of no concern to them. Faced with the infinite, they knew little of and cared less for the finite. But at some time in their recent career their genius had been seized by governments, not in the search for truth, for God, for the nature of man, but for destruction. Why had they, the scientists, everywhere in the world, succumbed so easily? Armed with truth and insight, why had they become harlots? Patriotism? Why, any of those young Russian boys, the schoolboys pulled from their classrooms to man tanks, was nobler than all the modern scientists in the world. They had faced truth and had suddeny refused to surrender to oppression, to madness. This could not be said of the scientists, who had used their talents not to save man, to advance truth, to search through the visible universe for the invisible Law which controlled all things. Had they delivered themselves over to prostitution out of mere mortal fear? No. They had suddenly developed the modern disease, the fatal disease, of the desire for flattery, of worldly importance, though God knew that it was not money they were after and not wealth after which they lusted. Flattery. Importance. Immediate attention. The desires of the wanton.

Some, in search of these foul trinkets, these gauds, these little paste jewels, had become Communists, not out of conviction, truly, but out of egotism. If the posturing actor, the demagogue, could attain tremendous amounts of newspaper space and publicity by mere babblings, by striking a dramatic pose, by lies and sonorous stupidities, then why should the scientist huddle in the shadows? The scientist had fallen into the most ancient of traps, and the most evil: the lust for power. He did not actually want to wield power; he simply wished to know that he had it. He too (and it was quite pathetic when you thought of it) wanted the vulgar applause of the mobs, the mobs who had murdered their prophets and their kings, who had stoned truth in the reeking market places, who eternally set up gibbets and guillotines for their own savage hates, who at the very worst had murdered their Saviour. For that offered power, for that shameful applause, some scientists everywhere had become Communists. If ever a man like these needed pity rather than anger, the scientist needed it. He should be pitied for becoming only a foolish man and not remaining a priest at the altar of truth.

Dr. Kadimo, himself, had said to one of these piteous and confused men on the eve of the latter's appearance before a Congressional committee: "Why? Why, in God's name?" And the scientist had looked at him with dazed eyes and had repeated: "Why? Why, frankly, I don't know. They—they seemed interesting people, and there are so few interesting people in the world, aren't there? Fewer than ever before in the world's history? I really knew nothing of their ideology. They—they merely appreciated me." And he had flushed and looked down.

"Why should you care if they or anyone else appreciates us or not?"

The poor man's face had appeared to fall apart disastrously. "I shouldn't have cared, should I? We never cared before. But a man does like some honor, doesn't he? After all, we are human, aren't we?"

"That's the trouble," Dr. Kadimo had answered gloomily.

How had he, himself, escaped being afflicted by the disease? First of all, he had had a childhood and youth of strict spiritual discipline. Second, he was of an old race and a cynical one, which never believed what men said. Third, his nation had been consistently violated by Russia over the centuries. Communism! The disorder and madness of the West! Strange that the oriental Russians should have contracted it. Had they been more susceptible, never having been afflicted with it before as all Europe periodically had been so afflicted, and thus acquired immunity? Why, even America, at certain periods in her history, had practiced communism. The disease of the West. The crime of the West. For Russia's misery now,

271

thought Dr. Kadimo, we of the West should plead guilty and ask for absolution. Before we die.

If Russia, fevered by her alien malady, should loose universal death on the world, the Western world deserved it. To be even a little more specific, who had hurled the first atomic bombs on mankind? Who, in fact, was the only nation ever to do so? *Mea maxima culpa,* thought Dr. Kadimo. There is no virtue in us, no faith, no real strength, no fortitude, no justice, no integrity, no honor. There is only the fear of the rabbit—the weak, quivering fear—that we shall suffer as we have made others suffer.

Now a fragment of a poem he had learned in his first American classroom returned to him. (Kipling?)

> *The tumult and the shouting dies;*
> *The Captains and the Kings depart;*
> *Still stands Thine ancient sacrifice,*
> *An humble and a contrite heart.*
> *Lord God of Hosts, be with us yet,*
> *Lest we forget—lest we forget!*

The winter wind thundered at the hotel window, and Dr. Kadimo, hearing it, heard also the singing of his father's violin. "Lest we forget—lest we forget!"

His restlessness became intense. It was as if he were wasting time while an enormous task awaited him, as if a man of overpowering importance were standing outside his door. But he did not know what to do. Aimlessly he pulled open a drawer of his empty dresser. A Bible lay in it. He took it and opened it. Its pages had not even been disturbed by those who had slept in this room before. Then Atino remembered that it was a "superstition" (was it?) that a man in distress, or a man with faith, could open the Bible at random and he would find something pertinent in it that was of immediate use to him. Smiling palely at himself, he held the Bible, then let it fall open in his hands.

"The beginning of sorrows . . . For then there will be great tribulation, such as has not been from the beginning of the world until now, nor will be. And unless those days had been shortened no living creature would be saved—for nation will rise against nation, and kingdom against kingdom; and there will be pestilences and famines and earthquakes in various places—the beginning of sorrows."

Atino Kadimo stared before him. The desolation prophesied by the prophet Daniel. It was standing at the world's door, the desolation summoned by man's crimes.

But still there were the men at the desperate outposts of the world.

Very gently the doctor replaced the Bible. He had been answered sternly. He had been told what he already knew. But he had not been given the answer as to what he should do. His long fingers trailed over the top of the dresser and encountered a small white pamphlet. Vaguely he lifted it. The Man who Listens.

Intrigued slightly, he opened the pamphlet after an approving examination of the photograph of the starkly beautiful white marble building on the cover.

"If you are in trouble and do not know what to do about your great problem, you are invited to come here to talk about it to the Man who Listens. Thousands of people over the past years have come and have been fortified and given hope. The Man who Listens has never betrayed a confidence. He never has. He never will."

Scientists had to be discreet and "top secret" in the world of today. Atino found himself instinctively shrinking. Then he laughed a little. No one knew he was here—— But, wait, was he actually thinking of going to talk to the Man who Listens? Nonsense. He was a scientist with a terrible secret that only seven besides himself knew in all the world, and not a girl in trouble, a workman without employment, an anonymous widow, a clerk overcome by debts. He was a scientist on the way to the Pentagon in Washington.

You are only a man, said a voice in himself. The voice was so clear that he started violently and looked about the room.

The day was rapidly darkening; the heavy, sullen wind beat at the windows. The snow had increased. But it was silent, too silent in this room.

Who was the Man who Listens? The doctor, still forcing himself to smile, searched through the pamphlet. The pamphlet informed him that no one knew who the man was. Some thought him a psychiatrist, a doctor, a lawyer, a teacher. Thousands had seen him. Others had preferred not to see him. No one had ever told who he was.

Automatically Atino put down the pamphlet.

The sense of urgency, however, was stronger in him, like a powerful force. It was like magnetism, like the pull of gravitation. His heart was beating rapidly; he could hear the pounding of his pulses in his ears. An actual physical distress was on him. What was all this? He looked at the pamphlet and could not look away. He felt as though he were smothering.

Superstition. Too, who knew who the man was? It was even possible he was a Communist, lurking in secret, listening. What would the Pentagon say of such indiscretion? What would his associates, the Dynamic Research Associates, say of it? If any word—— He could be denounced, held up to public infamy—a traitor. He could even be called a Communist—if a Communist in that building made use of what he might say.

But he could be discreet. Now why should I even consider going to this sentimental, out-of-the-way place, this melodramatic place? I thought I had become a one-hundred-per-cent American, yet my heredity, my blood, is speaking in me. The wolf at the edge of the forest. The storm in Chicago, which had made him come here, only for fresh delay and a new storm. Marooned with himself, alone with himself, voiceless, drifting, hearing only his frightful thoughts. Worse, he had not solved his own problem, even in this silence.

He would prove it all nonsense. He called the airport. All flights canceled, of course, indefinitely. The storm was only really beginning. He called the railroad station. Sorry, all reservations were filled; there was a long waiting list for cancellations. He then called the bus station; even if a bus left at midnight he would be on it. All reservations were filled for two days. He was marooned with himself, and what more appalling thing could happen to a man in despair? In one last effort he called the two companies who rented automobiles. Sorry, they would have none for him until late tomorrow.

I could walk, of course, he said to himself with humor. Only two hundred miles!

The Man who Listens. Atino looked about his room. The restlessness was like a fever in him, and the urgency was even stronger. He found himself putting on his coat. He would, of course, not give his name. Danger! Danger! He could conceal his face with his handkerchief. Danger!

The scientist in him, he told himself, wanted to investigate this absurdity.

"The desolation." The wolf at the edge of the forest. He could see the wolf clearly gigantic, astride the world, with ravenous fangs, with madness in his furious eyes. Atino ran from the room, taking his small suitcase with him, which he must never leave for a moment. He was stopped in the lobby. He said impatiently, "Dr. Atino Kadimo. My suitcase? It has some papers—— If you wish, I'll pay you now, but I'm returning. Here are my credentials. Thank you very much. No, no apologies, please. I understand."

The manager himself, craven with regrets, went out into the storm and called a taxi for the doctor. Atino found himself in warm moving darkness, his bag at his knee.

"Out to old John Godfrey's place, eh?" said the driver.

"Why, yes. Is it interesting?"

"Well, sir," said the driver, "I think it is. You know something? I went out there two years ago. I have a wife and a couple kids. I was always a big drinker, and then it got out of control, see? I was always on a binge, and I was in court a couple of times for non-support. Then I went to see the Man who Listens. I told him all about myself. And after that I didn't drink no more. No sir."

"Oh? He gave you excellent advice?"

The driver was silent for a little. "Well, now, come to think of it, I don't remember if he ever spoke to me or not. Maybe he did, maybe he didn't. They have a button there, see? You could open the curtains if you wanted to. But I didn't. I was kind of ashamed to, after what I'd spilled about—everything. All I know is that since I went there I ain't had a single drink. No sir. Not one. And I don't want any. Everything's fine now."

The doctor waited for the inevitable, inquisitive question: "You in trouble too?" But the driver did not ask it. Instead he said, "I drive lots of people there. Mostly from out of town. I took five people from that there hotel of yours today, alone."

"There is trouble everywhere," said the doctor with cautious conventionality.

"Mister, you can say that again!" said the driver fervently. "With all them atom and hydrogen bombs waiting to blow the world up. Not that it don't deserve it, at that. I sometimes wonder about the guys who think them up—the scientists, you know? When I was a kid I used to see movies

277

about the 'mad scientist.' Make your hair curl. Why, those guys in the movies was Sunday-school teachers when you think of the scientists now! I'd like to hit them with a wrench where it'd do the most good. Yes sir. Ever know a scientist?"

"I think I met one or two at some time," said Atino. He felt sick. "At school. My teachers."

"Glad I didn't go to high school. I might've got a few ideas myself about blowing people up. I sometimes look at my kids. Nice kids. Not them juvenile delinquents. Mass at least three times a week. Regina says she wants to be a Sister. Well, we'll see. And there's Jimmie. He wants to teach school. Well, sir, I look at them kids, and well——"

Here was one of those who manned the desperate outposts of the world. Not a maker of wines, a poet, a philosopher, a musician, an artist—only a father with children. The outpost he manned was the most desperate of all.

"Well, here you are," said the driver. "You got to walk up that path. See the building up there?" He added admiringly, "It don't matter if three inches of snow fall all at once. The paths're always cleared right away. Ready for people."

It was only three o'clock, but the sky was very dark. The driver said as he made change, "It's funny. This's the worst storm we've had for twenty-five years. That's what the radio says. The worst storm. Never saw anything like this myself."

Atino paused. "No storm like this before?"

"Not that I remember," said the driver cheerfully. "It's one big storm, ain't it? First time I remember that planes were ever grounded here, either."

278

Superstition. Atino, grasping his suitcase firmly, went up the path. He looked at the glowering dim sky and felt the sting of the blizzard in his face. It reminded him of home. He saw Father Rozniak again. "A stench . . . of violence and terror." How had Father Rozniak died in the fury of the first World War? Hunger? A bayonet? Exposure? He had known it was all coming and he had not been afraid for himself. He had been afraid only for his people. He too had manned a desperate outpost. Manning it, he had faced the wolf. He had not run away. Men of God never ran away anywhere. Cardinal Mindszenty. He had not run away. The ministers, the rabbis, had remained to comfort their people, though their people, risking everything, would have helped them escape. They had remained. A shepherd does not leave his flock— to the wolf.

But the scientists evoked the wolf. *Mea maxima culpa.*

The sitting room was warm and serene. There was no one there but Atino. He put down his suitcase for a moment and looked about him with pleasure. Then he remembered the warnings he had been frequently given. Meticulously he examined the furniture, the underside of tables. He lifted the rug in various places. He scrutinized the walls. He tapped everything. But why should anyone "bug" this place, where only the obscure and desperate came? Habit was sometimes hard to overcome. He felt a little foolish.

A chime sounded. He started and looked at the solid oak door. He grasped his suitcase and went

279

into the serene marble room with its shut curtains and marble chair.

He looked at the curtains suspiciously. Then he went to them and tried to pull them aside. They would not stir. He looked at the button and read the inscription above it. He pressed the button. The curtains did not move. Very, very mysterious and melodramatic. He sat down in the chair. He took out his handkerchief and covered his face, then remembered that if anyone had wished to see him before this he had already been seen. He removed the handkerchief.

He faced the curtains. A phrase he had read in the pamphlet returned to him: "All the time there is." All the time. He said to himself: But there is very little time now.

He sat and waited. He could hear no storm here, no traffic, no voice, no opening or closing of doors. If the man behind the curtains had "all the time there is," so did he. He would wait the time out and see who would become impatient first. He laughed inwardly at himself for coming here. The clergyman behind those curtains would discover a man of infinite patience. But was anyone there, really?

Atino bent forward, his head held sideways. He listened for a long time. There was no sound, but he knew powerfully that someone was there, and listening. The Man who Listens.

Then Atino heard himself say aloud suddenly: "I am from an old country."

He waited, angry at himself for having spoken. He waited. Then he sat upright. Had he really heard an answer—"And so am I"?

Atino jumped to his feet and examined the marble walls. Where did that light come from? Very interesting. He talked rapidly to himself, for his heart was thundering, and it must be controlled. He passed his hands over the walls. Solid. Nothing could be hidden. Nevertheless, he was frightened.

"Oh you of little faith! Why are you afraid?"

Atino swung around and confronted the curtains. "I heard you!" he exclaimed. "Who are you?" He sat down.

The room was silent. I am going mad, thought Atino. I did not hear a voice at all! I only heard something in myself. Or did I?

"There is a terrible storm outside," he said aimlessly in his distraction.

"Yes. A most terrible storm. It is just beginning."

"Just beginning," Atino assented. Then he sat up, stiff and yet trembling. Had he heard a voice again, or had he imagined it? He tried to recall the voice. It had been strong and full of echoes and sad. No. He had not heard the voice. It was only his own thoughts. Still . . .

Then he remembered another poem (Strange that he should remember poems today!) Francis Thompson? *The Hound of Heaven.*

> . . . *must Thy harvest fields*
> *Be dunged with rotten death?*

Not yours, O Lord, said Atino in himself. Only ours. Only ours. We have destroyed Your harvest fields. We have dunged them with rotten death. We will dung them again.

"That is why I came," he said to the curtains. "I must have an answer. Tell me what to do."

The silence waited. "I never hated anyone," said Atino. "I—we—discovered something. How to——" How to split, fuse, the atom, he continued in his thoughts. It was a marvelous discovery. We had discovered one of the secrets of God. Or had He given that secret to us? Why? For our knowledge, for our love, for our use, for our revelation?

"Yes," said the deep and echoing voice.

"What?" cried Atino. "Did you speak? Or am I going insane?"

He looked about the room desperately. He heard the echo only of his own spoken words. He was sweating. "I am a man in despair," he said without volition.

The room waited, and the light grew brighter, as if with encouragement.

"I was brought up in a very religious atmosphere," said Atino. "I was brought up in the fear of God. But that was in the old country. Few, if any, fear God now."

Silence.

"I love life," said Atino. "I love all life. Because God created it. I am a vegetarian. They laugh at me. But I never wished to destroy life. One knows that God gave the animals of the world to man, to eat and to hunt. But still, I could not bring myself to destroy life." He stopped, and then he said, "But I have destroyed life. I did not mean to do it. They took what we had to offer, to make life more glorious, and they used it for death.

Useless, malicious death. It was not necessary. A general told me it was not necessary. We were betrayed. Have you ever been betrayed?"

"Yes," said the voice.

Atino stared at the curtains. "Did I hear you answer?" he asked. "Or did I imagine it?"

Silence.

"The great Commandment," said Atino. " 'Thou shalt not kill.' "

He put his hands over his face. " 'Thou shalt not kill.' Above all, you must not kill. That is my problem. I don't know what to do! If I give—them—what we eight know—there will be more terror, more death. They will say to us: 'But if we don't have this, if *they* first have this, then we'll die.' If I say—if we say—this must not be used for death, then we'll be execrated. We'll be called traitors. Traitors to what? The code of killing, for killing's sake?

"Dear God," said Atino, "I'm not a murderer. Help me. If You do not help me, then the world will die. They've already heard something of what we are doing and what we know. That is why I am on my way. If you do not help me, Your beautiful world, Your garden, will be destroyed. My associates have given me all authority. I don't know why this is, why they gave me authority to speak for them."

He looked at the curtains with tormented eyes.

"Do you know that between Mars and Jupiter there was once a world, a planet like ours? A planet, like ours, with life upon it? God never created anything lifeless; He could not, for He is life itself. But that planet exploded. Or did it ex-

283

plode? Were there men like ourselves there, with death and hatred and evil and war in their black hearts? I know that many astronomers say that life would have been too cold on any such planet between red Mars and Jupiter. It might have had an atmosphere unlike ours. But must every life be like ours? Might not the oxygen we breathe be deadly to other creatures? The methane of the moons of Saturn may be breath of life to the inhabitants of the moons and Saturn. The breath of life is not only oxygen. We are too provincial. We insist on casting life in our own meager image. What our animal lungs can absorb must, per se, be what other lungs can absorb. What heat there is on this world must necessarily be the heat other creatures must need. What folly! What stupidity! Must everything be what we need, what we demand? Must everything be tempered, fashioned, arranged, heated, and cooled—in the universe—according to man's needs? Are there not others with other needs, ordained by God? God has established the boundaries of the worlds. Perhaps He intends, by other atmospheres, by other thermodynamics, to keep evil from spreading from one world to another—to bar man everywhere. To bar murder—everywhere. To keep it restrained, in its own prison."

Atino leaned toward the curtains, twisting his hands together, forgetting caution, forgetting everything but that he was a man and a soul.

"The way between Mars and Jupiter is full of immense debris, enormous, fragmented. It was a world. Did the inhabitants destroy that world?"

The silence answered him.

"And so," said Atino, "we can—we probably will—destroy our world too. Help me. I am only a man, and I am afraid. I was not born in this country and so am open to suspicion. By whom? By the provincials, by those who will not understand, or those who pretend not to understand. For their own wicked reasons."

He looked with passion at the curtains, straining forward. "Does goodness reside only on one particular continent, in one country? Are all other countries outside the pale? Who gave any country 'the leadership of the world'? Not God. Only the egotism, the pride, the folly, the stupidity, the meanness, the hate of any particular country. Are we all not men, the children of God? Where is there leadership—except in God? But one must not mention God these days! If you do, there are smirks and winkings and sidelong glances. There are intimations that you are mentally ill."

He groaned. " 'In God we trust.' That is on our coins. We in America pretend to believe that. We do not. We trust only in weapons and bribes and treaties and admonitions—as does our adversary. The old, old history—the history of death. What man ever stood on the battlefield and cried out: 'Thou shalt not kill!' Never, in the history of the world. Killing is our reason for living. We are all guilty, everywhere. None save God is good."

He clasped his hands vehemently together and extended them toward the curtains. "The United Nations. Oh, God. What have they done to prevent murder? To establish justice, freedom, love, under God? Nothing! A congress of quarrels, of self-seeking, of secret betrayals of men of good will.

285

They have stood silent before evil. When an affair of magnitude comes before them, they count the population of cats in the world! Dear God, it is quite true. Quite true. Dear God. Dear God! They won't even permit Your Name to be mentioned there. It might offend somebody!"

He stood up, violently trembling, broken. He went to the curtains. "Do you hear me? Will you let me see you? Will you answer me?"

He touched the button. The curtains flew aside.

He saw a great alcove, more than twelve feet high, more than six feet wide, curved like a protecting and hallowed shell, filled with light.

He saw in the alcove a tremendous crucifix of roughly carved wood, broad and wide.

On the cross was nailed the Son of God, the Son of man, true God, true man, carved of ivory, or perhaps of the finest white wood. More than life-sized it yet seemed formed of living and pulsing flesh, exquisitely tinted, majestic.

The figure was not of the dead Christ but of the living One. The head was lifted, held forward, strained to listening, suffering yet hearing, intense if agonized. The eager eyes were turned on Atino, listening. The crown of thorns stood on the heroic forehead, and drops of blood streamed from it. The hands bled, and the left side, and the twisted feet.

The ardent, anxious, self-forgetting, loving, and listening eyes, the eyes which knew everything, saw everything, understood everything! The Sacrifice, offered up of Itself. For man. For evil, plotting, whispering, malicious, blackhearted man. Man, the murderer. Man, the thief. Man, the betrayer. Man, the destroyer.

Pity and mercy beamed on the mighty features, and forgiveness. The pity and mercy and forgiveness extended not only to man but to all the worlds He had created. To all the worlds He would create.

The light glimmered on carved muscle and thigh and strained arm, on rib cage, on breast, on chin, on stretched leg, on bleeding foot, so that it was not an image there, but Life itself, suffering and flesh-forgetting and loving, and eternal.

"Yes!" cried Atino. "Yes! I should have known! The Man who Listens. You have never stopped listening. You listen through eternity. Dear God. Dear God!"

He was weak, almost fainting. He let himself down beside the cross and leaned his head against the feet. Instantly a powerful sense of ultimate protection came to him, and comfort and love and gentleness and comprehension. He knew he would not have to speak aloud. All his thoughts would be heard. The mighty cross and Figure stood over him, a Fortress, a Gate that hell itself could not force.

We have discovered something, said Atino in his mind, and pressed his cheek against the feet. During our secret experimentations in our laboratories. We have discovered how to harness the sun, its great energy, its tremendous power! We were not even looking for it, yet in a few hours we had it. We stood there, aghast, searching each other's faces. We had the power of the sun! My associates and I.

He looked up at the great head. It appeared to

287

have bent a little downward toward him. He could see the large and living eyes, listening and enormously bright.

We knew what this meant. Before what we had discovered, the atomic and hydrogen and cobalt bombs were nothing. Only firecrackers. We had discovered the secret of the sidereal universe! Did You give it to us?

The eyes appeared to fix themselves on him in assent.

Yes, yes, said Atino in his mind. You did. It was so simple, after all, as all that You have made is simple. Only man has complicated everything, made everything obtuse and complex, labyrinthine, devious. Out of his evil nature.

We had discovered the power of the worlds. Once again, as once man had been, we were little less than the angels. I cannot tell you of our exultation, and then our terror, and then our complete understanding of what this meant.

What should we do with this awful thing, this awesome knowledge? we asked each other. Dared we give it to the world? Dared we, remembering, give it? Would we not be traitors to You, to our fellows, if we divulged it? We shut our doors tightly for days, for nights, for weeks, while we hardly slept or ate and only whispered, our heads together, our eyes pleading with each other, asking, asking.

Washington knew we were working on something, but not what it was. Had we inadvertently given a hint at one time? One of us? Or perhaps our faces betrayed us to watchers. Or our shut doors had alerted somebody, and our silence.

We had discovered how to destroy the world, between one breath and another, to hurl its gigantic fragments into space, to destroy man and all his works.

Or we could control the power at will, direct it to any nation, while we ourselves were protected. We found we could throw up an invisible field to protect us. Any nation which has this secret can control all mankind. This is the terror!

He strained his face up toward the larger face bent down to him. Was there a terrible warning in the eyes now, even perhaps a divine anger?

Atino no longer thought of "superstition." He did not feel that the mighty Figure on the cross was only wood or ivory. It appeared to encompass all the universes from fingertip to fingertip, guarding, holding. A Force greater than all the constellations and stars and galaxies. "Dear God," he whispered, and bent his head to kiss the feet.

After a little he continued to speak in his mind.

One nation, with this, can rule the world, make all the rest of the world whimpering slaves, can desecrate Your world, can destroy what You have done and given. It can take from Your children the freedom You gave them, and the stature.

We do not trust anyone. Is America more virtuous than any other country? No. We cannot trust any government, for they are men and, being men, they are naturally evil.

But we do know that our discovery of Your wonder, Your great secret, could make an Eden of this earth again, joyous, without hunger, without lack of shelter, without fear, without pain, without hatred. It could abolish labor and disease.

289

It could open Your universes to man. It could finally reveal Your face. Your most holy face.

Atino was weeping now, like a child. The light seemed to grow stronger upon him, like the sun itself. It warmed his coldness, calmed his heart.

We cannot trust man, he continued. We cannot trust any government to use this power for the benefit of all men. No. What, then, shall I tell them when I am in Washington? Tell me what to do! For You, for my fellow men.

Tell me what to do.

He sat for a long time, listening, looking up at the carved face which seemed to be true flesh, both pallid and flushed, crowned with agony, listening, yet silently speaking in sonorous accents like the sound of remembered thunder.

Then Atino cried out in himself: Yes! Yes, of course! That is what I must tell the men in Washington who have sent for me. I had thought to tell them nothing at all because of the watchers at the desperate outposts of the world.

He himself listened, catching his breath sharply at intervals, nodding, turning up his face eagerly, nodding, clasping his hands vehemently together. Listening.

Yes, yes, it will be so easy to devise with Your help! A simple thing, as You have told me and shown me. How very simple! If they do not agree they get nothing, and the whole world may call us traitors and persecute us. But it will do no good. We cannot betray You and Your world.

A very simple device. I will tell Washington that they may have the secret—only if the secret is given to every nation in the world simultaneously. Only if they will permit me to show the men in the United Nations the device also, when I tell them what we have discovered. Only if they install the device You have shown me, first. First.

So simple. I shall tell them that before I give them the secret the device must be installed in the Pacific and Atlantic oceans, at the North Pole, at the South Pole. I can work this out in a few hours, tonight!

The device, installed in all those four places, will be guarded by ships of all nations, so that no one can tamper with it. Sunk deep in the waters, it will still be very sensitive.

If the power that I then give them is misused, is placed in a warhead and then tested secretly, then the devices will detonate every arsenal in the world, every stockpile of atomic and hydrogen bombs, including this new power of harnessing the sun. No matter how hidden, the wave lengths of the devices will find them, whether on land or sea or island. They will detonate them all. The whole world will perish in one breath. There will be no victors, no vanquished. There will be nothing left at all. There will be only fragments floating between Venus and Mars where once we had our orbit and our life. There will be universal death for man. There will be no more world.

Life. Or death. Man had that choice once before, and he chose death. Will he do it again? Only You can know. Only You. Will man choose to see Your face, or will he choose, in one instant, to die? Only You can know. I trust only You.

Yes, yes! The device is entirely clear in my mind now.

What can they do to me? We have been very careful, my associates and I. Eight of us. Each one of us has memorized only one eighth of the formula, one eighth of the calculations. You see, we didn't even trust each other if pressure were applied. There are no written records. We destroyed them after each had memorized his part.

When I leave here I will call my best friend immediately. But not from the hotel. I will tell him that all our associates must leave at once for other countries so we cannot be taken all together and forced to speak. Our passports are in readiness. We will run. Not for our sakes, but for the sake of the world, for the men at the desperate outposts.

Then only will I go to Washington. This storm! It has protected even the destroyers, for they are men too.

Atino Kadimo stood up, refreshed, strong, full of youth and resolution.

He reached up and put his hand gently on the wounded side. "You brought me to You," he said. He bent and kissed the bleeding feet. "So man can be protected, even against himself, from the wolf at the edge of the forest."

He looked into the deep, great eyes, and they seemed to smile at him.

"You came to save man. Dear God. You came, as the Salvation of the world. How great is Your love.

"You brought me to You through the storm so that I may repeat the words of Your Salvation.

"For the last time. For the very last time."

ABOUT THE AUTHOR

TAYLOR CALDWELL, born in Manchester, England, came to America in 1907, and has lived here ever since. After graduating from the University of Buffalo she worked as a stenographer and court reporter for the State Department of Labor in Buffalo, New York. Her first novel, *Dynasty of Death*, was published in 1938. Her other novels include *Let Love Come Last; The Balance Wheel; The Devil's Advocate; Never Victorious, Never Defeated* (recipient of the *Grand Prix* and the *Prix Chatrain*); *Tender Victory; The Sound of Thunder; Dear and Glorious Physician; A Prologue to Love; Great Lion of God; The Listener; Captains and the Kings;* and, most recently, *Bright Flows the River.*